After a fairly typical education, Jill trained as an SRN in nursing. A marriage and two children later, she began writing for her grandchildren in 2007. She self-published her first fictional novel in 2019. Due to health concerns, she moved into a care home where she still writes.

To my grandchildren and great-grandchildren

Sean, James, Sam, Skye, Jewel, Ava, and Authur

Jill Nutbeem

DEEP PURPLE

AUSTIN MACAULEY PUBLISHERS™

LONDON * CAMBRIDGE * NEW YORK * SHARJAH

A CIP catalogue record for this title is available from the British Library.

ISBN 9781035845965 (Paperback)
ISBN 9781035845972 (ePub e-book)

www.austinmacauley.co.uk

First Published 2024
Austin Macauley Publishers Ltd®
1 Canada Square
Canary Wharf
London
E14 5AA

For Jenny, for giving me such inspiring illustrations for my books.

Thanks must go to Sue and Kathy for their constructive insight, support, and encouragement.

Tucked away in a small backstreet of central London, a tiny cobbler's shop struggled to survive in a featureless row of hastily erected modern shops, gaudily decorated to hopefully encourage trade.

Elderly Oscar Harrison, a highly reputed cobbler of bygone days, sat smiling wistfully to himself, as he surveyed the untidy clutter of stock on the small, cramped shops, shelves. His whole working life had been spent behind this very counter that he was leaning against. A pair of pince-nez eyeglasses, complete with clips, perched on the bridge of his rather scrawny nose. His gangly, rather undernourished-looking body with straggly dark hair—a kind of handsomeness, with crinkly smiling eyes, made known the fact that he was still agog with wonder at the new designs, for ballet, pointes and tap shoes, that had come onto the market in later years.

Many a famous ballerina and danseur/principal dancer had peppered his shop with requests for his skilful mastery in hand-crated, top-grade ballet shoes or ultra soft leather slippers, with a soft sole, for the men, which made such a difference to their performance on stage. A ballerina's footwear can be Full-Sole, Split-Sole or Demi-Pointe shoes, made of a rigid box with several layers of cardboard—to take the weight of the dancer's body and glue, with the remainder of the slipper being made of leather, satin and cotton.

Oscar was only too well aware that nowadays the small local cobbler's shop was rapidly losing its valued customers to large manufacturing companies, who could produce the desired products in much larger quantities, distributing to stores throughout the country, with online availability, together with dance costumes and dance fashion accessories. His also highly desired tap shoes of varying styles for different professional dances, had now been solely taken over by a top-ranking manufacturer, who, once more, supplied many stores in the country.

Once his remaining stock had been sold and collected, his little shop that was now sold awaited transfer to the new owners and 'The Dancer's Dream' would no longer be his, but turned into an elite travel agency.

Gazing around him rather sadly his eyes came to rest slowly, riveting themselves on a pair of old and rather discoloured, bluish purple coloured tap shoes, skilfully designed and handcrafted by Oscar, for one particular customer, who had tragically died in a motorway accident. Although, several months later, after his first 'with sympathy letter', he had contacted the family again offering to send the tap shoes to them, as a sentimental gesture, for them to keep in remembrance of their son, but, having received no reply he had reluctantly placed them at the back of one of his shelves. They would need to be either sent to the family or discarded with the remainder of the obsolete, uncollected stock.

Over the next few days, most of his valued customers had collected their eagerly awaited footwear, lovingly tailored by Oscar for each individual customer.

Usually, his dancers would come in pairs or threesomes, some quietly thanking Oscar for their delightful shoes, whilst others more vocal or even humming the notes from their latest dance sequences. These last few days the general chatter had become whispers, as if there was some kind of conspiracy going on. Oscar caught the odd word or two, sometimes half a sentence—2 o'clock...Janet... pickup.

Smiles and sideway glances, one to another, were the norm these days, as the clock ticked down to the final day of business, after which he would lock the shop up for the last time. He planned to sell the family home which had now become too large for him to maintain any longer, with the four boys rearing their own families and Anita gone some three years ago. A small modern flat somewhere within walking distance of the theatres where he could still watch his elite dancers perform would suit him very well.

The final stages of shop clearance were hard for Oscar, but eventually, all was completed to his satisfaction. Shelves were cleaned and clear of stock, except for one pair of exceptional tap shoes, designed and handcrafted for an exceptional man. Cradling them now, in his calloused hands Oscar wished with all his heart that he could, at least once, have seen them on the feet of the man, destined for a great future in the world of dance. Life, though, was not always that orderly. Tragedies sadly happened far too frequently, leaving grieving, bereaved friends and loved one's behind, as was the case with this young man, reflected Oscar, shaking his head as if to dispel memories.

All too soon, it was midday. Oscar was closing the shop at 2 o'clock with the exchange of contracts having been made via the solicitors that morning. He would take the keys to the estate agents on his way home.

The new owners weren't expected to move in until later that afternoon. Time for a snack and a drink, thought Oscar, with a final sweep of the floor with his old but treasured broom that Anita had bought him as his first accessory when opening the new shop all those years ago now, that he could hardly remember the year that he had so proudly taken possession of it after his apprenticeship was completed, but, of course, you never stop learning, so Oscar kept himself up to date with the latest styles and fabrics.

Being a stickler for excellence he soon gained a glowing reputation, tackling a heavy workload, firmly believing that nobody else was sufficiently trained to deliver the expertise he did, proving himself right in his diligence to supply top-grade, hand-stitched dance slippers and tap shoes, with demand growing daily.

No sooner had Oscar finished his lunch and after his absolute final spruce up, than the bell to the shop tinkled violently, announcing a customer, to whom he would have to explain apologetically that he was permanently closed, as of now.

To his utter surprise, though, several well-known and well-loved customers appeared in the doorway, grinning unashamedly at the old cobbler they had come to respect and love ardently, for his skill and easy-going manner. His daily resolution was that nobody would go away from his shop, disappointed and that was how it was for over fifty years of hard, diligent work. Oscar couldn't think of anything else he would rather be doing.

"Please Oscar, come with us," implored a voice with a French accent, that immediately identified him as being Pierre, a talented danseur, taking on many high-ranking roles in well-known ballets, enjoyed by thousands.

"Yes, Oscar, please come," responded a delicate ballerina called Katie, who, Oscar lovingly thought of, as his granddaughter. They were about the same age, both with small features and tiny feet, for whom he had made many many pairs of ballet slippers, for Katie, of the varying styles that she needed for different performances.

"We have a surprise for you, Oscar," another voice exclaimed, this time belonging to a tall, lanky young man called Robert, currently away on tour with an award-winning dance company. Oscar was delighted to see him again after a gap of six months.

"What's going on?" gasped Oscar. "I'm just about to close the shop for the last time. Where are you taking me and what's the surprise?"

"Wait and see," giggled the company in the shop's doorway. "You won't be disappointed, we can assure you."

"Give me a moment, you scamp," laughed Oscar, beginning to understand their intentions. "I must put these tap shoes into a bag, then lock the shop."

Within a moment, Oscar had the precious shoes in his hands and the key inserted into the now slightly rusting keyhole. It's no good getting upset now, Oscar chided himself. It's been a great fifty years of a career I've always admired, as a master cobbler and I feel privileged to have played a small role in the lives of these delightful young people, giving their energy, time and expertise to dance, with performances demanding amazing skills. He knew the audiences loved them, often following one dancer's career and demanding encore after encore, despite the hours already spent on stage.

In the West End of London is an area, also called Soho or Theatreland supporting around forty venues for visitors from around the world to see shows, ballets, opera and a replica of Jacobean life in London. It is surrounded by the areas of Kensington, Westminster and Chelsea, close to the main shopping streets of Oxford Street and Regent Street.

Walking towards a parked car, with his company of his friends, Oscar reminded them that he had to deposit the shop's key with the estate agents, not far away from where they were now. Willing to oblige, the little retinue of cars drove Oscar to the office, where he eventually handed over possession of his beloved shop. They then drove on to the surprise awaiting Oscar, when the four cars, driven by either cast members or show directors, began to find parking spaces, Oscar realised he had been driven to Soho, an area of London close to theatre land, boasting today, a totally new look from times past when sex was for sale in most parts of the district.

Now more upmarket fashionable restaurants were drawing in the visitors, en-route perhaps to an evening's entertainment of a particular art form that drew them to London's theatres, where actors and actresses of professional standards performed their skills, often twice daily, to the delight of the ecstatic audiences.

As Oscar's car, driven by a well-known and respected choreographer pulled into the kerb, Janet, a dainty ballerina, leapt out from the lead car, to open Oscar's side door with a flourish, ushering him onto the pavement. Turning around, Oscar was made aware of a narrow doorway, behind which a flight of stairs led upwards. With Janet in the lead, Oscar claimed cautiously taking note of the colourful tapestry banners on both walls of the stairwell.

As he climbed, his eyes adjusting to the light, a wide beam of sunlight poured through a pair of wide-open doors, further up the flight of stairs, from behind which came a low murmur of voices with an added shout of laughter. It was all very intriguing with Oscar, wondering what to expect. It wasn't long before he found out! A tousled, red-headed young man, ran from the room shouting 'Great-grandpa', only to be caught at the top of the stairs, by a laughing Oscar, who narrowly escaped losing his footing.

"Please be careful, Dillon," called a voice that Oscar immediately recognised as belonging to his third son's wife, Priscilla, hastily charging after her grandson, trying to reach Oscar before Dillon managed to unbalance his great-grandpa.

"What a lovely, lovely surprise," chortled Oscar. "Are you all here to make sure I'm not feeling too sad on my last day at the shop?"

"That's right, dad, you've guessed correctly," said Adrian, Oscar's eldest son, coming to the top of the stairs, to give his father a massive hug. "We couldn't let you face this day on your own, knowing how important it was to you and mum—for fifty years. I'll wager you are still using that old broom that mum gave you as your first accessory for the 'The Dancer's Dream'. How she would love to be here with you and the rest of the family."

"Apart from her day of remembrance, a very memorable day, we haven't been able to see so much of each other because of work and distance and I am truly sorry about that."

"I really do understand, Adrian," returned Oscar. "The years flash by and I'm just so thankful that all four of you have found yourselves, such good wives, besides each one of you has given us grandchildren and even great-grandchildren that we've enjoyed watching grow up, finding their own paths in life. I have much to be thankful for. Now this—"

"Don't let's stand on these stairs much longer," replied Adrian. "All your friends from the dance world are scrambling to get in at the foot of the stairs. Come on in to say hello to the family, who can't wait to see you again."

With that, Adrian took Oscar's arm guiding him into an absolutely amazing room, so incredible that Oscar had to stop and take a deep breath of sheer pleasure, causing his friends to back up behind him. Opened mouthed he stared around him at the enormous room, highly decorated in the 17th-century Baroque style—extravagant, bizarre, dramatic grandeur of curving lines decorated in gilt and gold, belonging to another age, following the idealism of the Renaissance and Mannerism period of history.

Baroque came to England from a French word—'baroque' meaning irregularly shaped, at first used mostly to refer to pearls, eventually coming to describe the ostentatious, rococo, over-elaborate colours and designs of the artist, often depicting their own life-styles, strongly adopted by Roman Catholic churches, being displayed in many a pear-shaped dome. Seen, as well as in architecture and painting, in music, dance, poetry, sculpture and other art forms, using the same dramatic colours and lighting.

Breathing deeply, Oscar allowed himself to be drawn away from his gaping awe of the room and the length to which the drinks bar reached, to reunite with his ever-enlarging family. As he and Adrian approached the tables where the family were sitting, each member rose to their feet to greet a much-loved father, father-in-law, grandfather and those old enough, great-grandfather. There was Adrian with his wife Sue and children Naomi, Richard and Grace with their children Archie, Rose and Derek respectively.

Next came Clive with his wife Annabelle and their adopted twins, Martha and Mary, both engaged to be married. Third down the line was Timothy with Priscilla, his wife, with their daughters Camilla and Charlotte, who was the mother of Dillon—a young rascal, clearly very attached to Oscar. Fourthly and Oscar's last child was Michael, living and working in Singapore for a prestigious bank, with him, his wife Patricia and their family of four—two boys and two girls, going by the names of Martin, Dean, Sally and Anne. That this family of six had been able to attend his final working day was a great blessing to Oscar, who hadn't met with them since Anita's Remembrance Day three years ago.

What a sacrifice had been made on his account, he pondered, as he welcomed and hugged them all, deeply grateful for their love for him. Letters of loyalty and continuing love preceded today's technology whereby he could, after Anita was gone, speak to and see the family growing up, by a simple process of pressing numbers on his phone, to reveal smiling faces. What a Godsend, he muttered to himself as he uttered a silent prayer.

Patiently waiting to climb the stairs and join the party, now beginning to make a start, were many famous faces that Oscar had known and tailored their dance shoes, for, for more years than he cared to remember. Nothing was beyond him in terms of design, style and delicate handcrafting for just the right balance and support of ankles, heels and insteps.

It had been a great working life with no regrets, except, of course, that his dear Anita was no longer with him to enjoy the next phase of their lives together, but it wasn't to be and Oscar must make the best of things, as they were. Although he loved his extended family very much, there was nothing that could entirely compensate for his loss. He must find something to occupy his time and keep the memories fresh and lovely of his and Anita's time together.

Fortunately, he had found a suitable, bay windowed ground-floor flat, close enough to walk to theatre land, with ample space inside to even have a guest room for any wandering grandchild needing a room for the night or longer, if necessary. Maybe he could invest in a laptop and indulge his desire to write his autobiography. There were all sorts of possibilities to explore! His own home had finally been sold, with contracts being exchanged at lunchtime tomorrow, so he mustn't be too late getting to bed tonight, but in the meantime, he was determined to enjoy this wonderful surprise.

Very soon the party was in full swing with the large room hardly able to accommodate them all, as more came and some left for evening performances in various venues. All the food and drink consumed by the guests had been graciously supplied by dancers—of years gone by and more recent up-and-coming young stars, maybe treading the boards of London theatres for the first time, directors, choreographers, backstage hair and costume dressers, even scene shifters and the occasional composer.

It was a totally unexpected and amazing evening for Oscar, who was plied with food and drink, some of which he hadn't tasted before. He and Anita had led simple lives bringing up the children and caring, when appropriate for, homesick vulnerable young dancers suddenly thrust onto the professional scene, finding it hard to adjust to life in the big city and needing some homely comforts, sometimes with accommodation requests if unable to find anywhere else.

It was a happy, busy life, with the years rushing by at an alarming rate. Visits to the family were made as frequently as possible, with a couple of highlight trips to Singapore, which Oscar and Anita found far too hot for them, but a joy to see the children and grandchildren.

The morning following Oscar's retirement party dawned bright and crystal clear. He relished a little lie-in, stretching lazily—a luxury he rarely had. Memories of the party came flooding back plus the many conversations he had enjoyed with every member of the family and the large number of friends from the world of dance.

Most of the talk had centred around Oscar and his plans for the future, although he had asked a question here and there about Martha and Mary's forthcoming marriages and why they hadn't brought along their fiancée, to which they replied that they both lived in their home country of Thailand—from where they themselves had been adopted, finding it impossible to take time away from their respective colleges. Oscar then said how much he would like to meet these young men, to which Martha replied that they had every intention of inviting him to the weddings.

Talking about the forthcoming sale of the family home brought many a tear to the eyes of his sons, who had put this possibility to him within a couple of years of his loss of Anita, but, for him it was too early, knowing how much Anita had enjoyed bringing the boys up there.

Now, though, was the right time and funnily enough, he was actually looking forward to the experience, now he was fully packed up, with the help of his dancing friends. The exchanges of the three properties—one being a first-time buyer, each involved in Oscar's purchase, would hopefully take place, with the monies being safely in the banks of the vendors, then the move could take place. Making his way to his solicitor's office he was confident that his purchase was safe, so much so that he couldn't resist a slight detour to look again at his future home, liking it even more now, excitedly viewing the current owner's busyness in their house move.

As predicted, by Oscar, there wasn't a hitch and events moved onwards, with the removal date set for two days' time. With no regrets Oscar slept well, waking early on the morning of the move with last-minute packing up of bedding, for example, making sure all the necessary contracts and paperwork connected to the house were within easy reach of the new owners, who would find them complete. Anita had been a stickler for filing, with everything labelled for easy identification.

Once more, the keys to this home would need to go to the estate agents to enable him to collect all the keys to his new property. Promises of help with the move were flooding in, with even a couple of family members driving over for the big occasion.

There was one last thing that Oscar had to, sadly, undertake and that was to say goodbye to an old faithful friend—'Cocky', a robin, who had been the first thing Oscar had seen every morning when collecting the milk from the doorstep. Cocky always gave Oscar a nod of his head, after which he enjoyed his breakfast of worms that Oscar had collected the night before, followed by a drink of warm milk, lovingly heated to just the right temperature by Anita, that Oscar had now taken over supplying.

He wasn't sure whether the new owners would be interested enough to carry on with this tradition, as they were younger than himself and Anita, but nevertheless he had made it a matter of concern when they had viewed the house, seeming amused, but ready to comply, thought Oscar gratefully.

Quickly swallowing his last cup of coffee in his old home, Oscar opened the door, first, to two of his sons and their wives, then finally to the house removers—a local family company who had moved himself and Anita into this home all those years ago, shortly after their exquisite marriage ceremony.

There were tears and laughter during the course of that morning and afternoon, until they all collapsed into hastily placed furniture, later in the evening following a fish and chip supper in Oscar's new home. After eventually finding where the coffee, tea and sugar had been put into cupboards, in the kitchen, two of Oscar's daughter-in-law offered to make a tray of drinks, much appreciated by the group of helpers, who wanted to see Oscar settled into his new home.

It was gone midnight before an exhausted Oscar waved goodbye to his family and friends, tumbling into his old comfortable bed, revamped by the girls. Waking much later than usual, the following morning, it took a while before he realised where he was, but, by lying quietly for a few moments, yesterday's house move came flooding back into his mind, with it, thoughts of how much Anita would have welcomed a modern home like this, for the next phase of their lives together.

With a gentle sigh, Oscar clambered out of bed, made his way into the kitchen half expecting to see his wife already slicing fruit to add to the porridge she would be stirring, on her sparkling new cooker, that he had promised her for years, but somehow had not got around to purchasing it for her, yet hadn't received a word of complaint. The pair of them had just merged together so well, like a hand-stitched pair of ballet shoes, supportive and reliable.

Oscar checked the mail to see if there was anything he should be forwarding to the previous residents, whose new address he had securely written in his address book, although he had learnt to use his new phone and was contemplating buying a laptop, he knew he should learn to insert names and addresses too.

'Oh dear,' he sighed, I was never any good with the latest gadgetry, with modern technology being top of the list. 'What would Anita say about his fumbling attempts to get to grips—with even the language, used in the instructions he had been given, with the purchase of the phone that both Adrian and Derek had recommended he should buy as his first usage of a modern piece of 'gadgetry', to encourage an easier way to keep in touch with the family especially those overseas, as with Michael, Patrica and the grandchildren?'

Thankfully, he had mastered that exchange fairly well, enjoying the familiarity of seeing their well-loved faces and hearing them talk, at the same time.

With breakfast over and washing up finished, Oscar showered, dressing hastily in old comfortable clothes and wandered into his new garden. Not as large as his previous one, it would be easier to keep tidy. The young couple living here before had obviously enjoyed their garden, as they had transformed a small piece of land into a little haven of luxury. The patio was south-facing with well-kept borders of small but rambling plants, giving it the appearance of a spacious rockery, with York stone, easily laid slabs, between the plants.

The rest of the garden was mainly lawn, some of it being camomile, which gave off a delicious perfume when trodden on. One fairly large tree—a cherry dominated a central position in the lawn, with spindly overgrown side branches, that Oscar thought would be his first task tomorrow, otherwise all was neat and tidy. A small bird was holding forth on one of the branches and Oscar could almost swear that it was 'Cocky', his special friend that he sadly had to leave behind. But 'no' he thought, how could it be, his old home was many miles away?

Yet, the thought persisted, causing him to go back indoors to heat, to a lukewarm temperature, some milk, before returning to the garden, to offer the saucer to the small, but radiant, bird in the cherry tree. To his utter astonishment, the small bird inclined his head, flying down, to perch alongside Oscar, on the patio, stretching his tiny neck towards the milk, drinking appreciatively.

'Cocky!' exclaimed Oscar ecstatically. 'I didn't think I would ever see you again. You clever bird, however, did you find me?' The robin almost smiled, continuing to drink his milk, before flying back to his perch in the cherry tree.

After a light snack, for lunch, Oscar had a planned appointment with a furniture store in the heart of Soho, a favourite for him and Anita, when browsing happily for more modern contemporary furniture a few years ago, but inevitably had not gotten around to buying, although they had agreed on several pieces that they liked. Now, Oscar was determined to improve on those outings, actually intending to purchase some for his new home.

Would the children be impressed, that he had gone ahead, without consulting them? Or would they be slightly miffed that he hadn't asked their advice first? He would soon find out when they paid him a visit and saw his acquisitions. He was fortunate enough to have released a reasonable amount of capital, by downsizing, thereby having some extra cash to use if any of his young protégées, many in London for the first time, were getting lower salaries than expected, needed a little help, he would be pleased to supply their needs.

All his kith and kin had been well provided for, keeping him and his wife poor in the beginning, until their business had reached its full potential and they were established. Now, with a handsome amount in the bank, he was ready for any eventuality.

Pausing to gaze in the double-fronted shop window, his roaming eye was drawn to a rather handsome right-handed chaise lounge in velvet teal—a must in Oscar's eyes. The colour was perfect with his proposed colour scheme for the lounge and he remembered how he had admired it before, whilst he and Anita were having the occasional day out, enjoying a leisurely lunch, in their favourite eating house. Maybe another two-seater teal settee would complete the ensemble, with the floor-length curtains already hanging in a pastel shade of cream. A solid light oak coffee table, standing on a matching rug between the two pieces of furniture, wouldn't look out of place. Anita, he knew, would plump for cushions, so he would consider those too.

Determined to carry through these purchases this time, Oscar pushed open the heavy door to be greeted by a loud clanging bell. A middle-aged sales assistant approached, enquiring how he could help. Oscar made his way directly to the chaise lounge, perching himself gingerly on the edge, with the assistant urging him to try it to its full advantage. With his feet firmly planted on the protective plastic footrest, Oscar was instantly converted, agreeing on the price, then discussing his other thoughts for his spacious lounge in the flat. Which grandchild would claim it first, he wondered?

The salesman assistant was, of course, eager for a sale, suggesting some floor lighting for maximum effect to show off the chaise lounge at night which, in the daylight, Oscar was duly informed, would shimmer, giving a pleasant effect also. He wasn't too impressed with the sales pattern, his eyes, this time, alighting on a wider television than he had at the time, and, with more time to watch rugby matches despite his failing eyesight, he decided to indulge in that as well.

Toting up how much he had just spent, for his own pleasure, he was rather alarmed knowing though that his sons had been persuading him to do this for years, but he was always too busy. Anita hadn't seemed too bothered either, being busy herself looking after the youngsters and him, in the shop, whenever time allowed.

Arranging a delivery time, Oscar arrived home, but for the first time was a little lost. How to spend the evening, after gathering worms, for Cocky in the morning. Then it occurred to him that it had been some time since he had contacted the family of Trevor, the brilliant young tap dancer, who had a distinguished career predicted for him, but who had so sadly been killed in a tragic motorway accident.

Already, having offered the handcrafted tap shoes, to the family, as a remembrance gift of Trevor and receiving no reply, he had put them to one side, to remind himself to write again. Taking them out of the plain paper bag, Oscar gently cradled them in his roughened hands, then, sitting at his desk penned another letter to the family advising them of his move and new address, once more offering to donate the tap shoes to them, for Trevor's sake. Finding the correct address, Oscar folded the letter, placing it securely in the envelope for posting the next day, before finally entering their address onto his new phone.

After a week, during which time Oscar had taken delivery of his extravagant purchases, rearranging the room tastefully, a letter arrived from Trevor's family, in reply to his generous gesture of giving them the tap shoes, rather stunning him with their polite refusal of accepting the tap shoes, but thanking him for the offer. Oscar could hardly believe what he was reading, but never—the—less needed to know the reason for the refusal.

Reading between the lines it seemed that neither of his parents wanted him to go down the dance route, trying hard to dissuade him for two years before he finally made his move to London, to seek advice. Unknown to his parents Trevor had been attending dance classes in another town for two years, encouraged by his gymnastic mistress at school, who had recognised Trevor's aptitude for training regimes, his clear, concise, fluid and rhythmic movements and long supple legs.

He had so impressed her that she had used her influence at a dance academy, to give Trevor the opportunity to prove himself, in exchange for free tuition, during which time she had taken it upon herself to explain to his parents how progressive they considered Trevor to be, in the ability to dance. This had so appalled his Father that he had forbidden Trevor to attend the academy in the future.

Since then Trevor had completed his schooling, obtaining excellent grades in his exams that would take him on to college and university, but all Trevor wanted to do was dance and would, at every possible opportunity. In the end, opposition from his parents forced him to consider taking his chances in London—just one of the many hopefuls that Anita had nurtured.

Finally, Oscar had read that Sir Reginald Braithwaite, his two other sons and his brother had all been in merchant banking, having relished high hopes that Trevor would eventually follow the family tradition, becoming a merchant banker. His wife had strongly supported her husband, using all her powers of persuasion and love too for her son, to discourage Trevor from following a chancy career on the stage.

These powers to stop a young person from following such a dream caused Oscar to become speechless with rage, having just encountered such an outrage. Never in his fifty years working closely with dancers from all walks of life had he ever come across an incident such as this. What now? He would offer an apology for causing them any more pain than they had already been through, then allow the matter to drop. He would take possession of the treasured pair of tap shoes.

Finding some quite thick rope, Oscar plaited two strands together, then, pairing the tap shoes to hang vertically, tied the plaited rope onto the heels, without needing to spoil the style by inserting any anchorage for the rope, having given them a good clean and polish, bringing them back to their original colour.

Finding a white screw head already in place, in a prominent position in the bay window, Oscar hung the pair, where the slight breeze, from the top fanlight, caught the swinging shoes making a clacking noise as they joggled each other. Taking pride of place, when Oscar sat on the window seat, he sprawled, blissfully watching them, wondering whether, in the future, a new owner might be found for them.

The days and the weeks passed swiftly enough, with the boys visiting whenever they could, exclaiming thoughtfully about Oscar's choice of furniture, in the lounge. As predicted it was Dillon—the young scamp of the family and one of Oscar's great-grandchildren, who rushed headlong towards the chaise lounge, lying flat out, in the comfort of youth, lovingly stroking the plush velvet fabric, declaring it was the nicest settee he had ever seen. His daughters-in-law, although surprised, applauded his choice, sitting themselves carefully on the two-seater settee. Other chairs—not yet altered or changed, were available for the rest of the family to use.

Oscar's thoughts on writing his memoirs remained with him, but he understood he would need to buy a computer or laptop, which he knew nothing at all about, obviously needing instruction. He decided to contact the local council to see what was available, applying for training courses in his area.

During his enquiries regarding teaching how to operate a computer, from limited technology understanding, he also discovered a local author would be holding classes, very soon, on, of all things—writing an autobiography, just what he was looking for. It was a long shot, but Oscar applied for both the computer learning and the autobiographer's course from whom he hoped to draw on some salient points to put him on the right road to writing his memoirs.

In the meantime, Oscar kept in close contact with his up-and-coming young starlets and those with a more professional role, having already achieved star status. He missed their frequent visits to 'A Dancer's Dream', the careful measurements of individual feet whenever a new pair of ballet shoes, slippers or tap shoes were required, often at six to eight weekly intervals, the choosing of materials and the hours spent at his bench diligently applying his skills to achieve a first-rate shoe worthy of his professional dancers.

The theatre managers knew him as a valued and dearly loved, old friend, so there was always a warm welcome, for him, at the theatres when he decided to pay them a visit and enjoy the shows that he had so rarely seen. Seating for him and any friends he would like to bring along was always assured, with complimentary tickets given in respect of Oscar's services rendered for fifty years, many times over and above the call of duty.

Overawed, Oscar was taking many a delivery of flowers and cards, from his devoted clients, in appreciation of his dedicated care and attention given to them, during the years that he and his wife were in business. Often, tears would threaten as he recalled the names and faces of those he knew well, especially Trevor. His other main concern for his past customers centred around—where they obtained their new ballet and tap shoes from.

He knew there were several good manufacturing and marketing companies offering free personal measurement and fitting for every new pair of ballet or tap shoes bought from any of their outlet shops, with generous discounts given for those who were forced, by the closure of their retiring cobbler's, to seek a future supplier. Oscar investigated a few known ones that he had dealings with in the past, mainly purchasing fabrics or laces, finding them honest with their clients, upholding the promises they had made to them.

This was thankfully verified by many of his clients, who said though, they would return to him in an instant if he was still in business, but realising they couldn't turn the clock back had found a manufacturer with the closest of skills that Oscar had displayed. If in doubt, though, Oscar had made it clear, now his address had been circulated, that any time someone had a query regarding any shoe, purchased from him or not, he would always be available to answer questions. This was highly appreciated with one or two younger ballerinas taking up the offer, pleasing Oscar and the youngsters that the questions were answered satisfactorily.

The new television was a great success, with Oscar indulging himself in watching rugby on a Saturday afternoon. When the grandchildren visited, they were delighted that grandad had invested in a modern TV set that they approved of.

In the warmth of late spring and early summer Oscar would invite his friends, from the dancing world to his home, where, with a small group of people, he would cook supper on a barbecue built into the surrounding wall of the patio. He was settling into his new home well, having kept the bedrooms and kitchen much as they were, seeing they were his colour choice anyway and the beds and existing furniture fitting in together. The only thing to spoil his contentment was the fact that, even now, he was still missing his darling wife, Anita.

One sunny afternoon, when he had opened the windows in the lounge, to catch every breath he could, of a cooling breeze, Oscar noticed a young man of about fifteen gazing into the lounge, appearing to have his eyes fixed on the tap shoes swinging gently in the breeze, creating the same crackling noise he heard whenever he opened a lounge window. Realising that he had seen this young man on other occasions, but had not taken a great deal of notice, probably thinking that the boy knew someone who had once lived in the flat.

Oscar gave him a friendly wave, to which the boy, embarrassed, moved his fingers lightly, walking away from the flat, with, Oscar noticed, an easy swinging stride. Maybe, if he passed this way again, thought Oscar, he would invite him in for a drink of lemonade, asking him why he was so interested in the tap shoes. Perhaps he was interested in tap dancing himself or one of his friends could be? Forgetting the incident Oscar left the flat to meet a friend for lunch, catching up together on recent events, as they hadn't met since Oscar's splendid retirement party. The afternoon passed pleasantly for them both, agreeing afterwards to arrange another lunch together.

Nearing the flat, looking forward to a cup of tea, Oscar was surprised to see 'the boy' standing once more, peering in through his lounge window. Turning sharply 'the boy' began to walk swiftly away, but, intrigued, Oscar called him back, in an inviting way, to come inside and have a glass of lemonade. 'The boy' stopped, turned around and began walking back to Oscar, with a slight look of unease on his face. Oscar hastened to reassure him, chatting in a friendly way as he opened the front door, asking 'the boy's' name and where he lived. Relaxing a little 'the boy' accepted the lemonade glass that Oscar offered him, with a smile.

Opening up now Oscar found out that his name was Bradley and he lived not too far away and it was as he was passing Oscar's window, to meet a friend, that he saw the tap shoes. Being interested in dance, especially tap, he was keen to know to whom the shoes belonged. Did they belong to Oscar's grandson, he asked, with tongue in cheek.

"No," answered Oscar with a sad shake of his head. "They were designed and tailored by me for a brilliant tap dancer with a brilliant future predicted ahead for him, but tragically he was fatally injured in a head-on motorway accident, roughly one year ago now. His parents had tried to discourage him from following a dancing career, so he finished his education, after which he ran away to London. I offered them the shoes as a remembrance for them, but unfortunately, they refused the offer, so I have taken possession of them, hence that is why they are hanging where they are, so that I can enjoy them whenever I relax here."

Oscar stopped speaking to take a look at Bradley, surprised to see a pale-faced young man staring at him in amazement, then spluttering—

"You can't be Oscar Harrison, can you?"

"Why, yes, I am," replied Oscar, utterly taken aback by the boy's question. "Did you know who I was talking about when I told you about Trevor? Did you by any chance know Trevor or his family, in which case I'm sorry if I've caused you any distress."

"There's no need to be sorry," replied Bradley. "In fact, you deserve to know the whole story and I'm the one to apologise for not telling you who l was before you saw me loitering outside your window, several times now. You see, the first time I saw you I thought—from Trevor's description of you that you were the Oscar Harrison that he always spoke so very highly of—your skilful handcrafting of all the beautiful shoes—be they for ballet or tap, that you made so individually.

"He loved you very much Mr Harrison, because you see, Trevor was my Father, telling me much about you, the shop and the love and care you and your wife showed them, during the ups and downs of their careers. I was my parent's second son, the first being Oliver Braithwaite—the well-known opera singer, who I'm sure you must have heard of."

Now it was Oscar's turn to be stupefied, initially dumbfounded, as he stared once again at the young man sitting on the teal settee, with an announcement that caused his pulse to race. What an amazing turn-up for the books, knowing that Trevor's parents lived in the south of England, now here was Trevor's son, on his very doorstep in London! There were many questions Oscar wanted to ask, but before he began, he offered Bradley another glass of lemonade. Sitting comfortably again, Oscar felt he couldn't let the boy leave without finding out a little about him. Turning to Bradley—he asked, in a slightly husky voice:

"Bradley, you said you didn't live very far away. Does that mean you live here in London with your mother? And, by the way, I have heard of Oliver Braithwaite—a brilliant opera singer, if I may say so."

"I'll explain," said Bradley. "Shortly after arriving in London, my father shared a small flat with another young hopeful on the tap dancing scene. They both continued their training under the auspicious eye of musical directors, who would use the tap dancing skills of balance and co-ordination, as background dancers in shows, on TV or, if specialising in a particular form of tap dance, such as Irish dancing, some would freelance until 'discovered' for their talent and employed. Trevor, my father, was very interested in Irish dancing, which is why he asked you to construct this special brand of tap shoes, so I knew, as soon as I saw them that they were 'special'."

"What a discovery you made when you saw the tap shoes hanging in my bay window," responded Oscar, to Bradley's explanation. "It must have seemed like a small miracle and then to find out it was me, Trevor's old cobbler, who lived in the flat. What a surprise! Tell me, Bradley—did your father marry a dancer and, if so, how did your grandparents respond? Stop me if I'm being a prying old man, but do you see them at all and do they now understand your interest in tap dancing? I felt so sad for them when they refused to have the tap shoes as a remembrance of their son. By the way please call me Oscar. Mr Harrison seems so very formal and your father and I were on first-name terms for a number of years," continued Oscar.

"Thank you, Mr Harrison—I mean Oscar," smiled Bradley. "I would like that and please don't be concerned at asking me questions—I don't mind at all. It's so good to talk to someone who knew my father as well as you did. No, my father didn't marry a dancer. My mother was the choreographer of a show that he had been cast to perform in as a background dancer. She was slightly older than he was, so, having had some dance experience, immediately recognised his full potential, so took him on for further individual training.

"Having met on several occasions, both professionally and socially, they fell in love, marrying two years later. Oliver was born a year later, growing up in the world of dance, but, to their surprise had developed a magnificent singing voice, the exercises of his choral rehearsing, being much preferred to the role of dance. Casted for solo singing, he soon became known as a future lead tenor in opera, of which you probably know the rest, Oscar."

"But what about your grandparents?" persisted Oscar. "Also, are you being taught in a prestigious dance school to honour your father and further your love of dance—particularly tap?"

Bradley looked sad and replied to Oscar's question by answering, "Unfortunately my grandparents never forgave my father for running away and not following the family tradition of merchant banking. They knew of his marriage, but chose not to attend, sending instead a chintzy piece of porcelain as a wedding gift. It nearly broke my father's heart, but he learnt to forgive, praying that there would be a day of reconciliation, which never came and then his death in that awful motorway accident."

Bradley's face crumpled for a moment, as he rubbed his knuckles across his eyes before going on with the tragic tale. "We received a letter of sympathy, nothing more and no suggestion of a visit to us, nor an invitation to visit them.

My mother couldn't afford to pay the rent on the flat anymore, as, by this time I was well into my education, showing a great deal of empathy towards taking up tap dancing, as my father had done, but she was unable to afford dancing lessons. In the end, we had to give up the flat, moving in with my mother's sister and her husband."

"Stop," cried Oscar. "I had no idea all this was going on. If I'd known this before, I might have been able to do something to help. May I come and speak to your mother, please? I have just sold the family home to move into this flat for my retirement. My dear wife Anita died three years ago, so I'm living here all on my own, he said, as an idea was forming in his head."

Bradley looked strangely at Oscar as he said. "Please, Oscar, don't think I came here with any thoughts in my mind of asking for help, because I really haven't. It was the beautiful tap shoes that attracted me, in the first place and then to realise it was your home, was too big an opportunity to miss. I'm sorry if I've misled you and intruded on your retirement."

Bradley was obviously upset, getting up and moving away from the settee towards the front door, intending, whilst Oscar was deep in thought, to quietly let himself out of the flat and go home. The movement woke Oscar up from his reverie, to find Bradley about to leave the flat.

"Please don't leave just yet," pleaded Oscar with a lump in his throat. "Bradley, what shoe size are you? If you are the same size as your father, I would very much like you to have his new tap shoes that you can see hanging here, but only if you promise me, you'll allow me to send you to study at the most prestigious tap dancing school in London. You could continue your school work by day, whilst you attend dance training in the evening. Would that be too much for you, with homework as well?"

"Oh Oscar," gasped Bradley with a huge grin on his face—which was so much like his father's. "Thank you so much for the offer, but I don't think I can accept. It's most generous of you, but my mother would not allow it-she's determined not to be a burden on anybody. She's saving to be able to move us to a council property, so we don't have to rely on my aunt and uncle, although they say we can stay for as long as we like. You'd like them, Oscar—they are generous, like you and kind."

"I'm sure I shall," answered Oscar. "They have been very kind to you and your mother. If you would let me, I'd like to walk home with you to get better acquainted with the family. I have a proposal for your mother. Can you tell me her name?"

Bradley smiled with affection in his eyes, telling Oscar that her name was Annette and his aunt and uncle's names were Simone and Rupert. No, he said, he didn't mind Oscar walking home with him. He knew his mother would like to meet him, to thank him for his encouragement and thoughtfulness towards her husband.

Quite suddenly there was a clicking noise coming from the pair of tap shoes, causing Oscar and Bradley to glance at the swinging pair. Thinking there might be a breeze, Oscar got up to shut the window, but to his surprise, there wasn't a hint of wind to be felt. Looking at the tap shoes again, he saw they were swinging even more vigorously, appearing to have a will of their own. What was happening, as astonishingly the shoes began a rhythmic dance sequence, at the end of their rope.

Was there some sort of magic power causing the tap shoes to dance? This out of the known world experience was something that neither Oscar or Bradley had encountered before and to be completely honest, was a little bit scary. The two stood and stared at each other, absolutely amazed, wondering what to do. Should they take the shoes down and see what happens or leave things as they are, preparing to believe it was indeed a breeze? This sort of thing doesn't happen, in real life, reasoned Oscar, trying to think coherently and not dramatize the situation.

As the pair watched the shoes perform their magic, they were enchanted, having a strong conviction that the shoes wanted to be released from the rope that held them anchored in Oscar's bay window. Bradley nodded in agreement, moving forward to untie the knotted link in the rope chain, then stood back to see what would happen now. With a final swing, the tap shoes detached themselves from the rope, landing, in perfect control, on the lounge floor carpet.

Then began a thrilling display of spectacular Irish tap dancing in complete unison with each other. Oscar and Bradley thundered an applause. The next moment an even more extraordinary event occurred—the tap shoes suddenly appeared on Bradley's feet, beginning their dance sequence all over again, this time with Bradley having no option but to allow the shoes to take him where they will. A laughing Bradley didn't have a choice in the matter, although thoroughly enjoying the experience. Steps he didn't know he could execute just rolled from his feet and the Irish chuckle of sheer joy escaped his lips.

Around and around the lounge and into the kitchen, the tap shoes took Bradley, confirming in him the career he would dearly love to follow. A breathless Bradley collapsed laughing, onto the chaise lounge, but the shoes had other ideas, dragging him to his feet, this time employing a more sedate dance, to wind up the show. They then released Bradley, positioning themselves together in front of the fireplace.

Dazed by what they had just witnessed, Oscar and Bradley wondered what the next step was to be. The shoes obviously had plans for Bradley's future, intending to teach the young man all they themselves knew—a magic spell bestowed on them by a clandestine presence, hidden by its powerful anonymity.

By now, the afternoon was progressing into evening and Bradley felt he should be making his way home. Oscar then reminded Bradley of his promise to allow him to accompany him home to meet the family or arrange another day if it was now too late for any further discussion. Bradley was happy to respect Oscar's request, so the pair left the flat together, leaving the tap shoes in front of the fireplace, from where Bradley could collect them, after having spoken to Annette regarding her housing situation and a plan he had in mind for Bradley's future.

It was a pleasant late afternoon and not a long walk to Bradley's home, where they found Annette beavering away to cook the evening meal for the family. As Oscar and Bradley walked into the kitchen, Annette stopped what she was doing to welcome her son home, asking him if he had enjoyed his afternoon with his friend, to which Bradley replied that 'yes' he had.

Annette turned courteously to Oscar, asking Bradley who his friend was. When introduced to Annette as Oscar Harrison, he took her small petite hand in his gnarled ones, saying it was an honour to meet her. Hesitating only slightly, Annette offered Oscar a chair, obviously not too sure who he was, but prepared to make him welcome for Bradley's sake. It was now getting late and Oscar didn't want to put her into a position where she would feel compelled to ask him to stay for dinner, so he excused himself, asking her if he could meet with her again, at a more convenient time for her.

Annette willingly agreed, looking a little puzzled, suggesting a day next week that would suit Oscar very well. He then said goodbye to Bradley, offering him to visit anytime. Turning once more to Annette, smilingly wished her a good evening, followed by saying that Bradley would fully explain their association, which he said, was entirely platonic.

Waving his hand in a final salute, Oscar walked slowly home, going over, in his mind, the events of the afternoon and what the future could hold for Bradley. Arriving home and opening his front door, Oscar saw the pair of deep purple tap shoes, with black frontage, were still together in front of the fireplace. They didn't appear to have moved, let alone danced. Perhaps they were waiting for Bradley?

The few days leading up to the meeting with Annette seemed to be the longest of Oscar's life, so important was it to explain his ideas to Bradley's mother, to be able to set things in motion before the beginning of the new term and Oscar was not the most patient of men. Once he had an idea, as with designing dance shoes, he needed to act on it swiftly to reap the greatest benefit. He spent days meeting with some of his dancing friends when they had free time between rehearsals and the nightly performance. The conversation, he found, was stimulating, revolving around theatre gossip, which didn't interest Oscar very much, but who had been casted in another ballet, for example, was.

Finally, the suggested day to meet Annette showed on Oscar's calendar and as he was dressing himself in casual, but well-cut clothes, he actually found himself whistling a popular melody. It was a weekday, so probably Bradley would be at school.

Equally possible, Simone and Rupert, whom he hadn't met yet, would both be working. Bradley had said that Rupert was a salesman in a famous London bookstore and Simone was a community midwife, many times working over her hours when delivery was expected. Annette was therefore greatly appreciated, by offering to undertake being cook and cleaner in their home—a means by which she thanked her sister and brother-in-law for their hospitality, by taking herself and Bradley into their home, when unable to afford the rent since Trevor died.

Enjoying the afternoon stroll towards Bradley's home, Oscar had worked out a pretty convincing, acceptable plan for her and Bradley's future, that he hoped would pave the way to a beautiful, lasting friendship. On reaching her and Bradley's home, at the arranged time, Oscar found the kitchen door closed, but with an older-style car parked outside the front gate.

Annette obviously had a visitor that he was loath to interrupt, so, turning around he made to retrace his tracks towards his own home, intending to make another date and time the next time he saw Bradley, which he was sure wouldn't be long, when a sharp tap on her front room window, alerted him to look around.

Annette was waving at him through the window, beckoning for him to come to the front door, which she opened at his light tap on the door.

A much younger man was standing directly behind her, with his right arm gently resting on her shoulders. They looked comfortable together, which gave Oscar a slight flutter in his stomach. Annette was still a very attractive woman, with a lithe, ballet dancer's body, even though she had retired from her dancing and, then later, her choreography role in the theatre.

There was no reason at all why she shouldn't have her own company of friends, especially from within the dancing fraternity, as Oscar himself had found out, were the most friendly of people, who worked hard and played equally hard. It was good to know she had friends to support her, since she had lost her husband and her challenging attempt to give Bradley a good life.

"Please don't go away Oscar, I've been looking forward to your visit since we last met when Bradley introduced you," said Annette, holding out her hand for Oscar to shake.

"I must admit I was really surprised when Bradley called you Oscar Harrison, a name I'd heard so many times before, in admiration of your skills and the kindness we always received from you and your wife, Anita. I remember her well and I'm so sorry for your loss. Please come in and sit down, but before you do, let me introduce you to Oliver Braithwaite—Bradley's older brother. You may have heard the name in connection with the operas that he performs in, here and overseas." Annette laughed, turning towards her son, explaining how he had deserted the world of dance, to become professional in the world of music.

"I'm delighted to meet you, Mr Braithwaite," returned Oscar, who had a great admiration for Bradley's older brother. "I've seen you perform on numerous occasions, thoroughly enjoying the operas and the characters you play. Let me congratulate you on your success."

"Thank you very much, Oscar," replied Oliver. "Will you please though call me Oliver and I'm delighted to meet you too, to be able to say thank you, as well, for all you've given of your time and energy, to ensure success on the dance stage, for my father. Your work was so vital to everybody."

"Come on, you two," chuckled Annette, as she emerged from the kitchen with a tray of what looked like homemade lemonade, much sought after on a warm summer afternoon. "Enough of this mutual admiration society. Come through to the lounge and have a cool drink. Bradley will be home from school fairly soon and Simone and Rupert will join us for supper. You will stay, Oscar, won't you?" Annette asked him, fully expecting an acceptance, which she duly received.

Sitting comfortably in Simone and Rupert's lounge the conversation flowed easily, in the meantime of which, Bradley came in from school, greeting both his brother and Oscar warmly. Annette, by this time, was in the kitchen preparing the evening meal, as Bradley went to give her a hug, announcing that he had quite a lot of homework that evening.

"Before you disappear Bradley and if your mother could give us five minutes, I would like to talk to you all," asked Oscar with pleasure in his voice.

Bradley walked through into the kitchen and asked Annette if she could come into the lounge for a few moments, as Oscar had something to say. Once they were all seated again Oscar outlined his proposal, which was, if Annette was agreeable, to allow him to pay for and send Bradley to a prestigious tap dancing school, in London, that he knew the proprietor would be more than willing to train Bradley for a career on the London stage, especially, Oscar said, as his friend knew about and respected Trevor very much.

Oscar also went on to say that the new tap shoes he had designed and handcrafted, on Trevor's instructions, he would like to give them to Bradley, to get him started. Looking quickly at Annette, Oscar saw a puzzled expression on her face, as she thought over what had just been said, but Oscar hadn't finished yet! He explained the situation regarding the sale of his family home, with the purchase of the flat, that would suit him very well, as he was still in walking distance of the theatres where many of his clients worked, sometimes meeting them for a cup of coffee when they had a break between rehearsals and showtime.

His proposal for Annette was to help her pay for the rental of a council house, if that was still her intention. He heard a gasp from Bradley and a half sob from Annette. With a smile on his face, Oscar asked her if she would like to think it over, maybe discuss it with Oliver, to which she nodded. Bradley couldn't help himself, as if all was settled, throwing himself into Oscar's arms, then pulling himself up short, he stared at his mother, almost pleading for acceptance.

It was at that moment that Rupert and Simone came in together. Simone had been able to finish work earlier than expected, as all her expectant mothers were managing well, at the moment, and, unless there was an emergency, she was free for the evening, having met with Rupert for a coffee before coming home. Annette got up to greet them, as did Oliver.

Bradley said, 'hello' and then excused himself to start on his homework. Oscar stood as Annette introduced him to her sister and brother-in-law, excusing herself to finish the evening meal. Once more Oscar was invited to stay, this time accepting gratefully. He decided to leave the invitations to Annette for another day, when she would have had a chance to talk to Oliver.

The evening was spent companionably, all enjoying Annette's meal, with Oscar more than interested in hearing more from Oliver, but he was a humble man, not revelling in his own success, so would quickly turn the conversation away from himself. Rupert and Simone were more talkative, giving the dinner guests amusing anecdotes from their daily experiences at work. Altogether, a pleasant evening was spent by everyone.

Leaving at a respectable time Oscar said goodbye to his new acquaintances, thanked Annette for a delightful meal and evening, asking whether he could contact her again in a few days, to hear her answers to his proposals, to which she shook his hand warmly, saying she would talk with Oliver tomorrow, as he was staying for a few days of relaxation, at Rupert and Simone's invitation, together with some well-received tickets to a new opera he was starring in, as principal tenor, with good revues from the local press. Turning to Bradley, Oscar grinned at his expectant acceptance from his mother.

For the next couple of days, Oscar was in touch with his four sons to advise them of what he had offered Bradley and his mother, Annette. They all knew of his close association with his 'specials,' as he called them and his interest in them still, now that he had retired. Oscar had told them, sadly, of the loss of Trevor, a remarkable young man in the world of tap dancing and how his offer to have the new tap shoes sent to his parents was refused. He had also told them of his unexpected meeting with Bradley, to find out, to his delight, that Trevor was, in fact, his father.

Now, Oscar needed to explain the current situation of Bradley's mother having to move in with her sister after Trevor's demise, being then, unable to afford the best training for Bradley, longing to follow in his father's footsteps and become a tap dancer of some repute.

Therefore, Oscar went on to say how, after the sale of the family home and the purchase of the flat, there was enough money in the bank to provide excellent training for Bradley and a helping hand with the rental of a small modern council house for Annette, allowing her to move out of her sister's home, to one of her own. He hastened to add that the boys and their families would still be well cared for, as he had set up trust funds to allow them all a comfortable life after he was no longer around.

Flushed by his son's expressions of horror at the thought of their father not always being there and the love they expressed, nearly reduced Oscar to tears, of their trust in him always working for their's and other's good. As to his intentions, they said how proud of him they were, in his desire to help both Bradley and Annette. They felt he had every right to spend his money, also gifts, in any way he pleased, thanking him for his assurance of their future, but reminding him, at the moment, they were all secure in their present posts, hoping to remain that way for many more years to come—what a confirmation for Oscar!

His friend Jonathan Tate, the dancing school proprietor and skilled trainer in all styles of tap dancing, including Irish, would be delighted to take on Trevor's son, in his London studio.

Some evenings Bradley would visit Oscar, on his way home from school, giving Oscar an update on how he felt the situation, on Oscar's proposals, were progressing. Annette had already talked to Oliver, who, although feeling that he himself should make a similar offer, felt that Oscar was a trustworthy and reliable person, who had the respect of many influential people in the dancing world. His opinion was that Oscar wanted to compensate the family, in some way, for Trevor's death and how much his father would have wanted his son to succeed, also to somehow try to make up to Annette, Oliver and Bradley for the Braithwaite's hurtful behaviour, without being too judgemental.

Trevor had been surprised, but delighted with Oliver's success in the world of opera, supporting him every step of the way, so equally his desire was to see his second son successful in whatever profession he chose. To have him want to tap dance, as he had, would have brought tears of joy to his eyes, now Oscar was giving him that chance.

The purple tap shoes, now silent near the fireplace became alert and active whenever Bradley was in Oscar's home, either dancing together as a duet or on Bradley's feet, where they would perform the most intricate of dances. Bradley and Oscar roared with laughter at their antics and sometimes, naughtiness when they would pretend to hide when you could see them shaking, soundless, but with obvious uncontrolled laughter. It was a happy time, with Bradley too, awaiting his mother's decision.

One evening, Bradley visited Oscar with a huge smile on his face. Annette had talked, long and hard with him, the night before, saying that she had given Oscar's plans a lot of thought and had decided, for all concerned, that she would gratefully accept these gifts, from Oscar. She was anxious, said Bradley, to know how far away the dancing studio was, wanting to be able to visit her son and for him to come to her or meet her halfway when training became intense with limited time allowed.

Oscar was overjoyed, determined to talk to and thank Annette as soon as possible. To walk home with Bradley, that evening, seemed like the appropriate time, so after a final cooling drink, Oscar and Bradley walked happily together, to his home, to thank Annette for allowing Oscar's plans for Bradley and his mother, to go ahead. Annette must have been expecting them, as she had mugs and a plate of sandwiches laid out on the lounge coffee table.

Once they had their preferred drinks in front of them, the three chatted together, getting to know one another. Oscar expressed his gratitude to Annette for agreeing to the proposed plans, to which she was equally as grateful for the offer which would give Bradley the career he had dreamed of and now, thanks to Oscar, the best of training to start in September at 'Tate's dance studio.' Oscar explained where it was situated in a pretty part of London, off a main thoroughfare.

Easy to walk to, Oscar assured her, providing a council house was available nearby and, at half-term and summer holidays, Bradley could come home. He also told her that she was welcome at his home anytime and Bradley would show her where it was. Perhaps, he suggested she could walk down with Bradley, when he collected Trevor's tap shoes, then, maybe, he said, she could be in for a surprise—Bradley looked at Oscar and winked.

Two days later, Annette met Bradley after school to walk, with him, to Oscar's home, where the tap shoes seemed to be patiently waiting! Opening the front door, welcoming them both inside, with a refreshing glass of lemonade waiting, Oscar was pleased to see Annette looking around, with pleasure, at his newly furnished home. She particularly liked the chaise lounge, congratulating him on his colour choice.

Oscar smiled, indicating that she sat comfortably on the settee, with Bradley perched alongside. Placing the jug of lemonade and glasses on the coffee table, they were all surprised by a clicking sound coming from the fireplace.

Immediately, Oscar and Bradley smiled at each other, waiting to see what the tap shoes would do next.

Annette's face was full of bewilderment, as she caught the secret smile, then changed to almost fear tinged with amazement, as the mischievous tap shoes danced their way across the lounge, just clipping Annette's shoes, as she screamed, pulling her feet off the ground to avoid contact with them, suddenly realising she now recognised them as being the same ones that Trevor had ordered from Oscar, before his accident in the motorway horror.

But what on earth was happening now? How could dance shoes move on their own accord, unless they had batteries attached, but she hadn't seen either Oscar or Bradley move from their seats to begin operating them.? Annette sat and stared at Oscar and Bradley, as if they were aliens, wondering how they were going to explain this away, when the shoes decided it was time for Bradley to dance.

Without opposition, they were on his feet in an instant, heaving Bradley to his feet, dancing a merry dance in front of Annette, who was, by now, frankly terrified. Seating himself next to her, in the space Bradley had been occupying, Oscar slipped an arm around her now quaking shoulders, not being able to explain anything. Annette nestled against him gradually calming, as she watched her equally entranced son, perform a sequence that she had seen her husband Trevor dance on stage.

It was a tricky combination of routine tap dancing steps, tapped very quickly and methodically for maximum effect, culminating in a magnificent sweep of the lounge, before stopping, with a breathless Bradley, directly in front of Annette once more, who could not stop herself, but applauded loudly. Releasing Bradley, who plumped down on the chaise lounge, Annette regained her courage to ask Oscar what had happened.

All Oscar could say was that an unknown presence, carefully disguised as a client, had entered his workshop one day, interested in holding the tap shoes that Oscar had sadly put to one side after Trevor's death. He had attempted to restrain the person, to prevent the shoes from leaving his premises, when he/she ran from the shop, thankfully leaving the tap shoes behind. Oscar had returned the shoes to the shelf, half forgetting about the incident, until Bradley had appeared on the scene and the tap shoes had become 'live,' giving the pair of them a shock to their senses.

Now, explained Oscar, this drama would happen every time Bradley visited his home, as if to say they belonged to Bradley. Would Annette, Oscar enquired, allow Bradley to keep her late husband's brand new tap shoes?

"I feel as if they belong to him already, as a legacy from his father," said Annette, with a breath of sheer wonder in her voice. "They and Bradley's own skills should take him far in the dancing world, particularly of tap dancing."

"I thoroughly agree, Annette, returned Oscar, but I think I should borrow a workbench for a day or two and handcraft Bradley his own pair of tap shoes to begin his training with, keeping these 'special' fellows for practice, at home, that my friend Jonathan Tate, who owns and trains, in his studio, will find for Bradley."

"I'm willing for that, Oscar," replied Bradley, "and to show my gratitude I will take a job for the remainder of these summer holidays, to be able to pay you for them."

"If that would make you happy," chortled Oscar, "go ahead, but I doubt you will find anything worthwhile for these last three weeks of the holiday. Besides you have shopping to do—you will need to visit several dance shop outfitters for men, to purchase leotards, tights—without feet, warm-ups, t-shirts and shorts— perfectly acceptable. These can be of any colour unless there is a specific dress/colour code, which Jonathan does not expect his students to adhere to any particular style or colour. Freedom of movement is far more important to Jonathan than any of these. Anything else you care to add to your purchases, such as water bottles or backpacks for carrying garments in, is perfectly agreeable to me."

"Thanks a million, Oscar," Bradley answered. "I'll try not to spend all your hard-earned cash," he joked.

"Enough of that, young man," scolded Oscar. "By the way, I don't suppose you want any help spending that money of mine, do you?" Oscar asked hopefully, grinning at Bradley.

Bradley made a face, then replied, "I hoped you might ask that, Oscar. I really would be grateful for your help. I haven't bought such items before and your thoughts could be very useful."

With that sorted, Annette and Bradley helped Oscar clear away the refreshments, before making sure the tap shoes were back in their niche in front of the fireplace. Opening the front door, Oscar said goodbye to two of the nicest people he had met in a long time, saying to Bradley to call him when he was ready for his shopping trip.

Turning to Annette, he lifted one dainty hand, brushing it with his lips. Annette immediately blushed, giving Oscar another flutter in his stomach. Watching the pair walk up the road together, he once more wondered what the future would hold. Whispering Anita's name under his breath, Oscar told her how much he cared for Annette and would she mind if at some stage in their relationship, he asked her to marry him?—just for friendship's sake, of course.

Three weeks before the start of the first term, Bradley was at Jonathan Tate's studio, where accommodation had been found for him in a first-floor flat, sharing with Jonathan's youngest son—the same age as Bradley. His name was Terence, Jonathan told Oscar, but Bradley had yet to meet him. Jonathan had thought that the two lads would be company for each other—which time would tell!

During the coming weeks, Oscar had sought out the use of a wooden bench, where he often spent days buying the materials needed to construct the best of tap shoes, for Bradley to commence the hardest of times, for possibly years to come, preparing to follow his father onto the dance stage, tap dancing his way to success. When finally completed, the tap shoes, made of black leather of a modern style with metal plates, for surreal sound, front and rear, were truly magnificent even though Oscar said it himself. Bradley was enchanted, vowing to make Oscar and his mother proud of him.

Getting excited for Bradley, the pair had thoroughly enjoyed their day together, visiting and purchasing from, the modern man's dancewear shops, where Oscar had an ever-open cash card, to buy the best of dancewear for Bradley. Annette had been able to join them for lunch in a friendly bistro bar near the London theatres, altogether a happy day for them all. Then came the day itself when Annette and Bradley made their way through London to 'Jonathan Tate's Dance Studio.'

Welcoming his students at the door of the studio, Jonathan escorted twenty, fifteen to twenty-year-olds, including their families, through the dance studio into a large room beyond, where tables and chairs were set up, with two tables groaning with tempting morsels to eat. Invited to sit wherever they fancied the guests were served hot or cold drinks, according to choice.

This was so totally unexpected, that Bradley and Annette were speechless for a moment for a moment or two, until the silence was broken by a troupe of eight children, ranging between five and nine years, by their appearance, tapping their way onto what looked like a freshly erected stage. Whilst the music asserted itself into the first score, the dancers positioned themselves ready to begin their dance sequence, in tune with the music, picking up their routine on time, enchanting the audience with their expertise and the obvious joy on their faces, creating a fascinating atmosphere for the newly arrived students to ponder over. Was this the level of skill that Jonathan Tate expected from his dancers?

With the young dancers evacuating the stage, so Jonathan invited all present to enjoy their time together. Strangers began talking to strangers, united by their offspring's urgent desire to revive the long well regarded art of tap dancing, in readiness, they hoped, for the London stage and beyond. Jonathan mingled amongst the guests, already supplied with food and drink.

Stopping alongside Annette and Bradley's table, he sought the opportunity to encourage Bradley to enjoy his time at his studio, to work hard, prepared to honour his father's success, living up to the name of Braithwaite, both on the musical stage and his love of performing tap dance sequences to an appreciative audience. Proceeding to say that he and his son, Terence would meet Bradley, in the dance studio, after the introduction party, where he would introduce them both, taking them to their new accommodation together, hoping they would become the best of friends in their love of the dance.

As the introduction party drew to a close Annette and Bradley said farewell, for now, to their newfound friends, walking through into the studio to meet with Jonathan and Terence. Jonathan was heavily involved in saying goodbye to the families of the students, asking the students if they knew where their accommodation was, to make their way there, but to be sure to be in the dance studio by 10 AM tomorrow morning, somewhat later than usual, which would return to the normal weekday time of 8.30 AM, with another 10 AM start on Saturday and Sunday free for home visits or other social events.

Some of the new students looked rather shocked, whilst the second or third years had obviously heard this before, standing there looking rather bored. Gradually the students drifted away until there was only Annette, Bradley, Terence and Jonathan remaining, to be shown the boy's flat.

Smiling at Bradley, Terence introduced himself indicating Jonathan as being his father, assuring Bradley that he would soon get used to the long hours and enjoy the experience. He qualified by saying that he had been dancing here, under his father's tutelage since he was four years old, warning Bradley not to expect great results immediately, but, by being given all the help needed, with the extensive practice, he would soon find his feet—so to speak. Bradley was grateful to Terence for breaking the ice, vowing to make everyone proud of him. Little did anyone know about the 'specials' waiting for him at home to begin their long association with their original owner's son.

The four walked out into the late afternoon sunshine, following the pavements through to Soho, not very far from where Oscar had made his new home. Bradley and Oscar had yet to discover that fact, which could and did, result in some delightful times together. Their walk ended about a mile and a half further on, when Jonathan turned into a small, rustic avenue, an attractive part of London, opening the front door of a small flat and into an equally small hallway.

The next door showed the interior of a reasonably sized lounge, with the kitchen leading off the other end. Upstairs was left for the boys to explore and choose one of the same-sized bedrooms, either front or rear of the flat. A bathroom, with a shower that completed Bradley's and Terence's home for at least the following year—small—'yes', but perfectly appointed to have a friend or two for an evening of music perhaps or just a chat.

Leaving the boys alone to get aquatinted, Annette and Jonathan said goodbye, Annette reminding Bradley that he had told Oscar he would collect the new tap shoes tomorrow evening and could he find his way there.

"Thanks, mum," replied Bradley, giving his mum a hug and Jonathan a handshake of gratitude, before turning to Terence to inspect their new home together.

Jonathan and Terence then retraced their footsteps back to the studio to allow Annette time to catch her bus across London and home. She sank down onto her settee before getting ready to start preparing the evening meal before Rupert, Simone and Oliver arrived home. Her heart was with Bradley as she tried to imagine him and Terence in their new home. It was a whole new experience for him, away from her since Trevor had died.

Once back inside their home, both the boys ran upstairs to claim their bedroom each. Terence was a fraction of a second ahead of Bradley, making his way to the front of the flat, looking out onto the part of the avenue leading to the front door, leaving Bradley with his more appealing bedroom at the rear of the building overlooking a delightfully laid out garden, that had obviously been tended with love.

Bradley had no idea about gardening but made up his mind to do the person justice, who had created such a relaxing space to sit in on a warm spring or summer's day. He might even enlist Oscar, who had a nice-looking garden himself. Settling themselves in with their scant belongings didn't take very long and the boys had plenty of time to have a cold drink, that Jonathan had thoughtfully provided, as well as milk, bread, cheese, bacon and ham with jars of mustard, tomato sauce, mayonnaise, jam and spread. It was a veritable feast!

A walk was then called for, to wash down and settle their ham and cheese sandwich and the always appreciated cold lemonade. Locking the front door, Terence and Bradley decided to follow the avenue to see where it led, surprising themselves to find a small wooded area and pathway leading to a children's play park. As the local schools were locked still from the summer vacation, a few of the children, presumably from the avenue, could be seen, with or without their parents, making the most of the fine weather.

A small skateboarding ramp was set apart, proving to be very popular. Old as they were neither of the boys could resist a jaunt on the roundabout and swings, egged on by the grinning four to five-year-olds, hopefully with watching parents from the nearest flats and houses.

The evening, for the new friends, was spent listening to dance music, that Terence was pretty sure would be introduced to Bradley and the other new students tomorrow—a typical piece of music in which to highlight a few simple tap routines. Another sandwich for breakfast—this time of rashers of fried bacon, saw the boys vying for use of the bathroom—nearly a friendship dissolver, until they later, sensibly devised a workable routine, suiting them both. Nine-thirty AM, they were kitted out, ready for the first day of a new year and for Bradley, the start of an exciting future ahead.

By 10 o'clock the new and ongoing students, amounting to about twenty, gathered in the main studio of Jonathan Tate's Dance Studio, ready and eager to learn as much as possible today. Clad in the new outfits for the latest students with the ongoing tappers in their older familiar outfits, waiting for further instruction, from Jonathan, as to where they should make for, many were exchanging first names, buzzing with excitement.

Selecting four of the seniors, Jonathan asked them to take six of the new students, to one side of the studio, to help them re-adjust what some of them were wearing keeping their clothing well away from their feet and ankles, especially with a helping hand to tie those unfamiliar tap shoes. Whilst this was taking place Jonathan had his pianist strike up half-remembered tap dancing tunes to which, he explained, the newest enlisted boys and girls, would attempt to unravel that morning.

In awe and wonder, with mouths opened they stood or sat, mesmerised by Jonathan's passionate interpretation of the music, with the percussive sounds of the metal taps on the highly shining wooden dance floor of the studio sounding magnificent to their unharnessed ears. Following this impressive display of what he would like to expect from his pupils, by the end of their training, preparing themselves for a life on stage, he also knew that a few would become disinterested and drop out, possibly within a few months, leaving those who were dedicated enough to continue the strict schedules, a chance of stardom.

With no sign of discomfort, Jonathan then sent his ongoing students into a further studio, along the corridor, with instructions to co-operate with another pianist to practise a recently learnt, choreographed sequence for a new show that was being planned for mid-summer this year. Being strictly competent and disciplined, he knew he could trust them to work well together, whilst he spoke to the new students.

Shutting the outer door to the studio, Jonathan asked the remaining set of new pupils to sit on the floor, where, he explained, he would like to tell them, in words, the basic outline of what tap dancing was all about, its originality, orientation and expression the sounds of metal taps striking the floorboards made—the percussive noise that could be heard by the tuned or untuned ear.

Then, he continued, they would stand together and practise some of the sounds they had just talked about. Tap dancing, Jonathan went on to say, is a contemporary dance style, with the addition of metal taps attached to the toe and heel of a special shoe, usually high heels to begin with, making a rhythmic noise when striking the floor. Its origin was in America as a result of a fusion of many ethnic percussive dancing styles, the biggest influences of which are English, Irish and Scottish jigs known as clogging, alongside African tribal dances.

Styles of tap dancing emerged in the late 19th-century, but it wasn't until the 1920s that the taps were attached to the soles of shoes, in two places—toe and heel, using screws, making dance more popular, becoming known as 'tap dancing' when dancers in a show called *Shuffle Along* in 1921 was the first to include dancers wearing tap shoes.

The styles of tap dancing are classified under four headings; 1) Classified or spring tap, popularised through 20th-century films. 2) Rhythm tap—tap dancing shoes, creating their own percussions on the floor. 3) Musical or Broadway tap.4) Funk tap.

Listening skills are vital to develop, continued Jonathan, as you will need to use your musicality to listen to the beats. Multiple rhymes are used, so it is essential not to get confused. Also, there are different types of music, so try to adjust and tap dancers to make frequent use of syncopation standing choreography on the 1st or 8th beat count.

Remember too, pressed on Jonathan, the dance style is reliant on the leg, particularly on the lower leg, so please inform me if any of you have had a recent injury, as you never tap with a straight leg, therefore knees should be soft and relaxed when executing dance moves. Ankles should not hurt after a dance workshop, so again, please tell me if you experience anything abnormal.

To avoid anything going amiss, good posture is extra important in tap dancing, so it is worthwhile learning about Salsa dancing, developing better concentration which, is better in older children or young adults, but younger children do have somewhat more energy and stamina, warned Jonathan. Another important lesson to learn is that no two tap dancing instructors tap or teach the same way, but, whichever way you learn, timing and technique are essential to master, either with music, following the beats provided or without musical accompaniments, known as Cappella dancing, understanding that improvisation is another form of expressing tap dancing.

One last fact to give you, before we go on to the fundamental elements of tap dancing and that is being the name given to 'Hoofers,' a tap dancer who dances primarily with their legs, making a louder more grounded sound.

"To end this part of our learning session this morning," pressed on Jonathan, "and before we physically practise the art, we need to know these fundamental points on how the taps actually work. We dance instructors have a responsibility to teach this early on in our classes together. You will all have to understand the eight basic tap dance steps names and how to execute them, namely the difference between a toe tap and a toe tip and a two-shoe toe tip, also if a ball tap is the same as the toe tap.

"This may sound like double-Dutch to you at the moment but don't worry, all will become clear as we carry out the steps together. I have also drawn and written you all a guide, for you to read and re-read at your leisure, giving the names of the steps and how to execute them. Here we have barres with background three-way vision so you can see what your feet are doing and then your progression.

"At home you may not have the same vision available, so I would suggest you work in pairs, if you can, correcting each other, or, if another dancer is not around, maybe enlist your parents or guardians to oversee the practice, having been shown the guidebook. Don't expect perfection straight away as we will need many sessions together and in your practice at home, to see how much you have learnt.

"Now, let's all stand, shake about a bit to loosen up, then we'll have a cold drink with a comfort break before we continue."

In ten minutes everyone was eager to see more, watching Jonathan as he named and made the step, clearly and accurately, so there was no doubt in the minds of the new students. It was a pleasure to watch him in a demonstration like this. Calling three to the barre and mirrors, at any given one time, they all accounted for the steps as best they could with Jonathan coming to the rear of each student to correct or re-position the feet.

'Walk tall,' he would say, 'give yourself another inch of your height and you won't go far wrong. Your feet can follow, putting the two together once you've mastered one.'

It was a long, hard, difficult session, lasting until lunchtime. Bradley enjoyed it immensely, but was ready for a break now with the others. Some had bought sandwiches to eat indoors or outside and some were changing to visit a local eating house. Jonathan gave each option an hour to themselves, encouraging them not to eat too much, as the afternoon sessions, he said, could play havoc on the stomach, if too full.

He then proceeded to tell them he would be giving a talk later on, after the sessions, about the nutritional needs of a dancer, be it ballet or tap. It would make good sense to come along, he concluded, if you are serious about keeping fit and dancing your best ever. Several heads nodded in unison, obviously intending to be there, absorbing the advice they would be given for their own good only.

Bradley and Terence did eventually meet up for coffee, after lunch, that first day. Terence had a previous engagement at the dentist's for a wisdom tooth check-up that had been causing him quite a bit of pain lately. He would have liked at least two to be removed, so he could hope for a pain-free run-up to the summer show, where he and his father were performing a paired dance sequence, but the dentist was hesitating over the advisability of this, due to the impaction, which could lead on to surgical intervention at a local hospital, for dental work to be carried out.

He was a little despondent, therefore, when he met up with Bradley halfway through the lunch hour. Returning to the studio, for a 2 o'clock start, the second and third-year students were scheduled to rehearse once again, with Jonathan this time, for the summer show, introducing a brand new hip hop type tap dance, written and choreographed by Jonathan himself. Terence was wild about it, predicting an unreserved, brilliant response.

The new students were asked to practise the routine steps they had been shown that morning, under the guidance of the second pianist, in the smaller of the two studios. She intended to play simple, easy-to-follow rapping music, to which she would observe their willingness to attempt the stances. After a drink refreshed break, the two groups joined up together to continue their practice routines at either end of the larger of the two studios, with Jonathan keeping close contact with both groups, as he intended to introduce a very simple dance for the newest students, to show off their newly developed skills to the audience, again at the summer show.

All was continuing smoothly for Terence and Bradley for the next few weeks, with Bradley making frequent visits home to visit Annette, only to find, that unbeknown to him, Oscar and his mother had already been making arrangements to view council held homes in close proximity to both Bradley's dance studio and Oscar's new flat, bringing with them a few healthy meetings to theatre's and shows, often with Oscar's own past client's, performing, then introducing them to Annette backstage afterwards.

Their relationship seemed to be strengthening at each new outing or simply an invitation to afternoon tea at Oscar's flat. Hand in hand, the pair would walk up the road together, to where Annette was currently living with her sister and brother-in-law, Victor having returned to his own home after his holiday with Annette, tickled pink that Oscar and his sister were getting along so well together.

He would dearly love to see Annette with a degree of happiness once more, in her life. She had been so desperately unhappy after her dearly loved husband had died, leaving her all alone with Bradley. He knew how much he would miss his darling wife, Abby, if anything should happen to her or Jimmy and Lesley if anything should happen to them also.

Hurrying home now, he stopped along the motorway to buy Abby the largest bunch of flowers he could find, thinking he was the luckiest fellow in the whole world, just at this very moment. He had an opera role, in two weeks' time and needed practice time with the cast, also solo rendering at home, much to Abby's amusement, when she would join him for the final aria, being an opera singer herself. Now he wanted that same happiness for Annette.

Rehearsals were also going well at the dance studio too when suddenly disaster struck. Terence's two rear wisdom teeth began to exercise a large amount of pain for him, causing him to fall behind in his attendance at the studio. Jonathan hated seeing his son in so much pain, determined to complete his responsibility at the summer show, by performing with his father, on stage, at the theatre, hired for the occasion.

He was taking it very seriously indeed, giving rise to a great deal of concern when the pain became intolerable one night and he was whisked into hospital with badly infected wisdom teeth, needing instant drainage and surgery. Jonathan, who had gone with him, that night was warned that Terence could be facing several weeks of dressing packs, to be inserted daily, as an in-patient, narrowly missing a condition called sepsis, which, as Jonathan knew, could be fatal.

At the moment he was just so glad that the surgeons had acted so promptly, to save his son's life, giving a little thought as to how they could continue with the summer show, with he and Bradley being the central figures. Making sure that Terence was as comfortable as could be expected, sleeping soundly now, probably for the rest of the night, did Jonathan finally left the hospital to make his way home, with one last call to make—a letter to Bradley, at their newly acquired flat, to inform him of the events of the night, assuring him that the doctors had placed his son out of danger, expecting a full recovery eventually, given healing time.

Jonathan then took himself off to his own home where he made a warm drink, before falling thankfully into his bed, missing his wife Margot dreadfully—deceased by nine years, even more in the early hours of this morning, to express relief and thanks that their son was saved. He had an early start at the studio tomorrow, with time ticking down towards the start of the show. The newest members were learning their roles well and Jonathan was delighted with their enthusiasm and hard work to help make the show a success on opening night.

Two members had left the tap dancing scene, for good, within a few months of starting, unsure how dedicated to tap dancing they really were, being overwhelmed with the hard routines they had never expected. Once re-organising the remaining dancers, there was no holding them back.

Bradley, knew though, that Jonathan was not going to pull the show, with so much hard work being given to it already, but was equally worried about his central performance, with Terence, when suddenly Bradley had a whooping idea. Why not learn Terence's role himself, passing on as much as he could remember to the 'specials,' who, he felt sure, would adapt immediately to the sequences? After all, they were 'magic' tap shoes. Weren't they well able to cope with this or similar emergencies to save the day?

Jonathan had no notion of the shoes or how they might have come into his possession. He did know though that Oscar had negotiated a place for his recently gained friend, called Bradley, known son of Trevor Braithwaite, famous tap dancer who had died so horrifically in the motorway collision and to whom Oscar had sensed a great desire to assist this young man Bradley in his longing to follow in his father's footsteps, keeping his achievements alive for posterities' sake, encouraging other 'hopefuls.'

Bradley had to find the right time to approach Jonathan when he wasn't visiting Terence in hospital, at the same time ensuring all was well with the dancer's abilities and health, preparing for the summer show in ten days' time. Jonathan was delighted to report to his students that Terence was making a better recovery than the doctors had anticipated and should hopefully be able to attend the show where he should have been dancing with his father, but was, for now, confined to a wheelchair whilst his broken and desperately sore gums, finally healed for good.

He was looking forward with great pride to the show, wondering how Jonathan was going to replace their act together. This was where the big 'surprise' would come in to bring hushed, incredulous delight, not only to Jonathan, but to the entire audience.

Bradley had found that 'right' moment to bring a thrill and hope into the master tap dancer's heart. Sitting down quickly, after hearing the whole story from Bradley, he could hardly believe his ears, let alone Bradley's spontaneous answer to his imminent question of how to replace Terence's role in the show. It was a genuinely made offer and one Jonathan couldn't afford to refuse. He was utterly intrigued by the thought of actually meeting and dancing with so-called 'magic' tap shoes, made originally by Oscar for a very important client.

Quietly, over the next three days, after dance sessions were over, Jonathan would teach Bradley as much as he thought the young man could remember of the very complicated steps needed for the sequences, leaving the fuller version for the 'magic' shoes to figure out and execute correctly with, Jonathan's choreographed version of the dance.

It was arranged that Bradley would teach the shoes all he knew, that evening, bringing the shoes discreetly to the studio the following day, keeping them hidden until time for a rehearsal together, after the day's sessions were over and everyone had vacated the building, except maybe the one responsible for the 'magic' being transferred to the shoes. Would they now have an answer to the riddle or would secrecy still be maintained?

At last, the long day of rehearsals was over and it was time to bring the 'specials' into Jonathan Tate's world of dance. Transferring his workday tap shoes for the highly designed pair of shoes that he intended to use on the new dance sequence he was almost ready to start the rehearsal.

Oscar would have given his eyeteeth, Bradley knew, to secretly compare to those he had made ready for Trevor Braithwaite to collect the next day, in readiness for a brand new role, next week, that could have sealed his future as the world's fastest tap dancer performer of all times and these magnificent new shoes that his father was now wearing. He smiled to himself, thinking that the competition could have been 'hot.'

Unwrapping the bag Bradley had carried into the studio that morning, he displayed the shoes for Jonathan to see and admire. It was amazing to compare, but the two pairs of shoes were almost an exact match. However, there was one vital difference and that was that the rear or heel taps, on Trevor's shoes were actually in two very separate parts giving an extremely specialised authentic sound, being made of a new highly developed metal. Bradley had just a moment to whisper imploringly, to his father's shoes, to behave themselves, when Jonathan signalled that he was ready to begin the rehearsal.

Moving deliberately into position, much to Jonathan's amazement, the shoes took their place alongside him, ready to begin the instant the initial beats began. Then the recorded music started and they were off, tapping rhythmically together as if they had danced that way all their lives! With the beats being interpreted well by both pairs of shoes, the magic began with the excitement of the chase and the magnificent symmetry of a young lioness, front and rear legs in full propulsion, covering its intended prey at an astonishing speed—a story written and choreographed by Jonathan, particularly for his summer show—a sensation if ever there was one.

Almost falling over in seeing such a triumphal display of unabashed wonder, the story unfolded, to tell of animal magnetism pitted against man's wiles. Wow! He exhaled as silently as possible to avoid any distraction from the story being told in such dramatic dance form.

With the final scene enacted and the beat still hanging distinctly in the air, Bradley could not resist a thunderous affirmation of enthusiastic applause, whilst grinning at Jonathan's obvious delight. The 'specials' halted by the side of Jonathan, who applauded their skills. They then abruptly made their way towards Bradley, where again they stood quietly, awaiting instructions.

He thanked them for their splendid performance, saying how proud he was of them. Quietly opening the bag for the shoes to be conveyed home in, Bradley tucked them under his arm, saying goodnight to Jonathan first, when he was asked to stay for a moment to talk over an important new issue that was occurring. Jonathan then engaged in a moment of perplexity.

"I have another big problem now, Bradley," Jonathan confided. "If I use your shoes, which I dare not refuse, who do you think we could ask to take Terence's place, with the 'specials' on their feet, for example? It would be a privilege to ask you, but, being a raw beginner you have not gained the skills yet to enact the part with facial and body movements and the extension of the knees to carry off such a dramatic role and I think you agree, don't you?"

"Yes, I do understand what you are saying," conceded Bradley, slightly disappointed, but knowing the master was right. "From whom I've watched, in the seniors, so far, I think I could spot two who you might recommend for the role. They would need to know the whole story, of course and be prepared to accept that the shoes are the ones commanding the steps, but their experience too would be needed to support the essence of the dance."

"I know exactly who you mean, Bradley," replied Jonathan, with a hopeful note in his voice. "I will speak to both of them individually tomorrow to engage in their interest. They each have their own dances to perform, maybe finding my request too heavy a responsibility."

As Jonathan and Bradley left the studios together, they were both slightly aware of the light following them as they locked the front doors. They looked at each other wonderingly, then shrugged, each turning in their homeward direction.

The next day saw the pair, with the students, began another day of gruelling warm-up time, followed by assignments and rehearsals. Bradley was still giving the work everything he had to give, so sincere in his endeavours to make Annette and Oscar so very proud of him.

He had visited Terence only last evenings in the hospital, where he was responding well to the daily packing with antibiotics for his badly infected gums, following dental sepsis from impacted wisdom teeth, now removed. He was being allowed to attend the summer show and arrangements had been made for Jonathan to collect him from the hospital, settle him in his wheelchair at the theatre, then placing him in the care of his many friends. Bradley had promised him the time of his life and an utterly amazing finale performed by his father and who else? Was a mystery Bradley would not reveal?

After rehearsals the next day, which had exceeded all expectations, Jonathan asked Michelle and Louisa to stay behind as he had something very important to say to them both. They were both senior students awaiting selection for a new show, each with their own distinctive style of dance and body language. Jonathan began explaining why he had asked them both to stay behind, as he had something to request of either one of them and he wasn't sure which would take up the offer.

Showing them the 'specials' he asked them whether they knew whose they were, with both girls saying that they had seen Bradley with a similar pair, but did not use them in group sessions. No, replied Jonathan, they were quite right, but there was something very unusual about them and that was because they were 'magic' tap shoes moving under their own momentum, as he demonstrated briefly. Both students laughed and said they must be fitted with batteries, to which Jonathan proved they were wrong.

Then, to their utter amazement, Jonathan told them the complete story, beginning with Trevor's request to have Oscar design and handcraft the special pair of tap shoes that would have propelled him to a world champion role as a tap dancer. He then told them of the motorway crash in which Trevor had died, finally the realisation that the tap shoes had been 'magicked' whilst in Oscar's possession. Jonathan then told Michelle and Louisa how Bradley had come on the scene announcing he was Trevor's son, longing to keep his father's name alive for prosperity's sake.

Now he asked them to watch the complete repertoire of the 'magic' shoes, to be performed by them and himself, Jonathan, as the final execution of the evening. His problem, he told them, was to find a senior student with the stance and body language needed to enact the story through wearing the 'specials'. The shoes knowing, the role, who would dance hypnotically with one of the students wearing the shoes, as if their own. Both girls were dumbstruck by the performance and what Jonathan had just told them, under orders of secrecy for the time being.

Immediately, Louisa raised a cheer and spoke with a tremor in her voice, "I have much to do for the show, Jonathan, but this has grabbed my imagination, to a wild degree and I feel it could well be the role for me to undertake. I will need to fully rehearse with the shoes on my feet to make sure I can put as much into the role that it deserves."

Jonathan smiled at her and, turning to Michelle to gauge her sister's reaction, was rewarded with a smile of affirmation, telling Jonathan all he wanted to know. So it was arranged that they would meet again tomorrow, after the final rehearsal before the show on Saturday and go through the complete programme together, including the choreographers, the orchestra and the stage managers with their supporting cast.

After a long and tiring day, all was set for Louisa to rehearse her additional role, giving one of the best and most enthusiastic performances of her career— All in all it was a stunning success.

Saturday—the long-awaited day of the summer show dawned bright and clear. After a leisurely breakfast, the entire company, with costume dressers, hairdressers, stewards and refreshment suppliers arrived excited and eager to begin the proceedings. The orchestra moved into the pit beneath the front of the stage, rehearsing on their various instruments. Jonathan was on top of everything, with last-minute instructions, making sure everybody knew where they were to be at any given time.

His final, most important function before the audience began to arrive, was the collection of his son, Terence, waiting none too patiently, at the hospital, for his father to arrive to take him to the theatre. They would just about have time for a sandwich and a coffee together. So Jonathan and Terence enjoyed their final half hour, with a very excited Terence being seated, fifteen minutes later, as close to the stage as possible, for an all-round view.

Bradley came to see how his friend was, telling him how much he was looking forward to having Terence back in their own flat once more. Other friends took the seats allocated to them, by Jonathan, to take care of Terence during the performance, keeping him supplied with drinks and other refreshments, if required.

The theatre was filled to full capacity with all the tickets having been sold several weeks ago. At exactly 2 o'clock, the lights were dimmed and a hushed audience waited expectantly for the show to begin. Jonathan mounted the stage, standing in front of the regal-looking curtains, referring the audience to their programmes, giving the amount of hard work and dedication put in by the students, particularly, he said of the new students, whose work was exemplary and to give them extra encouragement.

He then introduced the orchestra, who stood and took the appropriate vote of thanks. Jonathan then hoped the audience would have a wonderful afternoon, before stepping down from the stage, allowing the music and filming of the opening of the curtains to begin and with a musical star-studded overture, the show began. Stage changes and costumes were exchanged at lightning speed without a missed beat or step. Everybody was working well with each other to make the show a success and what a show it was!

During the interval for refreshments and ice-cream, there was an excited buzz of conversation throughout the entire theatre, as compliments were exchanged from parent to parent who had students performing new and innovative dance routines with excellent choreography. Applause, after rapturous applause, followed each amazing dance with precision and enthusiasm, with the sheer joy of the dance giving credibility to the skills demonstrated that afternoon.

Terence sat enrapt throughout all the performances, dazzled by the skills of those he knew and with whom he would have danced that afternoon. He wondered whether he would have given the dances as much credit as his friends had, but was confident enough of dancing the finale with his father, reminding him that the sequence of events was drawing to a conclusion and the time was rapidly bringing the show to the grand finale.

After the closure of the previous dance, a shuddering drum roll announced that something spectacular was about to occur. The audience was hushed, as the regal curtains were drawn back for the final time, to reveal a dramatic scene of bush and scrubland, dotted by stunted trees. A gigantic roar of sound from the orchestra gave way to pounding heartbeats and the scene was set. Jonathan, with his partner, clothed in animal skins were positioned, on stage, ready and poised for the moment to begin. A further drum roll began the frenzied feet of a chase about to begin—a young lioness with a heart set on prey, with which to feed her hungry cubs.

As the story unfolded, in a desperate bid to escape, so the beat, with the tap, tap, tap, of the dancer's shoes, becoming more intense. Not a single movement in the theatre, as the audience sat spellbound listening to the rhythm of the dance and the dancer's body language re-enactment of the scene. A sudden thud and all was still.—the lioness had made her kill. Her young would not go hungry tonight. A huge profuse sigh from the transfixed audience said it all!

As the slow ripple of applause rose to a frenzy, so the entire company of Jonathan Tate's studio took the final curtain call looking exultant with the applause they were generating. Jonathan drew the audience's attention to the magnificent orchestra, who stood and bowed their thanks to the audience, whose applause had increased in volume if that were possible. Tired, but extremely happy, the dancers, stage crew, host, hostesses, costume dressers and general 'tidy uppers' retreated from the stage, with applause, whistles and catcalls ringing in their ears, so much so that some of the newest members of the cast, were reduced to tears of over excitement.

Jonathan gathered the people, who had made the show such a success, around himself, showering thanks and praise to all concerned, then dismissing them quietly, saying he said he would see them all on Monday morning, in the studio and to enjoy the rest of their weekend. With one accord they all clapped and thanked their 'master of the tap dance,' well-loved and respected Jonathan Tate.

A rather quiet but star gazed audience stumbled out of the theatre onto the streets where they were met by a horde of local and not-so-local reporters, who had somehow been tipped off that something rather special had been happening at 'The Royal,' in Southwick Street, that afternoon, which indeed it had. They were keen to hear directly from the audience spilling from the theatre, so, telling as much as they knew and had seen with their own eyes they spoke long and excitedly of the brilliant dance sequences they had just witnessed, particularly of the grand finale and the amazing feet of the dancers, that had enraptured them all.

The following day, the papers were emblazoned with the events of yesterday afternoon, at a very ordinary theatre in a London street, capturing the imagination of many. The days that were to follow had Jonathan tearing his hair out, with the requests from eager parents, to have their children enrol in Jonathan's dance studio. New premises and certainly more professional instructors would have to be employed if all were to be accommodated.

Backstage, however, the audience of yesterday was unaware of what was to take place, which could have caused them to be flummoxed even more! Oscar and Annette had joined Terence where he was still sitting in his wheelchair and where Bradley was joyfully exclaiming over the show, telling Terence the story of the 'specials' and the part Louisa had displayed within the shoes. Terence was simply flabbergasted by what he was hearing, determined to meet these very special tap shoes, now belonging to Bradley, once handmade by Oscar, for Bradley's father, Trevor.

He was not expected back on the ward for another hour and a half, so Bradley, following Oscar's suggestion, pushed Terence backstage to join his father, who received his son with a hug, saying how glad he was that he could be there and hoped he had enjoyed the show.

He said he hoped that by now Bradley had explained about the 'specials,' to which Terence answered 'yes' he now knew the whole amazing story and what a wonderful example they had set, to honour Bradley's father Trevor. Louisa, he exclaimed was first-rate for the role, congratulating his father for selecting her, also aware that Bradley had desired to have performed that role, with his father, having rehearsed it so many times.

By now the foyer, box office and the theatre had been swept clean, leaving the stage to be cleared of all the relevant scene changes and even discarded costumes, perhaps from an over-enthusiastic dancer, who may well have been wearing two outfits, for a quick scene change. Soon, all that remained was a rather large pile of rubble that would be put outside overnight, collected the next morning by the local council street cleaners.

All who were still on the stage were Terence, in his wheelchair, Bradley, Oscar and Annette, Louisa and, lastly, Jonathan, whose final act of the afternoon was to lock up and secure the theatre's bolts. All of a sudden two small bright spots of light appeared, in the centre of the stage, growing stronger by the minute, until two figures could be seen emerging in the centre of each light. The company, on the stage, backed hastily away, covering their eyes from the bright light emitting from these strange beings. They had now grown to about eight feet tall and were smiling.

"Don't be afraid," they spoke in high tinkling voices, smiling around at everyone. "We have come from 'His Royal Highness' the One True God, who has instructed us to give you a clearer picture of why you Bradley have what you call the 'specials,' in your possession now. That's a good name for them, by the way, as they are very special, even in being unique. We are angels."

They continued, "and the bespoke tap shoes made by a very talented man, for your father, Bradley, intended for his specific use, to bring great honour to himself and to put tap dancing firmly on the map, worldwide, but as you probably know man can dictate his walk in life, having been given free choice, by God, which was why Trevor took the decision to attempt to avoid a far worse accident than did occur, by making the fatal swerve, sadly plummeting down the embankment, to his instant death.

"God, though, who never forgets, still had future plans for Trevor's son Bradley, who has now been destined to continue with his Father's declaration and determination to become the world's fastest tap dancer, by requesting Oscar to apply the rear metal taps in two pieces, rather than one, to increase speed, appearing to produce two taps instead of one and with a deeper resonate sound.

"When Trevor was acclaimed as a world champion, thereby increasing the desire for tap dancing, thus entirely in God's will for His future plans. This is not to say only Bradley here has a future planned by God, but everyone on this stage and throughout the world, be they male or female has a future in place for them to follow, if willing to walk in God's provision for their lives. The decision is completely theirs to accept God's ways or not."

The angel who had asked Bradley for the shoes, gently handling them with care, now returned the shoes in the same way—fondly. Bradley wondered for a moment if the angel had somehow 'unmagicked' the shoes, then realised that if God was going to use them in a very special way, they would stay the same 'special' tap shoes, bringing honour and glory to God, at the same time to himself, the title that would have been given to his father.

With raised hands, as if in a blessing, the assignation appeared to be over, as the lights emitting from the angels were beginning to fade and with a final bow to their stunned audience, the angels had gone, leaving six friends on the stage, looking amazingly at each other, but unbeknown to them there was a flicker of faith in every heart. Nobody doubted where these beings had come from, having heard them loudly and clearly proclaiming God's Holy Name with such reverence and adoration. Heavenly was obviously their home, bringing the essence of it onto this very stage.

With a quick re-awakening, the shaken little group realised they still needed to put the rubbish out for the morning collection, locking and bolting the doors behind them, before reverently and thoughtfully making their way home, except Jonathan, whose final act of the night was to return Terence safely to the hospital, from where he would be discharged in two days' time.

Apologising to the slightly tutting sister, Jonathan made Terence a warm drink, before settling him comfortably into his bed, promising to collect him, as soon as he was given the final once over by the surgeon, declared fit for discharge, then being arranged a follow-up appointment, in three weeks' time to make sure he was maintaining progress.

The telephone was red hot as Terence gave his father the good news, then contacted Bradley just as he was leaving for the studio, but Terence wasn't high and dry quite yet, as Jonathan had plans of his own, that being, to have Terence at his own home for a few days, until he felt certain Terence could be trusted, back in the flat, enjoying life again with Bradley. Pushing the heavy wheelchair to the car to transfer Terence into the passenger seat, Jonathan suddenly felt a rush of sorrow for his loss of Margot, his deceased wife and Terence's mother. She would have been so practical, knowing exactly how to handle this rather awkward situation.

Terence, seeing the anguish in his father's eyes, sought his father's hands, squeezing them gently. He well remembered his mother, so understanding and consoling when he had scrapped his knee, whilst climbing a tree, for example. He missed her as much as his father did, with the pair of them often pouring over pictures of her on happy, carefree days at the beach.

Life had to continue though and without a sibling to reminisce with, he drew a certain sense of normality back into his life, by absorbing himself by gaining good pass marks in his school exams, then joining his father as a dedicated student, in the dance studio, where he renewed his trust in humankind, making solid friendships along the way, so by the time he had met Bradley, he was far from being lonely, giving help and advice to new recruits, helping them to absorb dance into their very bones, aspiring to reach the pinnacle of their future chosen careers.

So father and son worked well together with Jonathan fully aware that in a few years' time, if Terence was keen, to enrol him in the academy of dance, to commence training as a professional dance master, who could then enlarge the name of 'Jonathan Tate and Son, Dance Studio,' to a higher level of prestige than it had been able to claim before.

The dance workshops had begun again, in earnest, after the summer show and the summer vacation was very nearly forgotten, but not entirely. Since the spectacular ending of the show and the public interest it had aroused, Jonathan had been kept busy by craftsmen measuring adjacent rooms, in the studio's building, ready to be converted into a further dance studio, where the newly enrolled beginners, having started in September, had their first introduction to dance, in particular the art of tap dancing.

A recently qualified professional pianist had been employed, who had a good ear for dance tunes. She would be a fitting person to play ad hoc pieces as the need arose. After Jonathan's introductory talk and an example of tap dance, the young ones would join Angela, in the new studio, with its own barre and three-sided mirrors, to practise, under her tuition, using experts of well-known dance melodies, proving to be a great asset to the studio.

Well before the commencement of the new term, Terence had returned to the flat he was sharing with Bradley, a gift to the boys by the generosity of Jonathan, Terence's father, who, although subscribing to the bills, had the boys learn the skills of housekeeping by keeping them in somewhat short supply, thus having them account for every penny they spent on food, clothes and entertainment, for example.

Neither had handled their own living expenses before, so were eager to learn to control their somewhat rash expenditure of the past. Older now, they were quick to grasp the new challenges, so gaining Jonathan's approval and respect with, the occasional meal out, by their benefactor, to supplement their otherwise meagre supplies.

With the summer term now in full swing, Bradley had become a second-year student whose progress was monitored very carefully by Jonathan, as he maintained with all the students—first, second and third year. The more experienced the students became, the more they were expected to warm-up and rehearse their own dance routines, without being too much under supervision, unless they had secured for themselves a stage role, in which case Jonathan would encourage and rehearse with that student until they were confident dancing the role in front of an audience.

Closer to the start of the show, all the cast would rehearse together in the venue they be performing the show in, putting in less hours at Jonathan's studio, for which they would be refunded a part of their course fees.

An exciting event occurred for Bradley towards the beginning of the half-term. Jonathan had entertained a London company of stage managers who were recruiting for a 'Winter Special'—a dance show, being performed over the Christmas period and featuring many different types of dance, from overseas clog dancing, Olde England Maypole dancing, the Helston Flora day dance—the furry dance, the Morris Men, Country Dancing, modern-day HipHop, to traditional Ballet and Tap Dancing. Typical Welsh, Irish and Scottish dance would also be included in the repertoire. It would be a full programme of spectacle and drama.

These men were scouts looking for outstanding performers, possibly from many dance academies, studios, schools, maybe even young street boys performing their style of art. The venue would be large, with a salary being paid according to seating numbers and the experience of the artists assigned to a particular role. Jonathan could see their eyes carefully watching each dancer in practice mode.

A couple of third-year students were asked to dance to their chosen melody and were selected for two major roles in the tap dancing section. Asked if they would be available during this period, they replied in the affirmative, yet, still casting their eyes around the studio one more time, as the company applied their practice routines, they stopped when they spotted Bradley performing a rather tricky move—pens moved to pads and Bradley was asked to perform the same move once more, which he achieved to perfection—pens moved again to pads, as Bradley was asked the same question about availability.

Not sure of his mother's plans for Christmas, but not having heard of going away, assuming that Oscar would be with them, he gave his assent, with both the scouts agreeing he would be suitable to be part of the backup dancers. The three selected for the show were then told that contracts and letters of confirmation, with the name of the venue, the start of rehearsal dates, finally the show dates would be given to Jonathan for approval and signatures.

This would be a great challenge for Bradley, not having performed on a stage before, especially in front of an audience, when suddenly an idea began to grow. Why not use this opportunity to give the 'specials' a star role, namely their debut or launch. He would need to explain the origins of the 'specials,' to the stage managers and director, with the risk of being totally rejected and out of the show, but that was a problem for God to solve if it was the right time for His name to be declared, through the inspirational tap shoes, allowed to carry His name to those who were willing to listen.

It was a thrilling time for Bradley as he received Jonathan's congratulations with the full assurance that he would be allowed all the time needed for rehearsals, both in the studio and later at the chosen venue. Bradley then disclosed his thoughts regarding the 'specials'.

Jonathan could hear how determined Bradley was, but voiced caution, as this would be his first stage appearance as a completely unknown performer and to risk all, at the very beginning, may jeopardise any other opportunities for the shoes to proclaim their message from God. Bradley listened seriously, considering this sound advice from Jonathan. This could be a tricky decision to have to make, needing more than two heads to thoroughly think things through.

Bradley was a total novice when it came to asking God, in prayer, what he should do, but from somewhere within his spirit, that he was only just beginning to recognise was the part of him, connected to a Higher Realm, belonging to God, he found himself stutteringly ask a simple question, for guidance in this matter?

As the nerve-racking day drew to a final close, tap shoes were exchanged for outdoor shoes or boots, coats drawn snugly across still slightly heaving chests, although Jonathan always insisted on some gentle 'shutting down' exercises, along with a refreshing drink to get them home safely, goodbyes were called in conjunction with the slamming of the studio's outer doors. Reminding the students of the non-nutritional value of hot sizzling onions and burgers would have held little weight on their dash for home, as few would be able to resist the encouraging odours they would find drifting towards them.

Shrugging his shoulders in mock defeat, Jonathan and Bradley tidied up the odd leotard left on the floor, before they too put on their outdoor clothing, turned out the lights, finally locking and bolting the studio's outer doors. Saying goodbye and 'see you in the morning' before going their separate ways, Jonathan wondered what was passing through Bradley's mind right now and whether or not he would heed his warning, on considering the timing of introducing the 'specials.'

Hurrying home to tell Terence the good news of his selection, Bradley was met at the outer door of the flat by an equally excited Terence, almost dragging

Bradley into the kitchen, where he had obviously spent some time preparing their evening meal. It was getting cold announced Terence, so if we eat up quickly, I will tell you what I have discovered today.

Terence had been spending more time at home recently, as the operations on his wisdom teeth were still giving him pain, therefore regular outpatient appointments were continuing. He had developed an interest in cooking, being a dab hand at producing nourishing, tasty food, from leftovers and odd bits and pieces from the fridge and freezer, giving his father, Jonathan, reason enough to congratulate him on his endeavours, with special treats of meals out, with Bradley, to encourage this domesticity.

Tonight Bradley had a large plateful, of what could only be called a stew, with funny-looking lumps of what could only be called dumplings, thrust in front of him. Plunging his spoon in, at Terence's insistence, he found the flavour rather appealing if different, making him wonder what it consisted of. Terence grinned, slurping his stew with obvious enjoyment. Sitting back with a tummy rub, he appeared not to want a dessert, even if he had made one, which apparently, he had not.

"Now, come and sit in the lounge and I will tell you my news," Terence commanded Bradley, who had no option but to obey. His own news would need to wait until all was revealed by his friend. "I received a phone call today," continued Terence, "from guess who," and without waiting for a reply from Bradley, shouted, "Would you believe it, RAD—The Royal Academy of Dance. I wonder if dad knows about this yet, it may well still be in his in-tray?"

"What are you talking about, Terence?" Bradley quickly intervened. "Catch your breath and tell me what's happened. You're not usually as inarticulate as this. Have you been offered a role, by any chance, in a dance show, being put onstage next year?"

"Yes, I have," jubilantly answered Terence. "Oh, do listen, Bradley, it's a chance of a lifetime."

"Why don't you calm down now, enough to tell me what you want to say, from the very beginning," sighed Bradley.

"Alright," came back, with an exasperated look, from Terence. "It was like this. At about 3 o'clock, this afternoon, I was in the kitchen when the phone rang. The woman at the other end announced she was from RAD, saying she had been asked to contact me, with an invitation to take a star role, in a tap dancing show, being staged next year. Before I could reply, she asked me to listen to what had been proposed.

"Miriam told me there had been talks for some time, with the decision being taken that RAD would promote and sponsor 'The International Year of Dance' to be held in London theatres next year, as an invitation to those already friends and those not yet known, from overseas dance schools, the opportunity to celebrate together the common language of dance, without political or cultural barriers.

"The dancers, be they male or female would be offered homes with British dancers already in a show. Dates would be chosen and offered to them, with rates of salaries, rehearsal dates—usually between 4-6 weeks depending on the complexity of their dance, the time needed to learn the choreography and stage management, with a suggested timing for the programme.

"Both their own and British directors would work together to have the dancers perform to the best of their ability. Language could pose a few difficulties, but we will endeavour to match the company's director with a British one, who has a good grasp of the visiting country's language and dialects. Have you understood this, Terence?

"If you're wondering how we know of you, it's because of your father, who has made contact with us, in the past, to recommend you for professional training, a little later on, if you would like this. I hope I haven't divulged anything I shouldn't have. He's very proud of your abilities, by the way. Can you talk for another moment whilst I describe your role? This will all come to you in document form, for your final decision."

"Yes, of course," replied Terence, "but first a quick trip into the kitchen to give our evening meal a stir."

"That's fine, Terence. Do you enjoy cooking? It must be difficult in a dancing academy to always find the time and you can end up eating rubbish," added Miriam.

Terence hadn't found the breath to reply, as he was halfway towards the kitchen. On his return he sat down, intrigued to know who and why, he had been asked to dance this particular role.

"I'm back now and I'm listening," Terence invited expectantly.

"Don't be very surprised or even horrified by this, but we would like you to dance the role of Rip Van Winkle, a rather lazy farmer, in an American State, set against the background of The American Revolution of 1765-1776, a military struggle against British rule, affecting many changes in the lives of, happy as they were, Americans.

"You might not remember or even know the story of this farmer, who'd rather play with the village children than go into the fields to work. His wife so nagged him, that one day he escaped into a forest, where he met with some very strange dwarf men, who plied him with a potent, magical drink, whereby he slept for 20 years, waking to find the dwarfs gone and he had grown a lengthy beard. Humiliated and upset, he knew that it was unlikely his family would be around anymore and even if they were, they would be unlikely to recognise him, anyway.

"The country that would be sending this troupe are The Netherlands and the Dutch dwarfs will be played and danced by children of nine years and older. You, Terence, have the perfect height, colouring and expertise to do this role a lot of justice and it's completely justified, as there is an anniversary coming up, next year, of the signing of the Declaration of Independence, on 4 July 1776, thus ending the military campaign and British rule in America so, would be an appropriate time to perform this fictional tale.

"What do you think, Terence? Does the offer grab you? It could be your chance to become known and remembered. Other countries are putting in their submissions right now, so it looks as if it could be a great year. Would you like to be part of it?"

"It does sound fascinating," admitted Terence. "Me with a beard. How dad would love to see that! He still thinks of me as a child! I think I would like to attempt the role, so I'll say 'Yes please', Miriam. Count me in."

"Great," replied Miriam. "I'll be in touch again, very soon and everything we have said this afternoon will be documented for you, including venue, dates and rehearsal starts. Enjoy your role Terence and goodbye for now."

Bradley and Terence stared at each other for a moment or two, letting the news sink in, before Bradley broke the silence by telling Terence of his invitation to join a dance show at Christmas, this year, as part of a tap dancing background troupe, performing alongside many other forms of dance from, traditional ballet to street dancers and to include Welsh, Irish and Scottish dancers. Even an overseas clog dancing troupe was performing. I wonder, mused Bradley if this isn't part of the same initiative that Miriam was talking to you about?

Funny, though, he continued, your dad didn't seem to know much about the selection, as though he hadn't been informed. Maybe, as you say, he's been too busy to catch up on his inbox. I will talk to him tomorrow or are you coming in to tell of your good news? There is something else I was going to discuss with you tonight regarding the 'specials,' but that can wait for another evening. Terence agreed, rather reluctantly, but was itching to discuss this role of 'Rip Van Winkle,' already playing out in his mind the scenario or structure he would need to build on, to impersonate and capture the image of this man, when coming across these strange people.

How would he behave, for instance—alarmed, amused, inquisitive? Bradley smiled to himself, prepared to listen to Terence's thoughts as they centred on this one character. What about the angry wife? She would need to be of a strong type, annoyed with her husband for allowing his sons to work, when he should have been setting a good example, of honest, hard labour, bringing about a good harvest. His one redeeming factor, it seemed to be, was his great love for the village children, happy to spend his time reading and playing games with these youngsters!

Leaving Terence still mulling over his offered role of Rip Van Winkle, working out the moves, in his head, of the character of this man, challenged by how he could portray him, working at the same time with how the choreographer interpreted him. He was glad there would be an English director on stage with the national director, as Terence hadn't any knowledge of the Dutch language. Maybe though, if there was time, he mused, he could enrol in a Dutch language course, at least to understand the basics, being able to welcome these young dancers, making them feel at home, on and off the stage.

By now, Bradley had the coffee ready in the kitchen, so bringing it into their lounge he set it in front of Terence who mumbled an indistinct 'thank you' still deep in thought.

Having drunk his coffee, washed up his mug, said 'goodnight' to a bedazzled Terence, Bradley made his way to his room, hoping that Terence would not stay up too late, as he should arrive at the studio before his father to tell him not only about the role he had been offered but to ask Jonathan if he received the correspondence from RAD announcing the proposed 'International Year of Dance,' which Bradley was certain Jonathan would be very interested in being a part of.

A little later, as Bradley was nearly drifting off to sleep, he heard heavy, thoughtful steps on the stairs, discarded clothes being thrown, a rustle of bedclothes, then silence, as the pair slept, ready for another day of hard work in the studio.

The following day both Terence and Bradley were up in plenty of time to have scrambled eggs for breakfast, before grabbing their kit bags, containing sandwiches, fresh fruit, a snack bar for energy and a healthy bottle of drink each. They had plenty of time, so being a pleasantly warm day they decided to walk all the way, instead of busing it to just past the park, arriving a few moments before Jonathan came leisurely walking along with the keys in his hand, surprised to find his son and Bradley at the studio so early.

"What are you two doing here quite so early?" enquired Jonathan. "It's good to see you both so keen. How are you feeling today, Terry?" he asked. "Are you able to stay with us or do you have another appointment?"

"Thanks, dad," replied Terence. "I am feeling a lot better today. I'm on some new antibiotics that seem to be helping. If you like, I can do some work with the younger children, suggesting some practice they could try out during half-term."

"That would be very helpful, but if things get too difficult, just let me know and I'll get you a taxi home."

"Fine, dad, thanks, I hope I shall be alright though. By the way, I have some great news to tell you, but first I want to know if you've opened your post in the last few days," grinned Terence.

"Well," muttered Jonathan clambering into his instructor's gear, "I must admit I've been pretty busy getting everything ready for next term. Is there anything particular you think I may have missed and should see?"

"Let's have a look in your inbox, shall we," pushed Terence. "You might be surprised."

"Alright then," replied Jonathan. "I think we're already out here. It will be a minute or two more before the rush. Are you OK holding the fort for a mo?" he asked Bradley. "We shan't be long."

"Fine," grinned Bradley, thinking Jonathan was in for a big surprise and yet, he wondered, if he did know, when he had the 'scouts' in the sessions, last week, maybe even being aware that Terence was about to be offered this major role, wanting to keep quiet. So, Terence didn't think he had anything to do with initiating the offer through RAD's first. It was just the thoughtful way he behaved.

When the two came out of Jonathan's office a moment later, clutching a sheaf of papers, they were laughing, but Jonathan's face was a picture, Bradley did wonder if, in fact, he had been wrong. Terence looked triumphant as if he'd won the lottery, so maybe Jonathan hadn't discovered the papers before now. That was obviously going to be a secret between father and son, so Bradley remained quiet, opening the doors to allow the squash of dance students, to come into the main studio, to change and have a drink before warm-ups began.

The morning passed without incident for Terence and Bradley, in their respective areas of the studio.

Meeting up with each other, at lunchtime, Bradley asked how Terence had coped with the youngsters, to which he replied, that his father had taken over halfway through, but he had enjoyed the time he had with them. Those that stay from the beginning of the new term, through to the half-term, are the keenest of the new students, eager to learn the intricacies of tap dancing, willing to try their best to put them into practice, even laughing at the errors they very often made.

Walking towards the local park, where had agreed to have their lunch, Terence asked Bradley what he was going to say last evening, but hadn't been given the chance. Bradley laughed, saying how fascinating it was to see his friend so utterly absorbed by the role he was asked to play in 'Rip Van Winkle', in a forthcoming show, next year, for the 'The International Year of Dance.'

Now, he continued, I will tell you my news and by all accounts it seems to precede or is the commencement of the next year's shows that RAD are sponsoring. He then told Terence of the 'scouts' visit to the studio, the same day as Terence had received his telephone call, having identified two seniors to take leading roles and amazingly myself, grinned Bradley to be a background dancer, only because think I was able to execute a rather difficult move I had been practising for days.

Terence was thrilled for Bradley, explaining that the so-called scouts he had seen were in fact called 'talent scouts,' qualified themselves to recognise outstanding talent or up-and-coming stars when they saw them, often hired by dance directors in relation to dance recruiting, knowing exactly who and what was needed. Bradley told him that the show was scheduled for over the Christmas period, ending in the new year, a 'long run,' concluded Terence and could well be the opening introduction for 'The International Year of Dance.'

Bradley then introduced Terence to his idea of 'releasing' the 'specials,' for the initial reaction and attention, for the first audience to see them for themselves and the God-giving opportunity of hearing the complete story. There was silence, for a moment, then Terence congratulated Bradley on receiving such a well-deserved accolade but was equally as cautious as Jonathan about this first appearance.

If, as he pointed out, the directors did not take kindly to the 'specials' having this prime role, even if sympathetic to Bradley's explanation and also having faith in a living God, Bradley's career, equally any other opportunities, to tell the story, could well be jeopardised. These plausible issues hadn't really occurred to Bradley before, as, although being a bit impetuous, he was also aware of the importance of this task that, he felt sure, he and the shoes had been given, to proclaim God's word, through this important story, begging to be told.

Wondering what to do next, having had two cautious opinions about going ahead with his plan after he had talked with the directors, now he was not so sure himself. It had all seemed so clear to him at the time. His knowledge of prayer or talking to God, was itself simplistic, in the extreme, but instinctively he bent his head, uttering the words, "Please, God, tell me what I should do now?"

Terence was gathering up their lunch boxes, not really knowing how to help his friend, who, he knew was worried, anxious to get on with the declarations of the 'specials.' He realised he had been praying, but what would the answers be? Maybe it wasn't Bradley that God had committed the task of revelation too!? Could it possibly be Oscar, who had created the shoes, that God had intended to be His interpreter? Who would be more plausible to an audience, went through Terence's head, at that moment—an older man, with life experience or an inexperienced young man, even if he was the son of the acclaimed tap dancer who had died so tragically in a motorway accident.

He and Bradley walked silently, returning, to the studio, that afternoon, when Terence turned towards Bradley and asked whether he would consider meeting with Oscar, Annette, Jonathan and himself, to discuss the problem he was now facing. Maybe talking it through with those who knew the situation well, could help to clarify things in Bradley's mind, he wondered. At this point, the pair had reached the studio where the afternoon sessions were about to begin. Bradley promised to speak to Jonathan before he went home. Finding his concentration difficult during the afternoon, Bradley was pleased when it ended.

"Are you alright, Bradley?" inquired Jonathan whilst helping the youngsters into their coats. "Ready for the gathering group of parents waiting outside? You seemed a little distracted in some of your sequences this afternoon."

"Since lunch with Terence, I've had quite a lot on my mind," answered Bradley, busy collecting a small girl's coat and bag that had been hung too high for her to reach. "Could I speak to you before you go home, as I feel this is going to involve you as well?"

"Yes, of course," smiled Jonathan. "Anything to oblige. I need to change my shoes and pick up some papers from the office, then I'm all yours."

Coming out of the office, Jonathan saw a pair of worried faces.

"You two look as if you have the weight of the world on your shoulders," observed Jonathan.

"Well, in a way we have," returned Bradley. "I feel we are going to need all the help we can get, to determine where, when and how we let the 'special' introduce their story, that God wanted proclaimed. Now that we're into half-term, would you be willing to meet with Oscar, Annette and ourselves, to talk this through, if it feels right to pray to this God, which churches frequently do, to ascertain His will for the congregation. We may feel awkward at first, but we have always been encouraged to take our problems to Him?"

"Yes, that's fine by me, but I have a hectic week next week, but could come along, say, to Oscar's at 7.30 PM, if that suits him too, on Wednesday evening. By the way, Bradley, I shall be collecting soon, details of your contract, dates of shows, venue and when rehearsals start. I know it's nowhere near Christmas yet, but these shows are long-running, needing a lot of rehearsal time. I'll give it all to you on Wednesday and if you want some help filling in any of the forms, you only have to ask."

"Thanks, Jonathan," muttered Bradley, feeling that Jonathan was only giving this problem a cursory thought, but at least he was coming to the meeting. "I'll ring Oscar this evening to get his invitation for Wednesday evening and call you by no later than 10 o'clock, in case he's out with mum, is that alright for you?"

"Fine, by me," said Jonathan. "Are you two ready to leave and have a good half-term, but then, I'll see you on Wednesday evening. Perhaps we can manage a meal together before the start of the new term? Glad you got through today, Terence, without too much difficulty. How do you feel now?"

"I feel fine, dad, thank you," responded Terence to his dad's enquiry, then suggested that as he and Bradley, feeling rather peckish, had decided they were going for a double burger and chips, with lashings of tomato sauce, asked whether he would like to join them.

'Tutting' rather loudly at the proposed menu for their evening meal, Terence and Bradley were surprised when Jonathan said 'thank you' he would like to join them. Suddenly, Terence remembered it would have been his mother's birthday today, but as he was quite young at the time of her death, he had thoughtlessly forgotten. How like his dad to have said nothing, probably just going home to his now empty house, missing her badly, especially on her birthday. Was it too late to suddenly remember and give his father a hug of condolence or would it be better to keep quiet?

Then he remembered something else. The last time he had seen his mother happy and bright she had picked a flower from their garden, carefully showing him how to press a flower or a leaf, in the pages of a heavy book, leaving it to dry, but to keep forever, as a monument to the beauty of nature. Sinking his hands into the pockets of his old, rather tight now, favourite lumber jacket—his mother always bought on the large size to allow for growth, he found the folded piece of blue tissue paper that she had wrapped it in for him to keep. What if he could give it to his father, this evening, as a lasting gift from her, to both of them?

Bradley saw the agonised look on Terence's face wondering what had upset him so suddenly, then saw what he was holding something very carefully in his hands, when he suddenly realised that it may be the anniversary of his mother's death, in which case he would be an intruder at a very intimate time. With quick thinking, as they were strolling along, Bradley decided he really wasn't feeling too good and the thought of a burger meal was more than he could take, so would Jonathan and Terence mind if just made his way back to the flat now, have a snack and go to bed. He said he felt sure he would feel better in the morning.

Immediately, both his companions showed concern, saying they would walk him home and made sure he was alright. Bradley begged them not to, saying, when he felt poorly he was much better off on his own, not being fussed over. It took a while to convince them that he would rather be on his own and for them to continue having their meal together.

Eventually, Terence and Jonathan allowed him to leave, get home quickly, they said and go straight to bed. Jonathan added that if was not feeling well in the morning, not to come into the studio but see a doctor. Bradley agreed, walking away as if in some discomfort. Terence called out he would just have a quick burger, then he would be home as quickly as he could.

Bradley raised his hand in acknowledgement, hurrying around the corner, where he knew there was also a burger bar, bought one to eat on the way home, getting back as quickly as he could, in case Terence and Jonathan changed their minds, deciding to see him home, after all. Making himself a frothy coffee in the kitchen, Bradley hurried to his bedroom, to wait until morning, before approaching his friend again.

Meanwhile, Terence and his dad continued, in silence, towards their favourite burger bar, both concerned about Bradley, hoping he had managed to get home and into bed alright, although Terence, knowing Bradley so well, had a sneaky suspicion that his friend was faking when he said he felt unwell. He was perfectly well a few moments earlier and he knew Bradley had seen the look, on his face, when he realised he had not remembered that today would have been his mother's birthday. Just like Bradley, he thought, to come to his rescue!

Jonathan had been too absorbed in his own thoughts to have noticed anything untoward happening, staying a bit concerned still about Bradley, until Terence let him in on Bradley's secret ruse to let him and his father have some quiet time together. Jonathan was utterly taken aback, as he had no idea Bradley was role-playing, silently thanking him for this opportunity to be alone with his son on Margot's birthday.

Putting an arm around Terence's shoulder Jonathan hugged him, admitting that he wouldn't have expected Terence to remember his mother's birthday, as he was only a young lad, but claimed he was glad of his company this evening, nonetheless.

Eventually reaching the bar to order their preference—everyone in the area seemed to have the same idea-father and son sat companionably together, looking out on the still busy street, when Terence drew the tissue-wrapped gift from his pocket, handing it gently to Jonathan, saying it was a token of love, from Margot to both of them.

With unashamed tears in his eyes, Jonathan accepted the blue tissue offering, opening it carefully to reveal the exquisitely dried ruby pansy, that he knew Margot loved passionately, having planted them when they had, as newlyweds, moved into their first home. The pansies had matured and grown to cover, in their brilliance, a good sized part of the garden and now, here was her favourite, beautifully preserved.

As father and son gazed at the hardly little pansy, they both remarked it would be their best remembrance of an adored wife and mother. Carefully re-wrapping their precious memento, Terence and Jonathan finished their drinks, leaving the burger bar lighter-hearted than when they had arrived, in the knowledge that they were all united in a very special way.

The conversation, on the way to their respective homes, glad that somehow tonight had tightened the bond between them, in both love and respect, returned to the question of the 'specials' and the role they were destined to play in bringing comfort and peace to many, still walking in darkness and when, as yet to them, an unknown God, would reveal Himself.

Before going to his bedroom, that evening, Bradley had made a quick phone call to Oscar to bring him up to date on recent events, of both Terence and himself having been given stage roles, in a dance show, incorporated into 'The International Year of Dance'. Bradley added that his show was scheduled to take place over the Christmas period, closing in the New Year.

Oscar was naturally thrilled to hear the news and when Bradley spoke of his proposed plan to allow the 'specials' their 'debut,' on perhaps the last night of the show, having spoken to the directors and theatre manager in the meantime, he became even more excited.

Bradley then told him of the cautions he had received from both Terence and his father, with the result being to have a meeting, maybe for prayer, to seek God's timing. Asking whether it was possible to meet at Oscar's on Wednesday evening of next week, with Annette being asked to attend as well, Oscar was delighted to oblige. He knew, he said, that only God was in charge of this, therefore we needed to ask His plans for when the 'specials' began the story.

The next day Bradley told Terence how much better he was feeling, and, aware of a dubious look from Terence, he grinned back, hoping that father and son had welcomed the time spent together.

Owning up was a little too easy for Bradley, as he inadvertently let slip that he had telephoned Oscar last evening—adding quickly—before he went to bed, earning himself another dubious glance, adding that Oscar would be more than happy to host the meeting on Wednesday evening, as Jonathan had indicated it was his only evening free, from a busy week of planned meetings with other dance instructors, which were held not infrequently.

On seeing Bradley walk, with Terence, into the studio Jonathan's immediate concern was whether Bradley was well enough to attend classes that day, to be rewarded with a wink from Terence. When he was told of Oscar's agreement for the following Wednesday evening, it was even more evident Bradley had been faking the evening before, much to the gratitude of father and son. Feeling decidedly embarrassed by the situation, Bradley hastily changed the subject, taking an unnecessary length of time to change into his tap dancing shoes and clothing.

The week sped by, as there were necessary arrangements to be made, with final papers to be signed and submitted before the start of rehearsals for such a long-running show, such as the one Bradley had been selected to perform in. The venue chosen was a large Victorian theatre, slightly off the main theatre land, but still with star attraction. It was named 'The Blackbird Principle' theatre, with a large seating capacity, needed for such a large production.

By seven-thirty on the evening of the deciding meeting, the five participants were sipping coffee and nervously crunching on shortbread biscuits, in Oscar's lounge. The objects of calling the meeting were nowhere to be seen, as Bradley now used them in his and Terence's flat. As coffee mugs were emptied, Jonathan cleared his throat, saying that they all knew the reason why they were meeting that evening and, if Bradley explained further, hopefully, all would become clear.

Bradley remained seated, welcoming everyone in the room, then quietly repeated his desire to have the 'specials' given their own routine, after obtaining the authorisation of the directors and stage manager, of the Christmas dance show that he had been selected to perform in, as a dancer, on stage, a member of the background dancers, his first show to dance in front of an audience, fully accepting and understanding his acceptance or failure to be allowed to present the shoes, with the message that God had desired to be given, to many demoralised people, in the present world of destructive powers Win operation today.

He continued by saying, that, if they all agreed, this small group of friends would ask God to tell them His plans, for when, where and by whom should they present the 'specials,' tell the complete story, listen to the reactions by the audience and certainly the press, leaving the details to God, the maker of the universe and all creatures contained in it. As Bradley finished speaking there was a spontaneous move forward, to lean together, holding hands lightly but securely, bowing their heads in the presence of the Almighty, speaking in a simplistic, first-time prayer way, as in conversation to a listening presence.

This gradually became a dialogue, as prayers that were spoken were being answered. The first to admit to hearing from God was Annette, who had received a clear message that the shoes were indeed to be presented, to the public, in the evening performance of the day before the final closure of 'The Winter Special,' Jonathan then declared that God had told him that they were not to be concerned about the stage managers and directors refusing their request, as it had already been implanted in their hearts, as believers, that God was intending to speak to the waiting world, in a new way.

Gone was the anxiety, especially Bradley's, as the 'specials' were now in his possession and he felt the responsibility of them firmly on his shoulders. The question still remained though—who would present the 'specials' followed by Trevor's story, their magic powers given by God and the message He intended to share—was another answer this first prayer group were intent on finding—God's Will—encouraged by the answers they had already received.

After a few moments of awe-filled silence, Bradley uttered one name—Oscar. Looking slightly crestfallen, Bradley smiled at Oscar, confirming what he knew he had heard directly into his heart. Having known Trevor, designed the tap shoes according to Trevor's instructions and handcrafting them skilfully, the remainder of the group agreed with the decision, asking Bradley to verify, for the audience, Oscar's explanation of the 'specials' role, planned lovingly by God, to deliver His word.

On Monday, of next week, volunteered Bradley I will make an appointment for myself and Oscar, if he's willing, to arrange a suitable day to visit the directors (hopefully both will be there) and managers, to ask their consent to give the 'specials' their role to announce to the audience. The shoes would need to be shown with the complete unadulterated story. As God has told us, these men are already believers, so I'm certain we shall have no difficulty in obtaining their consent. Oscar said he was delighted to be able to accompany Bradley on any day that was decided.

Further coffee was declined by the remainder of these now closer-knit friends as they sombrely hugged each other, saying goodbye to Oscar and Annette, who would be walking together to Annette's home. The evening had been far more eventful than anticipated, giving them a good deal to think over.

The coming weekend had been set aside by Oscar and Annette, as, on the Saturday, the pair were celebrating Annette's birthday. Bradley had applauded their plans, as he could always take his mum out for a snack at lunchtime. In fact, he rather hoped that Oscar would ask the right question of Annette, as their relationship had been developing that way for some while.

Bradley was delighted, as he knew the pair of them needed love and companionship again after losing both Trevor and Anita. They shared a lot between them, even though Oscar was that much older, it didn't deter them from becoming good friends, then possible life partners. All that was needed was a slight push in the right direction!

These same thoughts had been in Oscar's mind as well, but, being a bit of a slow coach in the question of love, he wasn't sure if the timing was absolutely right. All his life he had been a stickler for doing all things at the right time, for all parties. He supposed it was a regime he was used to, as, being in the cobbler trade, particularly with the absolute correctness and fit of the dance shoes he adored handcrafting, he always had to be either exactly on time or slightly ahead of requirements for the many dancers who relied on that timing, as their very careers depended on it.

How much of that had spilt over into raising a family, maybe even annoying Anita, at times, with his correctness, Oscar wondered? The boys had never complained, nor Anita, come to that, probably shrugging it off as 'just being dad's way.' None appeared to have suffered, each child being treated the same way and they've all done well for themselves with good careers, nice wives, with children of their own, so why am I worrying now, though Oscar pensively? Maybe it was the thought of 'popping the question?'

He and Annette enjoyed looking around interesting shops in Soho, one day finding themselves in an oldie-worldie type one. Once inside, they were attracted to a counter containing trays of bold dress jewellery and couldn't help trying on some, with no intention of buying. A salesman had approached, insisting (in a polite way) on measuring their ring fingers.

It took a while to convince him that they were not buying. Whilst Oscar was apologising for wasting his time, Annette, in the meantime, was pricing up some rather unique water jugs. Joining her Oscar thought he had dropped a card at the first counter, and, as it was an excuse, made his way back to the jewellery counter, asking the salesman, who was still putting the rings away, the sizing of Annette's ring finger.

The salesman sniggered lightly but gave Oscar what he had asked for. Jotting the size onto a piece of paper, Oscar made his way back to Annette, who, all the while, had been unobtrusively hidden behind the water jugs, observing the paper being handed to him by the previous salesman, smiling to herself. She would accept if he was ready to ask!

Saturday came around very quickly, with the first thing on Oscar's mind was to telephone Annette, sending her his love on her birthday, reminding her to be ready by 7 PM, when he would collect her in the car and driver he had ordered for her celebration surprises. He had booked a table for them both at Annette's favourite restaurant, intending to allow her a free hand in choosing the menu, making sure beforehand that they had a bottle of champagne, on ice, to drink a toast with. Afterwards, Oscar had booked tickets to a show that Annette never seemed tired of seeing.

Reluctantly putting down his new phone, which he was still trying to get used to using, although Clive had recommended it, hoping it would encourage his father to keep more in touch with Michael and Patricia, with Oscar's grandchildren Martin, Dean, Sally and Anne, now in Singapore, with Micheal working for a prestigious bank that gave them a good life and hoping to come home for Christmas this year. The children, growing up fast, hadn't seen their grandparents since the year before Anita had died.

Oscar had taken Anita away for a rest, with Singapore being chosen as perhaps the last chance for her to see the grandchildren. It had been extremely hot that year and Anita had found it quite difficult, but glad she had come, as within six months of returning home she had been admitted to the hospital, dying six months later. The family had come to Anita's celebration of her life, but had returned to Singapore almost immediately for the children to get back, for a new term at the international school, they all attended.

Oscar had tried to keep in touch, but with a rather ancient telephone system, it was hard to keep the connection and the same when Michael had tried on many an occasion to ring his dad, but not always having enough time to say all he wanted to say. Clive had also told him he could use something on the phone called FaceTime, actually seeing, as well as talking easily to, the complete family. This Oscar was finding to be a great bonus, talking, and watching the children's demonstrations of their latest activities.

Before Oscar changed for the evening, he had one more shop to visit, this time to a well-known, modern jeweller, where Oscar was sure he would find exactly what he was looking for, that being an engagement and wedding band with which to give Annette an extra surprise, this evening. The helpful assistant realised that Oscar knew very little of his expectant wife's likes and dislikes, so, trying to be as casual as possible, he asked Oscar when his 'intended's' birthday was to which Oscar innocently replied, 'today,' wondering why that was important, until the assistant, smiling broadly, told Oscar that most ladies valued their birthstone, which he said, was diamond for this month.

Oh, thank you, stuttered Oscar, feeling a little foolish, because Anita had never bothered about that sort of thing. His eye fell on a very pretty ring of three fairly large diamonds, flanked by several smaller ones, looking like stars, set in a pretty gold band. Giving the assistant the ring size, which surprised him no end, he told Oscar the price, which to an inexperienced ear seemed rather high, but worth it to see Annette's pleasure.

The wedding band was a relatively easy choice, of which Oscar chose a low-carat simple ring that would reflect its beautiful shine for many years to come. Then a diamond necklace caught his eye, that would team magnificently with the engagement ring, becoming a must if he lost his nerve this evening. Leaving the shop with much lighter pockets than when he went in, Oscar was nevertheless pleased with his purchases.

Arriving home in time for a late snack, Oscar had plenty of time afterwards in which to contemplate the enjoyment of the evening ahead with Annette. It wasn't very long before Christmas was looming. Although Oscar always looked forward to his time with the family, this year promised to be somewhat different. For a start Michael, Patricia and the grandchildren were coming home this year from Singapore for the celebrations.

Although happily anticipating seeing them all, he also yearned to be at home, to be able to see more of Annette, but most importantly was his recently gained understanding of who God was, putting a slightly different emphasis now on how to celebrate the birth of Christ, of which he knew so little about, needing to attend a suitable church in which to learn. His thoughts were also with the 'The Winter Special,' and Bradley's expectations of himself being able to introduce the 'specials,' on the night before the final show.

By the end of next week, thought Oscar, we should have some of the answers. No more idling away the hours, it was time to change from comfortable loose day clothes to his good trousers and even better, a good jacket in which Oscar safely tucked away his reservation slip for the tickets to the show later. The elaborate boxes containing the rings and the flatter one with the diamond necklace, Oscar made sure were safely in the inside pockets of his jacket, he was just changing into. The necklace would be Annette's birthday present if he didn't have the courage to 'pop' the important question that evening.

Sure enough, at 7 PM promptly, the arranged car and driver, for the evening's entertainment, arrived. A uniformed young man rapped smartly on the front door of Oscar's flat, whereby the two walked the pavement distance to the car, with the driver respectably opening a rear passenger door for Oscar to enter the car. Pulling away from the flat, it was only a short while later that the driver performed the same procedure, politely ushering Annette into the rear of the car, alongside Oscar.

The restaurant was reached in plenty of time for Oscar to confirm the pick-up of Tim, to take them to the theatre before, laughingly, escorting Annette to their table, indicating that he gave her 'Carte Blanche' to choose from the menu, especially as it was her birthday. Taking her hand after their delicious meal, he chivalrously kissed it, at the same time murmuring, "Happy Birthday Darling," causing a ripple of merriment and 'knowing' nods, from the nearest tables.

Oscar decided to ignore this response, but Annette returned the gestures with a mischievous smile that lit her whole face. Finally, equally playfully, Oscar elicited a few more grins, by making a great display of trying to find something in his inner jacket pocket.

All eyes seemed to be on them, at that moment, wondering if they were going to witness a marriage proposal! Oscar's thoughts on this seem to diminish, as having already toasted her for her birthday, so Oscar placed a hand on Annette's arm, so preventing her from taking a second sip of champagne, whilst slipping the diamond necklace into her hands, whereby the glitter of the diamonds brought about oohs and aahs from the same tables.

Oscar played to the floor, so to speak, by opening the clasp to fasten them around Annette's slim neck, when a round of applause echoed around the restaurant. The chef and waiters, all of whom knew Annette well, stood quietly before presenting Annette with their own gift of her favourite perfume, the name of which they had managed to drag out of Simone, her sister.

Annette had not owned such a beautiful necklace before and she was overflowing in her thanks to Oscar, determined to wear them, at least when out together. The idea of him purchasing any rings after observing him return to the salesman in the Soho shop, had given her a slight pang of regret, but 'there's always next time,' Annette comforted herself with and they were a wonderful gift—the diamond necklace—a sure sign of his love, if a little shy of it himself, she thought.

Half an hour before the commencement of the show, that Annette knew Oscar was taking her to see, the name of which he hadn't divulged, she was anxious for the driver to appear with their car for the evening. A moment later having gathered up coats and bags, Oscar had the bill paid, waiting patiently now for the driver, who arrived apologising, but there had been a slight bumper-to-bumper exchange with another car, which had to be documented by the police, but the driver felt sure they would still be in plenty of time.

Making sure his passengers were comfortable, the driver added that he would be collecting another car, from his company, for the return journey from the theatre. True to his word, they drove steadily through the theatre going traffic, arriving in good time to collect the tickets and be shown to their seats. Thanking the driver for his consideration for their safety, watching him drive away, Oscar turned his attention back to Annette who was squealing quietly, in excitement, at seeing her favourite show, once more. Oscar did try to understand, as he could watch the ballets, that his past customers had danced in, over and over again, but he wasn't sure about a musical!

Enthusiastically, Annette tucked her arm into the crook of Oscar's, waited impatiently whilst he collected the pre-booked tickets, almost running, like a child, ahead of the usher, to settle and watch her CATS for perhaps the fourth time. Oscar was delighted to see her happy again, vowing to himself, that he would try to keep her that way, for the rest of their lives together. Anita, he felt sure would have applauded his intentions.

The show ended with rapturous applause, Oscar was convinced that Annette's had been the loudest! They were driven home uneventfully, paid and said goodnight to the driver, after which Annette offered Oscar a mug of coffee, but seeing that she was looking a little tired, Oscar kissed her gently, suggesting she glanced once more at the show's programme, then go straight to bed, to which she replied—yes sir—as he grinned at her response.

Tomorrow, Oscar eventually said, he was going to find a local church that, he hoped, may help him in his search to know more about God. Brightly Annette claimed she too, needed to know more, so could she join him, of which, of course, he was delighted. Having already searched the columns, in the local papers, he told her that the nearest seemed to be a Baptist Church, with the Pastor claiming you could never stop learning about The Heavenly Father. Starting at 10 AM, the pair arranged to meet at Oscar's at 9.30 with plenty of time to reach the church.

After a good night's rest, Annette arrived bright and sparkling, on Oscar's doorstep, the following morning, ready to walk with him to this Baptist Church he was so keen to visit, this Sunday. Oscar opened the door to greet her, brushing his lips tenderly against hers, as she returned the endearment, thanking him for making her birthday so memorable this year.

Linking arms, the couple walked towards the church discussing amiably the scant knowledge they had between them of what to expect this morning. Their recollections of attending churches were of weddings and funerals mostly, official, bearing little resemblance to the loving atmosphere of a God-given presence they had both known last Wednesday evening.

Surprised, Oscar and Annette found the Pastor, of the church, calling himself Stephen, waiting with a warm handshake of welcome at the open door, to greet his flock to morning service. Inside, the pair were astonished by members of the church milling around, having a cup of coffee and chatting with friends. Immediately, a youngish couple approached them, enquiring if they could get them a cup of tea or coffee, as they had a few minutes before the service began.

Accepting the invitation, Oscar and Annette were promptly served, whilst the couple who had offered the refreshment told them that they were members of the 'welcoming team' elected from being members of the congregation, to be on the alert for newcomers, making sure they felt completely at home and included totally into the service. Introducing themselves as Patrick—known as Pat—and Angela—better known as Ange Rather breathlessly Oscar and Annette hastily finished their drinks, to find themselves being gently propelled by Pat and Ange, to seats towards the centre of the church, followed by their newfound friends.

Looking as unobtrusively, as they could, around them Oscar and Annette seemed surrounded by a vast sea of smiling faces. The service was nothing like they had ever witnessed before, but strangely enough, they felt totally relaxed, listening intently to the message given, even attempting to sing the unknown songs and hymns. The Bible, from which the Pastor spoke, radiantly and with reverence, was almost impossible for them to understand, but helped by Pat and Ange, they began to recognise a little of what they had heard before. As for the prayers, they knew a little about them, didn't they?

The service ended with what Pat explained was an 'altar call', for anyone to come forward, for prayer, if they wanted to know more about Jesus, but Pastor Andrew had said simplistically there was to be no pressure implied, at all.

Oscar and Annette declined to stay after the service ended, as they had much they would like to talk about, but made it pretty clear they would be returning again, maybe next week. They were not delayed, shook hands with Pastor

Andrew, finding themselves with leaflets, in their hands, with invitations to friendship groups, home groups and Bible Study groups, most of which they put to one side, to read together, later.

Entirely satisfied, Oscar and Annette walked, with a lighter step, back to Annette's home, talking as if they were excited children, knowing that something wonderful was growing in their hearts. Jonathan, Bradley and Terence would be told, in the near future what had occurred this Sunday, but, in the meantime, their thoughts were turning to tomorrow, when Bradley would be arranging a suitable day, for him and Oscar to meet with the directors, stage and theatre managers of the Christmas show, putting their request, to allow the 'specials' their first time on stage, preparing the audience for a message from God Himself. What a privileged, unimaginable task!

By the next morning, Oscar was feeling pretty exhausted. The weekend had been such an eventful one from start to finish, that he rolled over luxuriously in his comfortable bed unaware of the clock ticking quietly, on his bedside table. Suddenly awake, with alarm bells ringing in his head, his mind struggled to clear itself. Then he became fully alert realising that today Bradley would be arranging a day for their meeting with the Christmas show managers and directors, requesting a time slot in which the 'specials' could be given free rein, for their own message to be interpreted, to the hungry world.

Having showered and dressed, Oscar felt alive again. Cocky was still waiting for his breakfast, perched on a low branch in the cherry tree, occasionally chirping loudly to remind Oscar that this wasn't Sunday morning and he was hungry. "Sorry, Cocky," yelled Oscar. "Breakfast is coming!"

With a swish of tiny wings, the friendly bird was perched on Oscar's arm, thankfully swallowing the worms and slurping the milk before flying off over the buildings—to where Oscar didn't know—

Time was passing too slowly for Oscar, who'd had his ear glued to the phone all the morning. Now it was 3 o'clock in the afternoon and Bradley still hadn't called. What could have gone wrong? He needn't have been concerned for much longer, as there was a tap at the door and Bradley walked in, with a smile from ear to ear.

Apologising for the delay, he told Oscar that the two directors had not arrived at the time of his first call, so he'd had to call again, in the afternoon. The pair had just arrived after having had to re-schedule rehearsal dates, because two young dancers had to complete a vital examination paper on the original day they were expected to fly to England, now arriving a few days later. All was sorted now, with rehearsals beginning next week, in a building near 'The Blackbird Principle.' theatre.

Bradley added he would receive the dates within the next couple of days. He then saw that Oscar was impatiently itching to ask the vital question, so, to put his mind at ease, he told him that he had briefly told them about some extra special tap shoes, handcrafted by an experienced cobbler and thought they might to see them, arranging a meeting, for both of them on Thursday afternoon, soon after 2 PM, if that was alright by Oscar, who was nodding his head emphatically.

It was Wednesday evening, when Oscar had begun to nod off in front of the television, that an unexpected call interrupted his thoughts. Hastily putting his new phone to his ear, Oscar realised that he couldn't hear the caller. Asking several times who it was, he suddenly understood that he was supposed to press the winking green light, to connect to the person at the other end of the phone. Feeling somewhat foolish, Oscar inquired again who was calling, only to hear a chuckle and a voice say, "You'll get used to it in time, dad and don't forget to 'hang up' by pressing the red button." Timothy's voice came through the receiver, clear as crystal.

"It's alright for you, son," twinkled back Oscar. "You and your brothers have adapted well to these new-fangled things. We didn't have them when you were very young and your mother and I managed very well with what we had, not seeing any reason to change. Anyway, to change the subject now, how are you all and that rascally great-grandson of mine?"

"We're all well, thank you, dad," countered Timothy, laughing. "I know we only spoke to you a week or so ago, but are you still keeping well and how is Annette? You told me then that it was her birthday soon. Did she enjoy the meal out and the show you planned to take her to see?"

"You're not usually so inquisitive, Timothy," Oscar retorted, smiling to himself, "but 'yes, thank you', we both had a very enjoyable evening."

"I'm glad, dad," Timothy tried again. "We are all pleased that you've found a close friend, with who you can share good times together, but without sounding like an anxious son, you haven't told us very much about Annette. Is Bradley, who you are helping through tap dancing school, her son, whose father was killed in a motorway accident? How about if you invited her for Christmas, with us here in Fareham, this year?

"It's been generally decided that, as we seem to own the largest house, the family would come here to celebrate, with everyone helping out. It will be a bit of a squeeze, but all the merrier, we'll manage nicely, as we usually do! I know Christmas is still a few weeks away, but as soon as Dillon understood Christmas would be here, he's pestered me nonstop to ring you, with the plans of asking you and Annette to join us, although on saying that, I'm concerned about Bradley, her son."

Oscar was immediately contrite, mentally kicking himself for not saying too much about Annette and Bradley, for the simple reason, that he thought they would disapprove or worse, not understand the attraction between them. He realised he had to put things straight between him and his family.

"Timothy, please forgive me," began Oscar. "I have been very selfish in keeping so quiet about Bradley and Annette.

"The truth is, I suppose, I didn't know your thoughts or the others, on me taking another woman out after we lost your mother. It's my fault. I should have known you all, only have my best interests at heart. Annette and I have a lot in common, as her husband Trevor, who died, was one of my most deserving customers, asking me to hand craft a very special pair of tap shoes, for him, that if he had lived, could have made him the fastest tap dancer in the world. I suppose his loss was so difficult, I found it hard to share yet another loss.

"As you've probably reasoned, Annette is several years younger than me and was a choreographer in one of the theatres that Trevor danced in frequently. There, I hope I've made my peace. Am I forgiven, Timothy?"

"Dad, I am so sorry if I've been hard on you tonight. I really had no idea how close you came to be, with the artists whose needs you catered for, for so many years. I should be the one apologising to you, for not allowing you to retain your own grief. Will you forgive me, dad?"

"Of course, son," replied Oscar, with a hint of tears in his voice. "Perhaps we should have had this conversation a long time ago. Now, about your kind invitation for Christmas. I would very much like to come, thank you, as we'll all be together again, after a few years without having Michael, Patricia and their four, who, I have been learning to speak to and watch their antics, whilst on my new phone.

"Who I can't answer for is Annette, as she will very likely have Bradley home. He has been given the opportunity this year, to have been given a role in a Christmas show, called *The Winter Special* rather like dance organza, and, I must admit I did tell him I would be able to see him, again, on stage, a couple of days before the end of the show, the week after Christmas, coming up to the New Year. Would that be alright if I left before we've finished the celebrations?"

"That shouldn't be a problem, dad, as by then I think we will all have had our fair celebrating, what with the New Year descending on us as well," mused Timothy. "By the way, dad, just to stop you thinking of a long train journey, I've happily volunteered to drive up to London and pick you up. I thought of coming the day before Christmas Eve, stay overnight with you, have a catch-up, then drive back to Fareham the next day, in time for Christmas.

"Actually, you'd be doing me a big favour. By the time I collect you the house will be full of presents to be wrapped and the final decorations to be put up, also full of the family vying for a place to deposit their food offering or wanting to cook, and, to be honest, I would rather be out of it. Once I've bought the tree, potted it, often decorated it as well, I am pretty redundant, unless I get roped into present wrapping, with young Dillon racing around in excitement. Wait a moment, he's clinging frantically to my arm, wanting to have a word, I think!"

"Hello, young man, how are you, getting excited, I expect?" answered Oscar to Dillon's 'Hello, great-grandpa;' can I come to London, with grandad, to bring you to our house for Christmas, please, please say 'yes.' I want to see you again, in your new home.

"He's scampering off to ask his mum, dad."

"Would you mind if he came, he'd be good company for me in the car and I know he can't wait until Christmas Eve to see you."

"No problem," laughed Oscar. "I'll buy a single mattress and I've seen a gorgeous Christmas sleeping bag that I'll buy him. Maybe let him bring his own pillow, to help him feel at home and he can sleep with you in the spare room. Does that sound alright?"

"Sounds good, dad, but I bet I know whose bed he'll end up in. I'll tell him he can come, as long as he's a good boy and does as he's told."

"Let him be," chided Oscar. "We'll have a great romp. Thanks for the call Timothy, I'll call you with an answer to your question, but, I doubt it, this year. I promise you'll meet Annette soon enough, OK? Give my love to Priscilla and the girls. Goodnight, son."

"Night, dad, sleep well and I'll speak to you again soon," said Timothy, ending the call.

Oscar made his way into the kitchen to make a hot drink before going to bed. He had enjoyed his talk with Timothy, but it had rather drained him, leaving him mentally exhausted. 'No time to ruminate on the past,' he told himself sternly. He had been rather wrapped up with seeing to the needs of others and his own children had almost been put onto the back burner, so to speak. He knew he had his own life to lead, but the family was part of that life too.

Falling into a dream-free sleep, Oscar slept well until the morning light filtered through his bedroom curtains. It was a fine day Oscar observed as he made his way to the kitchen window, to see if his chirpy friend was there and sure enough 'Cocky' was waiting patiently for breakfast. Worms and warm milk were soon dispatched, then with a small flutter of wings, he was gone. Won't Dillon just love him, pondered Oscar, happily wondering what today's meeting at the theatre would reveal.

Idly, but thoughtfully, Oscar decided he would find the new mattress for Dillon, perhaps buying the Christmas sleeping bag that had caught his eye. Dillon would soon snuggle into its soft quilty warmth, he hoped and not his son's bed!

Oscar's mind was not really on Christmas, but with meeting up with Bradley this afternoon. This close, though, he abstractedly wandered around the shops, keeping his eyes open for suitable gifts for friends and family. Finding himself not far from the Soho shop that had enticed Annette and himself, a few weeks back, Oscar found himself gazing in the window at the same water jugs that had attracted Annette's attention at the time. They were certainly colourful, in a bizarre type of way.

He certainly wasn't averse to them, so he entered the shop to enquire the price. Much sought after, he was assured by the eager salesman. A little pricy for a water jug, thought Oscar, but if Annette really liked them, who was he to argue! One down and about ten to go, decided Oscar, referring to his gift list, at least the cards have been written, ready to be posted nearer Christmas.

The mattress was easy enough to find, arranging a delivery for the next day, not so, the sleeping bag. Sadly, the shop had sold out, but not to be deterred, Oscar made his way to a well-known department store, where a similar, but just as appealing, sleeping bag was in stock. Picking up his purchases, Oscar decided to get home, have a toasted snack, then meet Bradley, as arranged.

So, shortly after the appointed time, Oscar, Bradley, two stage directors and the theatre and stage manager, Bradley was asked, not impolitely, the reason for having asked for this meeting. Untying the 'specials' from around his neck, he introduced Oscar as having been the cobbler who had designed and handcrafted the shoes, on the instructions of Trevor Braithwaite. Heads nodded, affirming that Trevor was known to them. Bradley then revealed that Trevor had been his father, arousing further interest.

Turning their attention to the 'specials,' the directors and managers remarked that they had indeed been skilfully made, but not unusually so, therefore, they asked what was the surprise element attached to them, which was the cue Bradley needed to launch into the full story. Listening enrapt, Bradley was asked to demonstrate his claim, whereupon he set the shoes down near the edge of the stage where the six men had been sitting, imploring them to not mess this up, but perform two of their best routines.

Bradley knew he had no need to be concerned, as he watched the pair give their best performances he had seen for a while. Tapping to well-known pieces, Bradley watched the faces of their hosts, absolutely mesmerised by the 'specials' routines, whilst anxiously checking Oscar and Bradley for any sign of tampering, but, of course, could find none.

Even after the dances, they asked if they could examine the shoes for any evidence of batteries or wires, without anything being found. As the four looked even more puzzled by what they hadn't found, they came to the same conclusion, together, that this could be the very reason they had been told in a prayer meeting that God was doing something special, very special, very soon.

Nodding in agreement, Bradley was asked to tell them more about why the shoes were so special, which was the ideal opportunity to tell their hosts about the visitation of the two angels from God, who, much to the astonishment, of the six who were attending to the final clearing up after the summer show, announced that it was indeed God who, through an unusual dispensation would 'magic' the shoes, that had been exclusively made for Trevor, his father, continued Bradley earnestly.

Since my father's death, he said, God then gave the usage and administration of the 'specials' to his son, who is here now, with the skilled cobbler who made them, to ask your permission to use them at the end of the evening show, on the evening before the final closure of the show, allowing God to use them according to His will.

It was decision time, as Oscar and Bradley sat calmly observing the faces of the four men sitting opposite them! Without a flicker of an eyelid between the four, the English director said, "If this is the will of God and we all sincerely believe it is, then we have no power to obstruct Our Lord, in what He proposes and when He wants to begin, so all we can say is 'Blessings' to you both and we will make a slight rearrangement of timing to the programme on that night. We are very privileged to be allowed to assist you in revealing His word, through the 'specials' and His chosen representatives."

After a prayer of praise and thanksgiving, the six men unselfconsciously hugged goodnight and without any more needing to be said, Oscar and Bradley left the meeting place, rejoicing in the goodness of God. Telling the others of their successful afternoon, Oscar and Bradley only began to realise how little it had been of their doing and, that, the acceptance had already been assured.

The following week Bradley was due to commence rehearsals, for the 'Christmas show,' with Jonathan generously offering to give any assistance needed, plus time away from the studio for the rehearsal times, so Oscar decided to ask Bradley if he had given any thought to Christmas shopping, before he was tied up with rehearsals and then the length of time that the show was running for. Bradley grinned a little sheepishly, saying that he had some idea of what to buy for the immediate family, but hadn't had time to purchase anything yet.

"Why don't the two of us have a day out together for some Christmas shopping and lunch," suggested Oscar. "If you have any youngsters to buy a gift for, we could visit Hamley's toy shop in Regent Street."

"Yes, I'd like that," replied Bradley. "I would like to buy a small gift for a couple of newcomers at the studio who are struggling a little, as a small encouragement. I don't start rehearsals until Tuesday, so could manage Monday, if that's alright with you, Oscar?"

"Yes, Bradley," replied Oscar. "Your mother may have told you about our excursion to church on Sunday, but I'd like to tell you my bit and what a revelation it was. Shall we meet up at your flat, say 11 AM?"

"That's fine," grinned Bradley, "it seemed a long time since we had a day out together, doing ordinary things. I'll be getting back to the studio now, as I can't skip practice time, now that I shall be given all the time I need off for rehearsals. I shall look forward to Monday though. Bye for now, Oscar."

Making his way home with the intention of ringing Timothy, when he was home from his job as headmaster at Tudor Academy, a local secondary school that his son had been headmaster of, for several years, hard work he claimed, but loving the contact he had with the children and the privilege of teaching, when time in the office, allowed. Having spoken to Annette regarding Timothy's and Priscilla's invitation for Christmas they both knew it would be impossible, as Bradley and Annette, with several other family members, would be meeting up for Christmas Dinner, in The Stag, another favourite haunt of Annette's and Trevor's.

The owner, with his head chef and regular waiters, loved opening up for small parties on Christmas Day. Although Bradley's show was being staged in the afternoon, as well as in the evening, he would have just enough time to celebrate with the family. Before being asked to join Oscar with his family, Annette had hoped he could have joined their little gathering, but he had firmly promised to be home for the debut of the 'specials'. Besides, he had a role to perform with Bradley.

Making his way home for a welcome cup of tea, Oscar remembered he must ring Timothy and Priscilla, to thank them for including Annette in their Christmas plans, but would need to apologise, on her account, that she would be unable to attend with Oscar. Picking up the phone when Oscar estimated it should be about time for Timothy to arrive home, he keyed the number, to hear his son's voice.

"Good evening, this is Timothy Harrison speaking. Can I help you?

"Good evening to you too, son." intoned Oscar, amusingly. "I'm phoning you, Timothy, on behalf of Annette, who thanks you and Priscilla for your invitation to the family Christmas celebrations, but sorry, as she is, it's impossible for her to come. Bradley, her son, will be coming home and other members of the family are joining them.

"Don't worry though, all our family will be meeting her soon enough, as I have recently received an invitation, from Clive and Annabelle, to attend Mary and Martha's double wedding, on 14 February in a Pwo-Karen tribal village, in the northern highlands of Thailand, where their prospective husbands Steve and Karin live. By the way, Timothy, have you two given any thoughts on what to buy as a wedding gift for each couple? I really have no idea, but hang on, I think maybe I have just got the right gift in mind."

"What is it, dad?" enquired Timothy, sounding intrigued. "If you have any bright ideas for us, then please let us know. We're stumped."

"OK, I'll tell you," confessed Oscar. "Where do you think the two couples will live when they are married? I do know a little from reading books on the subject that the wives go to live with the husband's parents, but I can't imagine our two accepting that tradition, they are modern thinkers and will want their own homes, even if they live in the same village as two couples? What about if I offer to build those two homes, for them, as their wedding gifts, unless, of course, they have other ideas?"

"That's a brilliant idea, dad," exclaimed Timothy, "but have you given any thought to the cost of two homes?"

"In a way yes," confided Oscar. "The homes or butterfly houses as they are known locally, because when finished they look somewhat similar to a native butterfly, must be relatively cheap, as they are built from natural materials found in nearby forests, i.e. bamboo canes used as the holding structures, interwoven with leafy branches from a wide variety of deciduous trees or palm leaves forming the rain repellent roofing and walls, all gathered and built by local Thai men who own and plant the fields, so building their own homes are taken naturally.

"It is subsistence farming, but which Steve and Karin will probably undertake, unless they have other plans. I have heard that Elephants are being introduced into Thailand to aid lifting and carrying, likely in use for pulling stumps of lopped trees, from the ground. If they're that forward-thinking, who knows, they could keep a few, hiring them out at a reasonable rate or in exchange for assistance in the fields when the crops are gathered, for sale in the local market or in cities such as Chang Mai.

"They are bound to need cooking utensils, pots and pans, etc., which you could buy locally when you get to know what they would like. I think we stay in Chang Mai for the first night after we arrive, so you could sound out Annabelle, she's bound to know their needs and purchase some items for their homes. I'm going to speak to Annabelle later on to find out where they propose living, the cost of labour and if we can get everything underway before their big day."

"Gosh, dad, you must have done quite a lot of reading to have become so knowledgeable of life with the hill people or the Karen's. I think though I'm going to have to come back to this interesting conversation another time, as I can hear Priscilla calling 'hello' to you, and, to me, that's suppers on the table."

"Alright, son, I'll let you get some food inside you," so returning Priscilla's greeting, then saying goodbye to Timothy, Oscar reluctantly put down the phone. He always enjoyed talking with his sons, but Timothy seemed to give him his full attention, possibly because he was a teacher, prepared to listen to his pupils.

Taking his empty teacup into the kitchen, Oscar made himself a light supper before settling down to watch a football match but woke up halfway through realising he had missed a goal, scored by the team he supported. What kind of husband would he be for Annette, Oscar wondered, falling asleep almost as soon as he put the television on. He wasn't seeing her this evening, as she and her sister Simone were having a 'girly' night washing and restyling each other's hair, as long as Simone didn't get an emergency call-out!

Tomorrow evening, though, Oscar had booked seats for a pre-Christmas ice show, promising a good evening's entertainment. Neither had seen a show live, on the rink, only when there was television coverage, so both were looking forward to it immensely, probably, thought Oscar, with a light snack and drinks beforehand.

Looking at his watch, Oscar realised he had left it too late to call Clive and Annabelle, to ask their advice about having two homes built, in the selected village, where Mary and Steve and Martha and Karin wanted to start their married lives, in Thailand. Tomorrow he would them give a call. If Clive was at work, Oscar hoped Annabelle would be at home. He reasoned that she would be more likely to know the couple's plans than Clive would. He had already acknowledged the invitation, which included Annette, but it wouldn't do any harm to confirm its arrival, besides he found Annabelle an easy person to have a conversation with. Sleep came easily that night.

Oscar made an early start the next day, as he wanted to speak to Annabelle before she busied herself with shopping or anything else that might take her out of the house. Cocky, as usual, was waiting for his anticipated breakfast, before he flew off until the next morning. After getting ready for the day, Oscar telephoned his son Clive's home, as soon as he thought it was a reasonable time, in the morning.

As expected, Annabelle answered the phone, sounding pleased to hear Oscar's voice, but wondered if everything was well, as he was calling not long after Clive had left for work, in the small but cosy café, he and a friend owned together, making a comfortable living for them both. Oscar hastily reassured Annabelle that he was fine, but had a question for her regarding Mary and Martha's wedding gifts and needed to find her at home to be able to discuss the advisability of what he was proposing.

Before beginning his questions, Oscar made sure that his and Annette's wedding acceptance had been received, to which Annabelle replied that it had and how delighted she and Clive were at the prospect of meeting Annette, who, they knew, were close friends with many interests between them. Laughing at Oscar's intensity with the matter concerning his two adopted granddaughters, Annabelle quickly brought her father-in-law back to the questions she knew he was hesitating to ask.

"You spoke, Oscar," she said, "about wedding gifts for our pair of future brides. Do you have anything specific in mind or would you like to discuss the options? It's very kind of you to think already of what the girls would appreciate for their weddings. I believe most of the guests are going to wait until they arrived in Thailand, to find something originally Thai, that the couples would like to have in their new homes."

"Ah, yes, new homes," muttered Oscar, not sure where to begin. "I will tell you now, Annabelle, of a recurring idea that I can't get out of my head. I have no knowledge of the young men's tastes, but I did wonder where both couples will make their homes. My idea is that my wedding gift to both couples could be to provide homes for them, but I wonder if they have other plans, rather than live in any of the Pwo-Karen villages. I immediately thought you might be the best person to ask."

Oscar heard a small gasp at the other end of the phone, then eagerly waited for Annabelle to reply.

"Oscar, you're the answer to my prayers," answered his daughter-in-law. "To tell the truth, I have been concerned about the very same thing and I do know that Mary and Martha would like their own homes once they are married. I understand the boys have talked to both sets of parents, who I understand, haven't been too offended at the decision, knowing how differently young people think today, about old traditions.

"Initially, the two couples said they would work in nearby towns to raise enough money to build their independent houses. Steve and Karin, both delightful young men who were at school together, grew up into hard-working lads and wanted to do their best for our daughters. I'm sure you'll get on well with them when we see you both at the double wedding, very soon Oscar."

"I'm sure I will," continued Oscar. "To get back to the question of homes, have you got time to discuss this now, Annabelle or shall I ring back at a more appropriate time? If this is the way to help both couples, we may need to act swiftly."

"Oscar, this is a very generous offer you are making, but even in the villages, it would probably cost 300-400 pounds each. We'll help too, of course, but the ceremony and flights are going to be pretty expensive to begin with, although overnight stays for our guests are not too costly in Chang Mai. Oh dear, Oscar, I sound like a terrible complainant, I am sorry, it's probably because it all seems so so far away, but we do want Mary and Martha to be happy and I think they will, with Steve and Karin."

"Then let me help. You'll make an old man very happy. It seems to me as if you've been worrying over this for some time," interrupted Oscar.

"I probably have, but Clive and I realised when we adopted the girls that one day we would likely experience these very same problems, as now and need to handle them wisely. Mary and Martha fully understand our anxieties, assisting us in many ways. They are brilliant daughters but are keen to fully explore their ancestry. Having chosen to marry Thai men, making their homes in Thailand, Clive and I will do all we can to support them in that decision."

"That's good. Now tell me, Annabelle, have the two couples decided where they want to live when they are married? Are they going to choose one of the Karen villages?" enquired Oscar, patiently waiting for his daughter-in-law to calm herself enough to answer his questions. He was very fond of Annabelle and knew that she and Clive had opened their home, as well as their hearts, to these two orphans, from a Thailand orphanage, but, if he was going to help in building homes for the betrothed couples, Oscar needed answers soon, so that the project could be started.

Annabelle sat staring at the phone for a moment, sipping a cup of coffee, before hesitantly answering Oscar's questions. "Sorry, Oscar," she finally spluttered. "I must admit, I've been feeling a little stressed out and your wonderful offer came as a complete surprise. I'm not going out until later this morning, to meet the girls, during their lunch break, to go through the responses to the wedding invitations to get some idea of the number of guests who are attending.

"I can discuss your offer with them and get back to you this evening if that's alright with you. I know they will be absolutely thrilled, as housing was a big concern, not being that keen to start married life with in-laws for too long. In answer to your question about where they would like to live, both couples are going to live in the same village and the boys will work on the land initially. It is only subsistence farming, but Mary and Martha are keen to mould into the village life of the Pwo-Karen, willing to subsidise the farming by making embroidery garments to sell to the increasing tourist trade or in the local markets.

"Fortunately, they are both creative, with designing and making clothes, being good with their hands generally. Art and design was the subject they chose to study at university, which will be a big advantage for them. They have chosen a village in which to settle. It's with the same hillside Pwo-Karen, in a mountainous region, surrounded by mixed deciduous trees and pine forests, both with high canopies to allow the light and sunshine through, always needed for the land, as well as the rain. The village is called Suay, a Thai name meaning beautiful, which sounds great. Clive and I can't wait to see it!

"Apparently, all further logging in the area has been forbidden by the government, so it should remain undisturbed. Although it's a fair-sized village, there is still plenty of land on which to build homes or farmsteads. Karin and Steve would just need to name their selected space to the elder of the village for the work of the building to begin."

"It does sound a lifetime away from our way of living, answered Oscar. Mary and Martha seem to have no difficulty there, knowing that Karin and Steve are where they want to make their future homes. You will all miss each other at first but knowing you and their wizardry with modern technology you will all keep very much in touch, as I'm learning as well, exclaimed her father-in-law enthusiastically. Since this idea came to me, I've been doing a bit of research into the life of the Pwo-Karen and the structure of their homes, which you and Clive have seen firsthand.

"As I understand it, all the homes are built from material from the forests; bamboo canes as the main holding structures, with leafy deciduous branches tightly interwoven between them for the walls and palm leaves, again tightly interwoven for a cooling, waterproof roof. The second level, usually the kitchen is laid with planking packed together. A veranda or living area, with open sides, is used for the tapestry and embroidery work done by the women. Steps to the upper areas are constructed from logs bound together with twine. Am I right, Annabelle?" enquired Oscar.

"Yes, you're right," replied his daughter-in-law, adding a few more interesting facts. "The homes cannot be built alongside each other, as in terraces, once a common site in industrial towns in our country. The reasoning behind these thoughts is twofold, firstly, because of the Thai belief in animism; that all objects have a spiritual essence, either good or bad, so homes joined together can allow an evil spirit to go from one house to another.

"To prevent this from happening, houses are built some distances apart. The second reason being held is that during the heavy rainfalls in certain seasons, so again strong rains can penetrate to another house built immediately next door, which seems a plausible reason as the houses, being constructed from vegetation from the forests will easily be absorbed by the close proximity of another house. The couples therefore plan to have their homes on different sites in Suay. I will tell the girls, this afternoon, of your kind offer."

"Good, that's great," enthused Oscar. "Thanks, Annabelle, for taking the time to talk to me this morning, I really appreciate it. Perhaps one last thing, would you ask Mary and Martha to ask the boys to find a builder in the village as soon as possible? I would be happy for them to start work as soon as they could and I'm more than willing to pay their asking price to build two homes, if possible, before the 'big event'."

"I will certainly do that, Oscar. I'll call you back as soon as the arrangements have been made and the girls will want to speak to you too."

With that, Oscar and Annabelle said their goodbyes. Oscar to have a cup of coffee, before taking Annette for their light lunch and drinks, after which he was looking forward to a delightful afternoon spent in Annette's company enjoying the ice show. He asked for a taxi to collect him shortly, then picked up Annette for their lunch at the ice rink, which boasted a cosy restaurant, to begin the afternoon with.

Annabelle, in the meantime, hurried through her household chores, excitedly anticipating her daughter's acceptance of the wedding gifts, a problem that had been so generously solved, by their grandfather. She knew it would give Oscar as much pleasure to build the homes as it would be for the two couples to receive them.

After a brief food shop, Annabelle, Mary and Martha greeted each other warmly, in their favourite coffee bar and after exchanging general snippets of news from around the workplace, then taking a look at the acceptances received, Annabelle gave the girls the greatest piece of news yet, that their future housing problems had been solved, by their grandfather wanting to give them a house each, in their chosen village, as wedding gifts. The girls' faces lit up with joy at this unexpected offer. Promising to thank Oscar as soon as possible, Mary and Martha said goodbye to their mother, to return to work, for the afternoon.

As expected, Annette was ready and waiting for Oscar when the taxi arrived. During the drive to the ice rink, Oscar filled her in on his talk with Annabelle, this morning and the fact that his offer had answered a huge question about homes following the honeymoon period, but that Annabelle seemed rather stressed by the organisation needed for weddings, so far away.

Annette was quick to understand, although, as both Annabelle and Clive had anticipated this problem ahead when they adopted Mary and Martha, the reality of it now was slightly different, as that, they themselves were so much older. This adventure was likely to be the topic of conversation for the Christmas celebrations at Timothy's and Priscilla's in just three weeks' time!

Driving up to enter the cosy restaurant, they put the weddings aside for a moment of relaxation in an unknown but pleasant area. The evening snack was delicately served, after they had a cocktail each, before following the audience being taken to their places in ringside sears, which Oscar and Annette could claim, as well. After a short period of music from the orchestra, lights flared across the large rink, placing the audience in spooky darkness, in anticipation of the body of the cast giving experts from the show before individual numbers were performed. It was indeed a magical entrance from the skaters, in a startling array of costumes and colours.

Settling back to enjoy the entertainment, Oscar and Annette were fascinated by the skill of the skaters, pirouetting on the ice-cold rink, in any number of different roles. All too soon, it was the grand finale performed by the entire cast. The audience clapped in enthusiasm, until their hands were raw, encouraging the skaters as they trooped away from the rink, many of whom would appear on the ice, again tomorrow evening or until the show had run its course. What an incredible introduction to the Christmas season, though the pair, making their way outside to await the arrival of their taxi.

Arriving at Annette's home, they both got out with Oscar paying the fare, with the intention of walking to his home after a cup of coffee with Annette. Once inside, they talked quietly about the evening, so as not to awaken the rest of the family, but to their surprise, Simone almost followed them indoors with an irrepressible smile on her face, at finding her sister and Oscar drinking coffee in the kitchen.

A heavily pregnant expectant mum had needed urgent attention earlier on that evening and having seen her safely admitted into the maternity unit of their local hospital, she herself was looking forward to a warm drink before joining her husband in bed. Setting the steaming cup of coffee in front of her, Oscar said his good nights, after saying he would next see Annette for this coming Sunday's service at Merryfields Baptist Church, to which she replied she would call for him on her way to the church. They were now regular attendees fully taking in every word that their Pastor spoke, committed now to giving their lives to Jesus, leading others to find the joy and happiness they had found as believers.

After Oscar had left, Simone looked quizzically at her sister, wondering, no doubt, thought Annette, when Oscar was going to propose. He had already given Simone every reason to believe that he loved her sister and, in due course, asked for her hand in marriage. Annette shrugged her shoulders laughingly, saying that you couldn't hurry a man like Oscar, but was sure it was only a question of timing. Simone too had shown a keen interest in the ecstatic happiness her sister and Oscar displayed on returning to church each Sunday. Annette had spoken briefly about her and Oscar's experiences since belonging to the church family but was as yet a little shy in sharing her faith.

The next day, being a Saturday, Oscar was looking forward to hearing from Mary and Martha that arrangements had been made to start building their homes. When his mobile phone sprung to life whilst Oscar was preparing some lunch for himself, it slightly startled him, but on putting the receiver to his ear he was delighted to hear Martha's voice, with Mary's in the background. He was equally startled to hear Martha say, "khaawp-khami maak."

"Hello, grandpa," said Martha, in English this time. "I just wanted to surprise you with a 'thank you very much,' in Thai. The word maak is equivalent to very in English and just to surprise you even more, a woman would say in Thai-kob khun ka or thank you. Mary and I, as well as Kevin and Steve, are overwhelmed with your wedding gifts to us and we can't thank you enough. We are in the process of finding a local village builder who would be willing to erect the two homes before the ceremony. Steve is quite certain he has found the right man and, with a friend, can begin building two conventional homes in Suay. A lovely village that I am sure you will fall in love with when you and Annette come out in February."

Oscar could hear Mary, in the background, thanking him exuberantly at her end of the phone line. It was always a pleasure to talk to his two adopted grandchildren, who were sparkling and bright whenever he telephoned the family.

"You are both and the boys, very, very welcome," returned Oscar. "You have made an old man extremely happy. I'm delighted at your choice of young men and both I and Annette are getting excited at the thought of attending this wonderful double wedding very soon. We send you all our love and blessings for happy lives, for the pair of you."

They then said their farewells sending each other greetings for an enjoyable Christmas. Thankfully Oscar had restrained from mentioning the fact that both Mary and Martha were marrying into animistic families, a fact that Annabelle had not spoken of, to Oscar, who wondered what her's and Clive's thoughts were or even if they had given it any real consideration, so keen were they to see the girls happily married and where they would make their homes.

With animism being an ancient religion Oscar wasn't sure how much it mattered in everyday life and whether the thought that everything, being animal, vegetable or mineral had a soul and therefore a spiritual existence would affect the relationships, at all. How easily could the girls unthinkingly offend their in-laws? Wondering if he could broach the subject to Pastor Stephen, after church, the next day, Oscar settled himself in front of the television set to watch his favourite football team, win their selected match, taking them into the finals of the football year.

Well timed, after the final goal had been delivered, Oscar's phone rang. Answering it quickly he was delighted to hear the softly lilting voice of the one person he always wanted to hear from, this time saying that she couldn't wait until tomorrow morning to hear how his conversation with Annabelle or Clive had progressed and whether Mary and Martha would accept their grandfather's offer of having new homes for them both, built as wedding gifts for the two couples.

Oscar was then able to tell Annette that the girls were ecstatic with the news, given by Annabelle, and, after work had rung him in a state of elation, showing their gratitude firstly, by thanking him in their Pwo-Karen language, startling him initially until he realised who it was, then thanking again, this time in English. Work would be starting very soon, with the girls saying that you, Annette and myself would love the village they would be built in and couldn't wait to see the whole family again shortly after Christmas.

With a sighing kiss down the line, the pair said their goodnights, hardly waiting until the next day when they would meet to walk to church. Oscar thought it was time now, the time to talk to Annette about the advice he hoped to receive from Pastor Stephen, after the morning service.

Sunday was a little chilly, but at least dry for their short walk to Merryfields Baptist Church, now their spiritual home. Pastor Stephen was, as usual, greeting his flock at the open door, but was more than willing to talk to Oscar and Annette, once the congregation had left and maybe after the clearing up, if they had time to wait for half an hour or so at the end of the morning's service and ministry, to those who would like to receive some guidance in their Christian walk with Jesus.

Oscar and Annette said they were happy to wait, for a chance to gain some advice on the question of animism, the spiritual and ancient culture of spirit worship, inbred into the lives of the people of Thailand. Annette had already prepared Sunday lunch for the family, to which Oscar was always invited. It was a good opportunity to have a catch-up with Bradley and today, remind him of their meeting tomorrow, for last-minute Christmas shopping trip, possibly to Hamleys, with lunch, of course.

Rehearsals were progressing well, with the show's opening date, in two weeks' time. Oscar had been happy to tell Pastor Stephen the complete story of events, leading up to the time of repeating the scenario once more and the part he was privileged to have played in the making of these remarkable tap shoes. Pastor Stephen listened without interruption, marvelling at the way God was working in these latter days.

Having little knowledge of what was to occur, on the evening of the shoes missive introduction, Oscar invited Pastor Stephen and his wife Jeanette to accompany himself and Annette to the 'Blackbird Principle Theatre,' on the arranged evening, to which the Pastor was pleased to accept the invitation, offering to drive the pair to the theatre himself.

It wasn't long before Pastor Stephen indicated that he was prepared and ready for the evening service and could give them a while of his time, inquiring if they would prefer the seclusion of his office or stay where they were, in the church. Oscar glanced at Annette, who smiled, saying she would be happy to stay in the church. Settling back into his chair, Stephen quite thought he was about to hear further evidence of the 'specials' abilities, but was surprised to hear Oscar talking about the forthcoming marriages of his two adopted grandchildren, Mary and Martha.

Knowing of the occasion, happening in February of next year, Stephen was further surprised by Oscar's questioning regarding the ritualistic religion of animism, inbred into Thai culture. He had not realised there might be a problem here, but knowing of Oscar's recently found faith, he was now not too surprised. The two girls were very likely to be marrying into animistic families, causing Oscar some concern as to where they stood in regard to their Christian, although not regular attendees at church, upbringing.

Stephen listened to Oscar's way of thinking, drawing on lectures he had heard at Baptist Bible College, after obtaining his bachelor's degree in religious studies, prior to training. This could be tricky, he thought, as he attempted to answer the questions Oscar was asking.

"It's been a while since I've been asked that question," smiled Pastor Stephen, "but together, with God's help, I'm sure we'll get some answers. Initially, the way I can remember being taught is that animatism and animism may appear to be the same thing and, in fact, both beliefs are often found in the same culture. There is a difference though and that is that the belief in animism is that only objects in the natural world have extraordinary powers—as in spiritual deity—whereas the belief in animatism does not have a personality—it is impersonal—as in "it" rather than a "he" or she without human characteristics, over which people have some measure of control.

"This will also tie in with Polytheism—belief in more than one God—Theism—a supreme being, distinct from creation and Dualism—opposing gods. The disadvantage of animism is that an animist's life is inclined to be spent in fear with the result that they believe that every wrong that is done to them, is their own fault and where guilt comes in. Monotheism however is a belief in one deity, the threefold perfection of the Trinity—one of God the Father, Son and Holy Spirit—three persons in one Godhead, called also the Trinity doctrine.

"Our God that we serve and worship and now having been granted forgiveness through Jesus' ultimate sacrifice for us. I hope this isn't too complicated," smiled Pastor Stephen looking at some degree of puzzlement on Oscar and Annette's faces.

"I'm sorry, Pastor, I think you've lost me," confessed Oscar, as Annette nodded in agreement, "but I can see, a little, where you're going with this. We as Christians can see God in many everyday things, such as a gorgeous rose, wild buttercups, a beautifully maintained garden, where seeds have been sown, but you bring growth by bringing sunshine and rain, seeing your part in the reproduction of life, even in a lovely painting, we can see your hand at work in the artist. Is that right, Pastor?"

Pastor Stephen nodded his head, as in agreement, before suggesting, "As from scripture, that we think more of things from heaven than we do of things from earth. Maybe," he continued, to Oscar and Annette, "you could carry a few portions of scripture, in card form, with beautiful sights and then some lightweight Bibles printed for those using another language, again with helpful images of God's beauty. I can approach the Bible Society for you, if you like, taking anything they are likely to provide.

"Another thought may be to ask them what they see and set their lives upon, in the number of items having a spirit entity, even I've heard of words being one, asking them to turn its spiritual force around to see something amazing and beautiful, rather than demanding and possibly ugly. You do need to realise too, that these entities might not welcome having their appearance concealed or turned around the other way.

"Thinking about it, they could demand recompense, but ask your future grandsons by marriage, what image would they rather see and enjoy, then help them resist any fallout, in protective prayer. I hope I haven't confused you or even made you feel a bit out of your depth, but you know I am always at the end of the line, even in faraway Thailand. I really don't mind being woken at 3 AM for any urgent help needed."

"We're really grateful for this talk, Pastor Stephen," followed up Oscar, trying to move things along so as to not make the Pastor any later. "Thank you too for your offer to contact the Bible Society for us. To be honest, I wasn't even aware there was one. We'll let you go now and think seriously about all you've said. Maybe we can be in touch when we know what they can offer us, so thank you again."

With that Oscar and Annette got up from their seats ready to leave the church, to hear Pastor Stephen say, "You two both seem to have evangelical zeal. God Bless you both."

Walking home from Merryfields the pair had a lot to talk about, knowing they were taking on a larger task than they were equipped for, also knowing that God was on their side and if this was the correct way to handle the situation, as Pastor Stephen had indicated, they would somehow receive the all clear, to proceed.

Maybe a talk with Clive and Annabelle or even Mary and Martha, if they had considered the matter, could be the first step, but to appear to be overzealous, to the extent that the happiness of the two couples were at stake, caused them to think again. A gentle, loving irreproachable manner, once the marriages were officially certified and their homes used in their marital status, might be considered the best way forward. This situation clearly needed a lot of prayer support.

Arriving home slightly later than usual, Oscar and Annette found Simone and Bradley busy putting the finishing touches to the Sunday lunch, that Annette had prepared earlier, being at a point where it was almost ready to serve. A slightly raised eyebrow from Bradley brought a smile to Simone's face as they hurriedly washed their hands to sit down, as a family to enjoy a delicious lunch.

With the clearing and washing up tackled by many hands, Annette was happy to make the coffee, in readiness for a comfortable afternoon exchanging events of the week, until Simone reluctantly had to leave to attend to an early delivery. Babies rarely considered the correct day of the week on which to announce it was their time to see the world for the first time. Thanks to the right time to place the call to Simone, all was well, with a brand new baby emerging safely, to his delighted parents.

Satisfied, but tired, Simone returned home to be greeted by a welcome cuppa and a slice—but small—of Annette's delicious lemon cake drenched in lemon juice. By now, heads were beginning to nod, as Oscar glanced at Bradley to see if he was ready to make a move back to the flat he shared with Terence. Bradley smiled, suggesting that they share a taxi together, being cold and dark by now.

With his mobile in hand, he organised a taxi to come as soon as possible, giving his mother a hug, thanking her for inviting him for the day, although he knew he never needed an invitation. His long-awaited show was due to open the day after tomorrow and with two performances a day, at the weekend's he wouldn't have much time for visiting. Rehearsals had gone well and the company was as ready as they could be for such an extravaganza, ahead of 'The International Year of Dance'. Excitement was rife, with intense rehearsing in all the countries who were taking part, to celebrate the common language of dance, without prejudice in any form.

No sooner than the good nights were said, the taxi arrived, taking Oscar home first, who then paid the ongoing fare, against protests from Bradley, to get the young protégée home safely, after arranging to meet the next day for their shopping day out in, London's Oxford and Regent Street.

Meeting the following day the pair enjoyed an early morning cup of coffee before hitting the frantic shopping 'buzz' of Christmas present buying, replayed in every town and city around the world.

This year, however, Oscar and Bradley were viewing the 'great event' from a slightly different perspective. Bradley needed a few more gifts than Oscar, which they found fairly quickly and reasonably priced, before making their way to the famous store of Hamleys, which had promoted Bradley to buy a few items, to encourage some of the first-year students, who were floundering a little under the pressure of a day at school, with learning the somewhat complicated moves of tap dancing, which they professed to thoroughly enjoy.

The store, when they entered, was a mass of customers eager to buy the latest toy of the year for their expectant offspring. Negotiating the seven floors, that Hamleys boasted, was a work of art, but eventually one level gave Bradley a few ideas, thankfully within his price range, well made so they wouldn't break too easily even if not handled gently, by younger siblings, perhaps.

Oscar also found some interesting small toys as Christmas tree gifts for the younger members of his typically sized family, with his and Anita's original four sons. Gradually making their way downstairs to the ground floor, through the still large number of people entering the store, they were relieved to see daylight outside, emerging once again onto Regent Street. Cars, buses, taxis and mainstream shoppers were hurrying past at great speeds, having finished shopping or left work in the frantic rush to get home in order to collect children from various schools or arrive home before husbands or wives came in from their daily work assignments. Such was any busy city at rush hour time!

"Do you fancy a meal before we make for home?" Oscar asked Bradley, as they had only eaten a light lunch, keen to visit Hamleys before it became impossible to manoeuvre easily through the shopping crowds.

"Sounds good," answered Bradley. "Have you any suggestions? I don't know this part of London as well as you do."

"How much do you know of Italian cuisine particularly Frittata's, rather like our English omelettes, but with a delicious blend of eggs, feta cheese and cherry tomatoes or any other ingredient you fancy, served with a tossed green salad or if preferred, sliced avocados or fried roast potatoes making more of a meal than a snack? If you like the sound of that, young Bradley, I know of just the place, just around the corner."

"You're making me feel hungry already," grinned Bradley. "We're in Oxford Street now, so how much further?"

A short walk from the centre of Oxford Street, Oscar turned right and there in front of them was an appealingly small, but charming entrance to the shop within.

"Here we are," chortled Oscar, ushering Bradley into a bright interior, where they were shown to a few select number of tables, welcomed with a smile by a typical Italian chef, cleverly rotating frying pans and deeper utensils, happy to keep his customers enjoying his expertly served dishes. A wine list was offered, but declined by Bradley, who needed all his faculties alert for his role on stage the following afternoon.

Oscar and Bradley thoroughly enjoyed their meal of Frittata's with the fried potatoes, avocado and a delicious tossed green salad containing peppers, garlic and other spices, ending with cheese and bacon muffin. A simple meal fit for a king, announced Oscar, to which Bradley heartily agreed.

Well-fed and content with today's achievements, the pair collected the bill, then hailed a taxi to take them to their respective homes. They went their separate ways but Bradley knew Oscar and his mum would be in the audience the next day, much to his delight. The time was nearing for the special message God had prepared for the world to hear and the start of the 'specials' notability.

Until the evening when he would collect Annette for the show, his day was free, but with a strong desire to revisit some of his previous precious customers. He knew their haunts, being made welcomed every time he looked in on them, too often hearing changes in roles, meeting new dancers that he would be introduced to and just revelling in the smell of lasting greasepaint, even to the odour from last-minute rehearsal time before the next performance. New choreographers were appraised for their devotion to their dancers.

This had been Oscar's world for so many years that to disengage from it now would be heartbreaking. So Oscar sat and listened approvingly, sometimes being asked to comment on a new kind of shoe for ballerinas, causing him some concern, from the knowledge and skill of handcrafted shoes proving for many years to be of the best support for the principal dancers. He had resisted calling Bradley for a 'break a leg' jest, that all would go smoothly for the first night, instead, had a healthy snack and a smooth drink delivered, knowing that he would have little time to think about any nourishment before the buildup to tonight's opening.

The show had been well advertised for many weeks before, with the names appearing of well-known performers. Bradley's name was featured much further down the programme, as a background dancer. Enough fame for the moment! Oscar was early to collect Annette, who, as normal, was ready and eager to get to the theatre, as soon as possible, to watch her son's first performance on any kind of public stage and was feeling immensely proud of his achievements, so early on in his cherished career.

By the time booked tickets had been purchased and the main guests being of public dignitaries from the many countries involved in this long production were assisted to their seats, Oscar estimated, by peering around, that it looked like the numbers were steadily increasing.

Jonathan and Terence weren't too far away, with Terence, with his fingers and possibly toes, crossed. No human luck was needed tonight, but the graciousness of God to direct His own show.

At exactly 7.30 PM, a long band roll was heard from the orchestra pit and the heavy blue draped theatre curtains were drawn back, to reveal a large stage troupe of those performing this evening. Announced by both directors of the show, the audience was promised a spectacular evening of dance, asked to follow their programmes for each exhibit of any one particular dance belonging to their country. Sit back, they were told and enjoy the many variety of dances performed for you this evening, all from aspiring countries around the world.

"The Winter Special" was indeed an inspiring show, appealing to young or older people in the family. Being the first night everything was running to a timed precision of overlaps between sets removed and reset for the next act, whilst the dancers were emerging from the wings, gathering themselves into position, as the orchestra played the first chord to commence the dance. Changes seemed to be operating smoothly until a popping noise was heard from one or two of the overhead lights.

Immediately the stage was plunged into darkness, with oohs and aahs rising from the audience, until with a flourish, backup lighting, although a little dimmer, relit the stage. There was just a brief pause as the dancers gathered themselves together to resume the dance, supported by applause from the audience. Slightly ahead of time, an intermission was announced, so that the theatre's electricians could work to restore full lighting.

The audience was assured it was a relatively minor fault, then offered free drinks, to be served as they were seated until the programme was continued. It was a generous gesture, much appreciated by all in the theatre, some of whom were relying on public transport, becoming a little alarmed by the delay. No sooner, though, than the prickle of alarm, an announcement was made that the fault had been detected and repaired.

Apologising for the interruption, the voice announced that the show would be continuing on its time schedule, which allowed for minor problems. Relieved, the audience began to relax in readiness for the remaining acts which gave them every reason to loudly applaud the patience and resilience of all concerned. Bradley's role, with the background dancers, seemed very polished, keeping in exact tempo with the main tap dancers so that the rhythm was perfectly timed.

Meeting up with him after the final curtain call, Oscar and Annette were eager to know how his first stage performance had satisfied him in his ability to tap dance and remembering, how, as a young child, he had watched breathless as his father Trevor had poured everything, of himself, into his brilliant performances, giving young Bradley the yearning to follow in his footsteps. This was just the early beginning of an illustrious career!

Tired, but immensely happy, the three of them hailed a taxi, waved, with delight, to Jonathan and Terence, who they knew would have not missed the show, thoughtfully allowing Bradley and his family to have this special night together.

The days were now hastening towards the Christmas season when Oscar and Annette would need, with family commitments to be apart for a short while, until the evening before the final night, when the 'specials' would touch the human heart, for God's word which, would be given through these 'specials,' a pair of tap dancing shoes, about to be used in such a way by, God the Almighty, to speak to a hurting, helpless, betrayed world.

With 'The Winter Special' continuing to attract large audiences at every performance, Bradley was kept very busy, hardly having time to wrap his Christmas gifts and do his utmost to keep in touch with Oscar, now a firm friend as well as a benefactor.

During the times they were able to meet, either for a coffee, not too far from the rehearsal site or if more time, a cosy evening at Oscar's, quite often with Annette joining them, when the evening began with a melody of remembered and more modern, upbeat modern music, being Bradley's choice. Inevitably the conversation would revolve around the 'specials,' or relaying to Bradley, Pastor Stephens' sermon from the previous Sunday.

This would encourage further discussion, with Bibles being opened to find the correct place in scripture, from where Pastor Stephens had been inspired to give the intended message to the congregation.

Very soon it was the day before Timothy and young Dillon were driving to London to collect Oscar, driving him back to Fareham, to celebrate Christmas with the families, some of whom Oscar hadn't seen for a long time, but now, becoming more familiar with his new phone, would call, with Face Timing quite competently, especially those in Singapore, who were thrilled to show him their latest exploits, to which he would applaud enthusiastically, keeping them all closer to him in his heart. Now, this year, he would see them in the flesh, noting, of course, how they would have grown.

Having wanted to show Annette his gaining of new prowess' in the kitchen, he was determined to invite her for a last meal together, for a while, to produce a slap-up dinner, with no expense spared or talent! Beginning early, Oscar had carefully written himself a minute-by-minute time plan. This was proving successful until a tap on his front door alerted him that Annette had arrived. He hadn't, on his work list, given himself time to leave the kitchen and greet her, so waited for her to come into the kitchen, only to find Oscar covered in steam, with his pince-nez slipping from his nose. This was causing him not to see her.

Stumbling in the direction of her entry, into the kitchen, he fumbled for her and with them both falling about laughing, greeted each other. At the same time, of which, Annette skilfully whisked off a saucepan lid, allowing the steam to escape, almost preventing some beautifully prepared vegetables from being incinerated into a mushy state. An action noticed by Oscar, who had been slightly inattentive, not giving himself time on his list, to allow for how quickly vegetables could be easily overcooked.

If not, the most perfect dinner they had ever eaten, Annette was complimentary of the success of the meal, in particular the tenderness of the piece of beef that Oscar had attended to meticulously, to ensure it was cooked well enough for both of them and indeed, with the splendid gravy, he had slaved over; it seemed as if he had passed with flying colours, at least by his dearest friend and that was all that mattered to him, on this lovely evening, with Annette by his side, already bringing in the bowls and cream that Oscar had already prepared.

There was to be an additional surprise for the start of Christmas, which was a masterpiece of an out-of-this-world fruit flambé alcohol-based, of course. A very adventurous move on Oscar's part, thoroughly impressing Annette, as it was supposed to, both enjoyed it immensely. How had he managed that complicated dessert, puzzled Annette, as the pair tucked in together?

Pushing Oscar to tell her where he had learnt this French skill of burning off the alcohol in a pan first, before adding the fruit, was an intended secret that Oscar would keep to himself. Eventually, the evening drew to a close, with Oscar fetching a taxi for Annette to drive home in. Telling themselves they would contact each other on Christmas Day, the pair embraced, knowing it wouldn't be too long before they would be witnesses to the 'specials' first onstage presentation.

The final clearing up from the surprise meal was fairly easy as, Annette had slipped in several times during the evening, whilst Oscar was engaged with something else. So by the time Oscar was prepared to get stuck in, he had found very little left to do, Closing the front door after Annette had left, he also closed the kitchen door, to start afresh tomorrow. The bed was calling, with Oscar finding he could hardly keep his eyes open—the long-term effects of the flambé almost drowned in alcohol, for which he felt just a simple regret.

Once his head was on his pillow though, he knew he would be feeling better tomorrow, looking forward to seeing his young scamp Dillon—whom he adored—and who was coming, with his son Timothy, to stay overnight, before driving to their home in time for the coming celebrations.

Waking early Oscar set about having a good tidy-up before Timothy and Dillon arrived, probably needing something to eat, especially Dillon who was always on the lookout for 'snacks,' to appease his almost constant hunger. Moving quickly into the kitchen, Oscar peered out of the window to see Cocky patiently waiting for a rather belated breakfast, head on one side inquiringly. What a joy it would be for Dillon tomorrow morning, thought Oscar, to meet this delightful little bird.

With a light lunch ready and waiting and the promise of a fish and chip supper, after which Oscar was looking forward to a long father-to-son catch-up, if, of course, Dillon was willing to snuggle down early enough with his brand new Christmas sleeping bag, a programme on television caught Oscar's eye providing a stopgap before his son's arrival.

Suddenly, there was the sound of a car drawing up outside, giving a brief toot-toot. A car door opened and closed, followed by a knock on the front door. Oscar was there in an instant, opening the door to a very excited Dillon running into his arms, shouting Hiya Great-grandpapa, before disappearing from view into Oscar's lounge, flinging himself dramatically onto his favourite piece of his great-grandpapa's furniture—the chaise lounge—long enough to have him lie full length upon it. A happy Dillon raced back into the hallway, as Oscar was relieving Timothy of his sheepskin jacket, calling for Dillon to do the same and calm down before an accident should happen.

"Great-grandpapa," called young Dillon, from the centre of the kitchen. "You've got some lovely food on your kitchen table. When can we have lunch? I'm hungry."

"As soon you, my young man, have calmed yourself down to eat anything, otherwise in your excitement, you could choke and then would we be, with no Dillon to enjoy Christmas with," returned Oscar in an amused, but firm voice.

With that rebuke Dillon perched himself at the kitchen table, with his grandfather taking the seat beside him, ready to help with the lunch, if needed. Oscar, having given Dillon a glass of milk, proceeded to pour Timothy and himself a very welcome cup of tea, relaxing in each other's company.

After a long drive with Dillon in the car, Timothy was grateful for the silence of Oscar's lunch being eaten and enjoyed, but it wasn't long before Dillon had finished, fidgeting to leave the table, at which Timothy suggested a nap in the new sleeping bag Oscar had told him had been purchased, waiting for its occupancy by Dillon, who gleefully shouted his delight when he saw it, climbing in without hesitation.

Once Dillon was having his after-lunch nap, Oscar and Timothy quickly cleared up the mess in the kitchen, put the kettle on, before sitting down to a frothy cappuccino that Oscar had perfected as one of his general accomplishments in the kitchen, partially to impress Annette, but also to prove that he was a competent cook. Family news and general catching up were exchanged between father and son, particularly the pleasure Oscar felt at the thought of seeing his youngest son—Michael and wife Patricia, with his four grandchildren—Martin, Dean, Sally and Anne—having been living in Singapore for the past eight years.

Timothy was pleased too as he hadn't seen his younger brother since four years ago, when he and Priscilla took Dillon out to meet his cousins. Camilla and

Charlotte were unable to manage the time away from their local government office roles, as local elections were drawing closer, with both girls needing to be there for the primaries of the election, at least. They both had important jobs to do in line with election procedures.

Just as Timothy finished talking about the forthcoming visit, the shrill call from Oscar's phone stopped the conversation, enabling Oscar to answer. It was Annette reminding Oscar that if he and Timothy were still talking, they would do well to look at the clock, which Oscar did, with a glance telling him that if he wanted his surprise to go ahead that afternoon, he should be ready to leave in ten minutes.

Leaping up with a start, Oscar quickly thanked Annette for her intervention, then turning to Timothy he announced that he had planned a little treat for the three of them that afternoon. Explaining, he said that as it was the Saturday before Christmas, Bradley—his young sponsored tap dancer and friend—had an afternoon matinee in the show called the 'Winter Special' which would be his first stage performance, in the background dancers. He had thought it might be a distraction for Dillon, so had obtained three tickets for this afternoon, with the show about to begin in half an hour's time, which meant getting Dillon out of bed quickly, into his outdoor coat and shoes.

Whilst Timothy was so engaged, Oscar rang for a taxi to arrive in fifteen minutes. Dillon looked sleepy after his nap but cheered up when his grandfather told him they had a Christmas treat this afternoon, after which they would buy the promised fish'n chips that Bradley had requested for supper. With the taxi almost screeching to a halt outside Oscar's front door, the two men helped Dillon to sit down, reminding him to be still whilst the driver was concentrating on the quickest route to get them to the theatre on time.

Without a hint of speeding, the driver pulled up outside the theatre door as the box office was opening. Thanking and paying the driver Oscar hastily drew the already purchased tickets from within his jacket pocket, propelling them through the dimming theatre lights, to seats that he knew would give them the best view of the stage. Dillon could hardly contain his excitement as he rarely was taken to the theatre, but as the orchestra played the encore, he settled down, with his hand in both his grandfather's and great-grandpapa's hand, jiggering in time with the music.

As each dance finished, Dillon would shoot up in his seat, waving goodbye to the performers. Oscar pondered on what Dillon would make of the 'specials,' act, on stage here, in just a few days after Christmas. It was that thought that linked Annette and Oscar, even though, by tomorrow, they would be far apart for a while.

Then onto the stage came the troupe that would perform the dance, of which Bradley was a part of their background dancers. Watching carefully, when Oscar pointed out Bradley to Timothy and Dillon, they both clapped enthusiastically when the dance was over and the stage was emptied in readiness for the scene changes to appear, swiftly and strongly clearing and resetting the scenes for each set of performers from many different countries, as a prelude to the 'International Year of Dance.'

Halfway through the performances, an interlude was announced, a time in which an ice-cream or even a drink could be purchased and enjoyed before the orchestra struck the chords again to announce the start of the second half of the show. Dillon, Timothy and Oscar opted for the former, licking their lips in appreciation.

All too soon the finale was upon them drawing together excerpts from the completed show, indicating the depth and dexterity of dance in all its forms, followed by a rousing cheer and applause from the audience. The curtain call gave vent to shouts of delight, as known performers were recognised and given a further clapping of adulation. The orchestra was invited to stand, with their instruments, bowing to the audience as they were given their due amount of praise.

It was a sensational show, that would continue nightly until after Christmas, which, by then Oscar would have returned home from Fareham, ready and expectant to attend, with Annette, the evening performance in which Oscar himself would make the announcement regarding the introduction of the 'specials.' God's Will was about to be done.

Tired but happy with his unexpected Christmas treat to the theatre, Dillon was full of chatter as Oscar asked their taxi to wait, whilst he took the orders from Timothy and Dillon for their fish 'n' chip supper that evening. The service was quick and efficient, considering the theatre audiences were emptying onto the streets, with many hungry families making for the most convenient food outlets.

Back in the taxi again, Oscar carefully handed the delicious-smelling boxes, containing their suppers, to Timothy, whilst he re-snapped his seat belt, giving the driver instructions to get them home. Warming up once indoors, having shed their outdoor coats and shoes, the three generations of Oscar's family lost no time in getting themselves seated at the kitchen table and with the food on warmed plates, with only one interruption from Dillon asking for another helping of tomato sauce, the simple but enjoyable meal was soon reduced to empty plates. Coffee for the adults and a glass of milk for Dillon, taken through to the lounge, gave way to satisfied sighs.

Curling up on his great-grandpapa's lap, Dillon was contentedly humming some of the tunes he had heard that afternoon. Timothy and Oscar took the opportunity to engage in some small talk, but keeping an eye on an active five-year-old was tiring, being hard now to keep awake before it was a reasonable time to suggest bedtime for one very sleepy young man. To encourage Dillon to snuggle into his new sleeping bag, Oscar whispered that by going to sleep quickly there would be another surprise waiting for him, in the morning.

Dillon and Cocky would get along well, thought Oscar, before drawing the curtains and reducing the light to a faint glow, just in time to hear a faint 'night night' from the depth of Dillon's pillow. Kissing the tousled head of his great-grandson, Oscar rejoined his son in the lounge, ready to watch a film they had both seen advertised, having been given excellent reviews from by producers.

Whilst Oscar was settling Dillon, Timothy had slipped into the kitchen, tidying up and washing the plates they had used for supper. He had then prepared two steaming cups of coffee for himself and his father, setting one down on the table nearest Oscar's chair, to which he returned, sinking into the cushions with a sigh of relief. Was he getting too old to take on a five-year-old, he wondered, grinning at Timothy, who wasn't so far behind, age-wise?

The beginning of the film was good, as expected, with the pair exchanging comments as the scenes progressed. Within a short while, there was a strange silence between father and son, until Timothy raised his head, asking Oscar what had happened.

An entirely new feature film was running, as with a guilty smile at each other they both realised they had slept through at least one and a half hours before the commencement of this most exciting film they were likely to see that Christmas. Priscilla kept a tight rein on the television programmes, aware that Dillon was all ears, picking up phrases and language, hopefully not used in the company of children.

Yawning and groping their way to their bedrooms, quietly, so as to not wake Dillon, Oscar set his alarm clock earlier than usual, as he didn't want Dillon to miss any of tomorrow morning's routine with Cocky, who would only stay for the short time it took him to devour the worms and warm milk that he so enjoyed and expected, before flying away to who knew where?

Waking to visit the bathroom during the night Oscar peeped into his spare room that he had made ready for Timothy and Dillon's sleepover, surprised to find young Dillon fast asleep, taking up most of the bed having manoeuvred his grandfather close to the edge, so making a favourable niche, under Timothy's left armpit, as close as possible to his grandfather's beating heart.

Struggling to stifle a laugh, Oscar returned to his own bed, thankful for peace and solitude, but equally grateful for the close relationship Timothy and Dillon had between them. His 'boys' had not disappointed either him or Anita, being held in high regard by friends and employers alike. How fortunate he and Anita had been, well aware that many families had difficulties to try and overcome, often lined with heartache.

Morning came all too soon, with the strident ringing of Oscar's alarm clock. He was determined to let Timothy have a lie-in this morning before the long drive to his home later on today, probably after a light lunch again, so hurried with his morning routine, arriving in the kitchen even before Cocky perched in the cherry tree. Getting together a tray containing milk, a pot of tea and coffee, with freshly made toast, marmalade, jam, plates and knives.

Oscar carefully carried the loaded tray to the door of Timothy and Dillon's room, placed it on a chair in the corner, calling before knocking none too gently on their door that the toast was getting cold and Dillon's surprise would soon be here. A moment later Oscar heard feet padding across the floor and the door opened by a now tousle-haired Timothy, who blinked owlishly at him—without his glasses being on—muttering was it morning already.

Turning his head, Timothy saw the still-sleeping Dillon sprawled across the bed. Rubbing an aching arm he fully opened the door at Oscar's insistence that the toast was getting even colder, thanking him profusely for his kind thought to prepare breakfast in this fashion. Hearing voices, Dillon woke up with a start, looking exactly like his grandfather—tousle-haired and sleepy. Coaxed into fully waking up, the three Harrisons tucked into tea and toast, with milk for Dillon who, very rapidly wanted to know all about the surprise, so with Timothy making his way to the bathroom, Oscar led Dillon into the kitchen.

Dillon grimaced whilst he watched his great-grandpapa pick up a dish with what looked like worms, a saucer of milk, before walking outside into the garden.

Intrigued, Dillon followed, wrapping the coat, Oscar had given him, tightly around his shoulders. Then the surprise happened—a small robin flew from a branch of a tree—onto his great-grandpapa's arm, wolfing down those horrible-looking worms, before accepting a drink of milk from the saucer, held out to him.

Oscar put out his hand to Dillon, inviting the boy to come and meet this new friend, explaining to him that his name was Cocky, as he would cock his head on one side when about to get fed as if to say thank you. Dillon was fascinated, moving closer, before hesitantly extending his arm towards the robin. Cocky seemed to weigh the boy up then, with a little flutter of wings, landed on Dillon's hand, almost looking him in the eye.

Oscar quietly motioned to Dillon to stay still or Cocky could be frightened and fly away. Boy and bird stood like statues until Cocky decided it was time to make a move, gracefully flying low over the surrounding rooftops, until he was lost to sight. Dillon realised he had been holding his breath with this exchange between the two of them, then gasped his delight at a smiling Oscar.

His excited talk for the next hour, questioning Oscar on how and when Cocky had become his friend, where he lived and where he went when he flew away, much of which Oscar didn't know himself, but with Dillon now so interested in bird life, vowed to buy some children's books on the very subject, assuring his great-grandson that he would, as soon as he visited again, try and find an abandoned. Birds' nest to show him and pictures of birds' eggs from which the fluffy baby birds, once hatched from the egg, would grow into birds as big as their mummy and daddy and one day have babies of their very own.

By now, the morning breakfast tray was cleared, with Oscar and Timothy doing a final clearing up, packing the car with Dillon's new sleeping bag and clothes he had worn yesterday, along with a tin of meringues that Oscar had diligently made with Bradley one wet Saturday afternoon when Oscar had said that he would like to make something for Christmas, that he could take to Fareham, as a special treat.

Oscar had, with a lot of practice, perfected his skill in meringue making, which together with some clotted cream could be sandwiched together for an afternoon tea. The airtight container that Oscar had carefully filled with meringues, was perfect for keeping this confectionary in tip-top condition to be given to Priscilla, on their arrival later on in the day.

Timothy didn't want to wait much longer before beginning their drive to Fareham. Although the distance wasn't that far, Timothy would rather not catch rush hour, coming into his hometown.

Dillon was getting a little restless, also wanting to be on the road, so Oscar soon rustled up a sustaining snack with soup and drinks, enough to keep them from becoming hungry on the way. Drinks of coffee or squash could be taken in suitable containers that would allay the thirst, sipped at a quick pit stop.

With the meal soon over, Timothy and Dillon gathered their few belongings together, whilst Oscar packed the clothes he would need for his days away with the family, not forgetting his rather old walking boots and warm outdoor coat, as he knew his sons and their wives often went for a walk after the Christmas lunch, so he was well prepared.

It was a family time of year and special, even more so for Oscar this year, as, with Annette they had made their commitment to follow Jesus, bringing them to the main event of their future lives, that of the introduction of the 'specials' to an unsuspecting audience, at the almost final end of the 'Winter Special,' when he would give the shoes the freedom of the stage and with Bradley would any questions that arose. The message he knew could be received with very different views, but God would be totally in control, with Oscar and Bradley simply utilising the only object through which God had chosen to give a clear message to a very needy, hurting world. What a night that would be!

Loading and packing everything into the car, including space for themselves, was quite a task, but after a few rearrangements, all was ready. Timothy only stopped to fill up with petrol and buy Dillon a small promised box of Smarties, so very shortly they were soon on the motorway, heading for Fareham. The forecasted sleet and snow had not happened as yet, pleasing Timothy, who would rather not face those driving conditions so far away from home. He wasn't accustomed to long drives, but with the weather good at the moment, the miles passed quickly.

Oscar was in the passenger seat, company for Timothy. Dillon was happily munching on his sweets, having been reminded to share, but once offered, he returned to the comic, he was enjoying. Looking around a few times to make sure all was well, Oscar was amused to see Dillon's head nodding and before long, the little boy was fast asleep with his head cushioned into his new sleeping bag.

Timothy and Oscar motored in silence for a good few miles, Oscar not wanting to distract Timothy, perhaps causing him to lose concentration. The car radio played quietly without waking Dillon and although it was cold outside in the car, the warmth was beginning to cause drowsiness. After a few more miles, it became necessary to look for a lay-by in which to pull over for a brief rest and drinks for them all. Timothy soon spotted one ahead and indicated in plenty of time he pulled over safely, switching off the car's engine, resting back against his seat's headrest, with a gentle sigh.

"Not far to go now," remarked Timothy to his father-in-law who nodded his head whilst removing the drinks containers from within the well of his seat, which were keeping his feet at a peculiar angle, so for a moment he wriggled his toes before offering his son his choice of nourishment. Choosing a coffee, Oscar extricated the flask pouring the hot liquid into a mug for Timothy to sip and enjoy for a while.

At that moment, Dillon woke with a yawn and stretched, asking if they were home yet. When told they were nearly there but had stopped for a drink before driving into Fareham, at the risk of joining the rush hour. It wasn't that time yet but would be if they stayed in the lay-by for too long.

Asked whether he would like a drink he answered with, "Please great-grandpapa, I would like an orange squash."

Delving into the bag again, Oscar served Dillon and himself with a plastic glass of the refreshing fruit juice. Back on the road again, it was only a short time before Oscar was seeing directions for Fareham—a lively market town in the county of Hampshire. Dillon emerged from the comfort of his sleeping bag, beginning to recognise where they were and before long Timothy was pulling into his and Dillon's own driveway.

Priscilla appeared at the front door, hugged the whirlwind figure of Dillon who had rushed indoors to a warm welcome home from his mum, who threw her arms around him telling him how much she had missed him, even after only one night away. Greeting his aunt, who had loosely grabbed Dillon's coat collar, to apprehend him, he made a rapid tour of the house, then back to the front door, ready to escort his great-grandpapa regally into the house to show him the room in which he would be sleeping, during his stay with them.

Finally, everybody settled again with Timothy gratefully drinking a cup of tea, Oscar made to examine the decorations and the tree, of course, with the soppy family spaniel getting under everybody's feet until satisfied his family was complete once more.

Priscilla had prepared a warm and nourishing, old-fashioned beef casserole, complete with wonderfully garnished dumplings that drew a host of praise and compliments, with second helpings of liberal servings. Much of the trifle dessert she had made, especially for Dillon, was regretfully refused, although the young man in question made a short shift of his served portion, licking his lips like a cat when asked if could eat some more. The remaining trifle would hopefully be safe in the fridge overnight!

Priscilla had been absolutely delighted with Oscar's surprise homemade meringues that looked unbelievably light and airy, that, sandwiched together with some of the ample supply of freshly delivered Cornish clotted cream that Oscar had also bought, would be offered on the next day's menus, probably after the family's walk on Christmas afternoon. By the time supper was cleared away and Dillon persuaded that despite his nap in the car, he must be tired and ready for bed, all who were travelling to stay with Timothy and Priscilla had arrived, much to the delight of Oscar. The remainder would come on Christmas morning when the family would be complete.

The happy chatter of meeting altogether again, echoed around the house, whilst Dillon's mother remarked that Father Christmas couldn't visit and fill the stockings until every little boy and girl was in bed nice and early on Christmas Eve, which soon had Dillon saying a swift 'good night' to his aunts and uncles before making his way, a little reluctantly upstairs with Charlotte, his mother.

The remaining members of Oscar's family gathered together in groups, greeting cheerily those they hadn't seen for some time. Giving particular pleasure to them all and especially Oscar, was to see his youngest son Michael with Patricia, his wife and their now rapidly growing children—Martin, Dean, Sally and Anne, all looking wonderfully healthy and tanned. They had only flown in from Singapore early this morning having collected the car to drive the short distance to Fareham, so were feeling a little jet-lagged, ready for bed. Having eaten at the airport, they assured Priscilla, who was quite prepared to cook them a meal, along with others who may not have eaten.

Supper that evening was going to be more snacks and finger foods, along with a delicious punch that Timothy always made, but this year because of collecting Oscar the main ingredients had been prepared by Priscilla and

Charlotte whilst Timothy added the final touch of a special recipe of his, always arousing comments and congratulations at Christmastime.

"How are you all getting along, out there in the heat of Singapore," asked Oscar to Michael, placing a fatherly arm around his son's shoulders?

"We're doing fine, thanks, dad," returned Michael. "Patricia and I do have some news for you, though. The bank is undergoing some changes at the moment and if the proposed change takes shape, Patrica, Anne, Sally and myself should be coming home to the UK in a few months' time, as the senior managers have requested that I be selected as the Managing Director of their latest up and running branch, in Manchester, doing well by all accounts dad."

His eyes were twinkling somewhat, but as Oscar suspected, with a hint of sadness.

"That all sounds very impressive, Michael, but what do Patricia and the children think about it all?"

"We've discussed this a lot, as a family, as it would mean Martin and Dean staying on in Singapore, attending an international school of further education. The school system in Singapore has seventeen schools—of which we are one— offering the UK curriculum, which we accepted and don't want to interrupt. Both the boys are busy with courses, taking them into their A-levels and bringing them back to Britain, even in the next few months would deprive them of reaching their objective in any university course they would want to follow back home.

"They are both keen on science, leading them into numerous possibilities. Neither Patricia or myself want to thwart any of these ambitions. The girls though are excited at the thought of coming to Britain—being their nationality— although having been born in Singapore."

"Well, I never," exclaimed Oscar, which was all he could think of saying after Michael's impassioned reasoning, almost as if trying to convince himself he and Patricia were doing the right thing, by the children., who obviously had their own opinions on the matter. "You seem to have thought this matter through the two of you, but what about Patricia's position as chief librarian in your local library?" continued Oscar, who was intrigued by the sound of this move back to the UK.

"That's also been taken care of. A library not too far from where we shall be looking to live has a vacancy for a senior assistant librarian. Patrica would like to reduce her hours anyway, as she's keen to learn to play another instrument, as well as the piano, with the intention of joining a local band. Full-time work at a library would limit her time to learn this instrument, hopefully playing at different venues and besides dad, she's not getting any younger, so after raising the youngsters I think she would like to slow down a little."

"I must admit it would be nice to have at least some of you back in Britain again, but don't you exert more pressure on yourself, because as you said of Patricia, you aren't getting any younger either. Now, shall we join the others for some food and drinks before we want to fall into bed? By the way, has Father Christmas visited upstairs yet?"

"I assume so chortled Michael. The mince pies and carrots that Dillon left by the fireplace, have gone anyway."

Christmas Eve was always a chance for a good catching-up time and the talks, jokes and the latest news, plus companionship altogether went on well into the night, so Oscar fell into an exhausted, but happy sleep when his head finally hit the pillow. Timothy's home was quiet at last, until an excited Dillon announced, with an excited shout from his bedroom that Father Christmas had come, bringing a lot of toys that his mummy, aunts, uncles and great-grandparents, had asked him to deliver on his sleigh.

It was an early morning wake-up call that mummy's and daddy's all over the world, where Christmas was celebrated, had to endure from a toddler up to the younger teens, who weren't too old to enjoy the excitement of discoveries in stockings or bulky bags when they woke early on Christmas morning. Timothy, Priscilla, Camilla and Dillon's mother Charlotte had known at least three years of this somewhat rude awakening on 25 December and were well prepared.

Leaving most of the family still dozing Priscilla made her way downstairs and into the kitchen where she busied herself making tea and coffee for the early risers. Timothy and Charlotte had sleepily followed Priscilla downstairs, Charlotte first looking in, on her jubilant son, preparing to wake his aunts, uncles and cousins. Charlotte suggested he wait a little longer until everyone was awake with either a cup of tea or coffee, ready for a festive day ahead. Dillon agreed, as long as it wasn't too long a wait, he said.

Oscar, in the room next door, heard this exchange between his granddaughter and her son, smiling to himself as he remembered another very special person that he would have liked to have shared his Christmas Day with. He would telephone her as soon as possible before she left to attend Merryfield's Baptist Church, alone this year, but in the company of her Christian family, who knew of Oscar's family's, traditional Christmas gathering. Perhaps next year things would be different!

If everything went according to expectations, he and Annette would be man and wife, making their own Christmas plans, so that both families could meet up. The largest event yet was still to come—the presentation of the 'specials' by which God was going to give a unique message to the world, an awe-inspiring word, thought Oscar that could very well change the course of history itself, qualifying what had already been written in His word—The Bible—Who could imagine what an Almighty God may have to say! In only a few days' time, the trembling anticipation would be over and he would understand the grace of God in a hushed universe.

Oscar quickly got out of bed, desperately feeling the need to pray. Falling to his knees, a moment of profound love engulfed him and he sought God with all his heart.

Wiping the tears of pure joy, from his face, to avoid questions, Oscar opened his bedroom door almost colliding with many of his family merrily wishing each other a Happy Christmas, making their way to one of the two bathrooms that were so necessary for large house parties such as this.

Tapping and pushing open the door of Dillon's room, he found him engrossed in a new toy he had asked for as a Christmas present. Sitting on the side of the bed, Oscar watched with a great tenderness in his heart, at this child's enjoyment, experimenting with his new toy, making it come to life in his hands, then gleefully showing the results of his labour to his great-grandpapa, who laughed and applauded the busy little hands that had been so quick at making this latest acquisition, work for him.

Hearing people moving around, Dillon was out of bed in an instant and grinning at Oscar still perched on the side of his bed, he gathered up the remainder of the stocking and gift bags running full pelt into his grandad who picked up the struggling boy, hugged him, then releasing him on a warning that he or somebody else could get hurt if he fell or ran into something.

Looking slightly crestfallen, Dillon agreed to walk from now on as there were a lot of people about. Shortly afterwards Charlotte came into Dillon's room to help him get washed and dressed, saying that the family were waiting for Dillon to join them before having breakfast or opening any more presents, being keen to see that their presents had made one little boy, very happy.

Very soon a happy buzz of oohs and aahs were heard as presents were given and opened. After this, breakfast was a rather stand-up affair, collect your cereal, toast and marmalade, tea or coffee and chat in either lounge or hall, as the kitchen was out of bounds except for Priscilla and the girls who needed the space in which to get the Turkey in the oven and to prepare the remainder of the meal, usually eaten quite late in the day, so that those who wanted to attend the local church could stay on afterwards for the Christmas mince pies and coffee or tea, without feeling the need to rush back for an early lunch.

Oscar had retreated into the study once he had eaten, to give Annette a call to send her all his love for Christmas, remembering that Bradley and the rest of the family would be there as well and his greetings were sent to them too. Bradley, it seemed had taken over the reins in the kitchen, persuading Annette to attend Christmas morning service at her and Oscar's family church, so he cut the call short knowing that she needed to start making her way there.

Timothy surprised Oscar by announcing that he felt inclined to attend their local church for the 10 AM service this year, to accompany his father and if anyone else would like to join them they would, of course, be very welcome. A few startled faces gave the overall impression that a few more would be coming along as well, once they had thought about it and so eight of the Henderson families found themselves walking along to the local parish church, that before, would probably not have realised was even there.

Embarrassed smiles were exchanged as they wondered what was in store for them. As at Merrryfield's the door leading into the church, from the porch, was open and a slightly rotund middle-aged minister, with penetrating blue eyes, stood on the threshold gladly welcoming the steady flow of parishioners and visitors alike, into the warm, rich hay-scented interior of the church. Extending his hand, the minister smiled deeply into Oscar's eyes, as he introduced, in turn, each member of the family.

Shaking hands with them all, they were greeted with a smile, hoping he said that they would enjoy the service. Turning now to meet other folks coming into the church, Oscar also made to lead the way, along a central aisle to where the pews were beginning to fill with Christmas worshippers. Children, clutching a parent's hand happily playing with a much sort after toy, that may well have been received earlier that morning.

There was an air of happy festivities permeating throughout the building. A large side space widened right, from off the aisle, but what caught Oscar's eye was the largest, most imposing reconstruction of the stable, he had ever seen, where Jesus had been born to Mary and Joseph, in a town called Bethlehem, two thousand years ago. The crib or manger was centrally placed with a doll-sized image, residing there, representing the Christ child.

Mary and Joseph were kneeling by the crib, as were the three Kings or Wise men, who had been told to follow the natal star that they could see in the sky, from their lands far away and which would hover over the place where Jesus, the new king, could be found. They had bought important gifts that would have a part to play in His life, here on earth. The animals that inhabited the stable were clearly seen, in the act of feeding.

A lantern, held by Joseph, lit the scene, as Oscar and his family paused in their walk to a pew. Martha, Mary and Charlotte were among those with Oscar, peering wide-eyed into the stable, when the inexplicable happened. The fixed, plastic features of the occupants of the stable began to soften, with the mouths of the animals moving, as if in the act of chewing. The facial muscles of the Kings were slowly moving until each was smiling.

Watching bemused, Oscar and his family looked at the Holy Family, who were themselves smiling contentedly into the eyes of their audience. Whatever was happening here? Could it be a trick of the light, but no, the only light was that emitting from Joseph's lantern, not casting any shadows, to account for anything unusual happening. Seven shocked faces turned towards Oscar, looking for an explanation, but he was at a loss for words.

And then Oscar heard it, then the sound of the wind, moaning as if rushing through a corpse of trees, then silence—that seemed to Oscar to last for eternity—and beyond. Immediately Oscar's thoughts were churning, taking him back to the reading in the Old Testament of the Holy Bible, when a man called Moses was given The Ten Commandments, inscribed by God, onto large sheets of stone. Moses hadn't heard God in a quiet whisper, but in the strong wind and fire, on the mountaintop. These commandments, given to the Israelite people who had spent forty years in the wilderness after their escape from Egypt, are the very same for us today. Oscar trembled.

Glancing at his family Oscar could see they had heard the wind, but looking then at members of the congregation filing in for the service, amazingly there wasn't a trace of fear, anxiety or complexity on any face, just a calmness as they shared a pew with family and friends in anticipation of the coming service. Moving away from the open stable, Oscar gently moved his family back to the central aisle, and, walking somewhat mechanically, as if unsure of their footing, he ushered them into an empty pew, each sitting in silent thought.

The Reverend Greg Wilson welcomed the final stragglers into the church that Christmas morning, before closing the heavy oak door behind him. After fifteen years of ordination, he had unhesitatingly known God was calling him to serve in the parishes of Fareham. His wife Judy, who ran the Sunday Schools and the work with the elderly, was equally convinced and so the pair began their work in the parish they felt called to lead.

Sometimes it seemed like an uphill struggle, but when a new curate was appointed the way became clearer. There was a radiancy attached, not just to the church building, but to home groups and the sharing of meals. Bible study groups were introduced bringing light not only to the mind but in the parishioner's eyes and behaviour towards one another. No longer were pews reserved for one particular family, for, as the seats were taken, so pew dwellers willingly offered to share.

With a smile, as he passed each pew, Reverend Greg Wilson made his way along the aisle towards the altar standing in the chancel. Glancing into the stable, his eyes seemed to lock onto the serene blue ones of the baby Jesus. Whatever had happened here this morning was nothing short of a miracle, instigated by God, whose very presence here was almost tangible. Not knowing what had occurred at any given moment, nor did he need to know, but one thing was certain, at least one person here this morning had received an encounter from God and whose pathway in life may have been changed forever, for something far far better.

Reaching the chancel step and mounting them The Reverend Greg Wilson turned to greet the congregation welcoming them once more to this Christmas morning service, before proceeding with a traditional service of well-known carols with the exception of a new song for Christmas, written by a lesser known Christian songwriter.

This song, presenting Jesus as King of Kings and Lord of Lords, direct from the writings of the Prophet Isaiah, was a joy to be able to teach it that Christmas morning, with the organist and choir giving it a rousing introduction. Scripture readings in accordance with the liturgy of the day followed, after which Reverend Wilson climbed into the pulpit to once more narrate the Christmas story, giving thought to events happening in the world beyond these four walls and how, as Christians, we make a response.

The service ended with an unprecedented cheer for the arrival of baby Jesus; the choir filed out and with the children clutching their new Christmas toys; the congregation walked back to the heavy oak door to exit via the porch, after shaking hands and a Merry Christmas greeting to Reverend Greg Wilson.

Oscar was nearly bubbling over with excitement as he and the seven members of the family who had joined him in church, made their way outside, standing uncertainly together. Their faces too were glowing with an inward light, yet with a touch of fear and trepidation of having experienced such a tumultuous happening. Timothy's response was to soundly shake his father's hand, whilst Martha opened her mouth to utter one word 'Wow' not an altogether right response to Father God, but the only one that seemed to her, to sum up the elation she felt.

As the family began the short walk back to Timothy's and Priscilla's home where cocktails or tea and coffee would be waiting, there were more revelations to come. Charlotte admitted she felt as though a troublesome weight had gone from her shoulders with a sense of peace and tranquillity in its place. Her face was bright and happy, and Oscar hadn't seen her display before. Michael and Patrica, home from Singapore, spoke of confirmation about returning to the UK, something which had been bothering them since realising they would need to leave the boys, Martin and Dean, to continue their education in Singapore.

They knew without a shadow of a doubt that, although their friends would be at school with them, there was that added assurance that a higher power would be watching over them. As Michael and Patrica were speaking the remaining family members were nodding and smiling in their direction, agreeing totally with their understanding of God haven spoken into their lives. With such a recent encounter, Oscar found himself being asked many questions, especially how he and Annette had found their faith and believed in God.

Dillon, as anticipated, made a bee-line for both his grandfather and great-grandpapa, giving each a hug to welcome them home. The others came in the front door on a quieter note, but with a smile on each face, radiating an inner peace. It could have been a sombre moment, arriving home from church, instead, those who had stayed at home, caught the light of excitement in the eyes of those who had been to church and without hesitation asked what had happened in the service that morning. It was Martha, encouraged by her sister Mary, who launched, with enthusiasm and a lightness in her voice the events of the morning and what they had all witnessed whilst looking into the replica of Jesus' birthplace, in Bethlehem.

For a moment there was utter silence amongst the families, then a bemused number of questions began, with Timothy finally suggesting that they accept the fact that God was trying to get their attention and instead of asking why, perhaps they should pray instead.

With a murmur of agreement from the still bewildered Harrison family, they, as one bowed their heads, admitting that they knew, for themselves, that they had fallen far short of God's standards, but were now asking for forgiveness, with a chance to start afresh, on newly directed pathways. Echoed by a unanimous "Amen", there was an even deeper sense of family love for one another than ever before. Christmas celebrations continued with an awesomeness and joy of understanding the true meaning of Christmas.

The Christmas roast Turkey with all the trimmings, plus a delicious cooked ham, was served a little later this year with the complete families managing to all become seated at Timothy and Priscilla's large farmhouse table which they extended into the lounge. All were in a heightened sense of excitement, with Oscar being asked to commence with a prayer of thanksgiving that hadn't, in the past, been included as part of the proceedings. Oscar was honoured and delighted that this year had just a significant meaning for them all, including a small five-year-old boy who sang out the 'Amen' at the end of his great-grandpapa's prayer to Jesus, that he was yet to learn more about.

Once more the kitchen was inhabited by many willing helping hands to clear and stack away the plates and dishes from the dishwasher, before indulging in a welcome cup of home-blended coffee and Christmas cake if anybody had room to eat anymore. Oscar's homemade meringues and local farmhouse clotted cream had been consumed yesterday with exclamations of how light and fluffy they were.

Very soon it was time for an excited Dillon to gather together his new toys and articles of clothing, say goodnight to his aunts, uncles and cousins, then take hold of his grandmother's hand, this time, drag her upstairs for her to read him a bedtime story before settling down to sleep cuddling the latest favourite toy. Kissing the drowsy tousled head of her grandson, she was filled with an even greater love for him than ever before. Although not in church this morning Priscilla knew that what had happened there was a wake-up call and she felt her heart bursting with an overwhelming thrill of happiness within her. Life was certainly about to enter a change for the whole family of Harrisons.

Leaving Dillon's bedroom, Priscilla made her way back to the lounge where her two daughters and Timothy were involved in a family game of guessing what character was stuck on one's forehead, a game called 'Heads Up,' not dissimilar to charades and bringing about a lot of laughter. Watching the interaction with the other players Priscilla found several long-held resentments dissolving into a much-needed sense of forgiveness. Seeing her, Timothy moved into his, seat inviting her to sit down and smiling contentedly she joined him, becoming wholeheartedly immersed in the game.

After an hour or so of entertainment, some of the younger members of the families began to tire, after which their parents suggested they may like another hot drink and then perhaps, bed, an appealing thought as the log fire that had warmed the rooms so efficiently earlier on, was beginning to lose its robust heat.

Soon only a few stalwart members of the family were left, hugging the remainder of the fire, some wanting to talk more about the events of the day and how they should continue their lives, with this new understanding of God or Heavenly Father, as Oscar called Him. Concerned that some may have an inkling of a judgemental God, who would find fault with many things they did in their everyday lives and punish them for it, Oscar, although tired himself knew he had to try and explain a few things that, for the moment they would perhaps not know about.

So, began an impromptu Bible Study, with Oscar recalling the gospel story of how both the old and new testaments of the whole Bible point to Jesus and His coming to earth as both God and Man to show mankind the way back to knowing a loving Father, who we had become separated from, by sin or our failure to live up to God's standards, which we cannot do on our own merits, but by Jesus being an intermediary between His and our Father and mankind.

This, Oscar said, was called 'Grace,' an unmerited, spontaneous favour shown to us by a loving Heavenly Father—God. Faces that were perplexed at first began to smile as Oscar underlined how much God loved us all individually and knew the way our paths in life would take, even before the very beginning of the world. A few more perplexed looks encouraged Oscar to suggest a prayer to this recently known Jesus before they all made their way to bed. Tomorrow, he suggested we could talk some more and so once more heads were bowed to acknowledge a Holy God, with a true yearning to know more and to say a heartfelt thank you.

Climbing thankfully into bed, Oscar prayed for guidance for tomorrow, when his family would question him again. His heart was filled with joy as he drifted off into a peaceful, trouble free sleep. Tomorrow he must report all these things to Annette, knowing he would be seeing her again very soon and then the 'specials' debut at 'The Winter Special' dance show, now extended into the NewYear, so the actual day for this great event would be at the evening performance on New Years Day. Bradley had telephoned him with this update just before they left for Fareham, the day before Christmas Eve.

Boxing Day for the Harrison families was usually a quiet one, with most sleeping in after a late night before, but today was rather different, with many awake and downstairs early, to help Priscilla rustle up breakfast for those who were already up, with a new vigour in their behaviour. Although it was a cold day, Oscar included, decided it was dry and bright and that a walk would be a good idea. Wrapped up warmly against the bitter wind, a flurry of activity coming from the rear of the group, caused the walkers to turn towards the sound, which was the small body of Dillon hurtling up to them, desperately trying to drag on boots and coat at the same time.

"Good morning, young man," laughed Oscar, scooping the breathless boy into his arms. "I thought you were still in bed and asleep. We were only going for a short walk and didn't think to wake you."

Holding onto the hands of both his grandad and great-grandpapa Dillon happily decided this was where he wanted to be, despite his mother urging him to take his scarf with him if he wanted to catch up with the walkers. Serious talking was now a little difficult as Dillon managed to dominate the conversation with his childhood chatter, not really expecting an answer.

Back at the house again, with welcome hot drinks waiting, they found the rest of the family cheerfully contributing their services in preparing an early lunch so that the afternoon could be spent in family talks, with much in speculation of Martha and Mary's forthcoming weddings only a couple of months from now. Both the girls were eager to discuss Oscar's offer of building two new homes for the couples to move into when they came back from honeymoon. He was pleased to hear that the two local men were more than happy to begin the constructions within a week or so, to have them ready in time for the couple's return.

Oscar had managed to telephone Annette to talk over the events of the day before, which he hadn't had time to tell her about when he had rung to say a 'Merry Christmas' to them all, just before the Christmas meal, yesterday. He also wanted her opinion of his thoughts about telling the family about the 'specials,' and how they were going to be used by God for His global message.

Annette was typically thrilled about Oscar's family having heard the gospel and was pretty certain that the family would wonder why Oscar hadn't told them before, when they heard what God had to say via the tap shoes in a few days' time. Thinking aloud, Oscar came to the same conclusions, determining to do something about it, that very afternoon.

The two reception rooms in Timothy and Priscilla's home had been opened up into one large lounge, to accommodate everyone and with log fires in each one. The atmosphere was getting decidedly warm, with conversations gradually slowing down. By now it was nearing the middle of the afternoon and reviving cups of tea were definitely being called for, with Oscar suggesting he and Timothy disappear into the kitchen to prepare a tray of refreshments for them all, after which, he said, he had something very important to tell them. Priscilla seconded the idea, saying it wouldn't be long before she and the girls would be getting supper ready.

Soon, most were sipping beverages of their choice, eager to hear what Oscar had to say. He began by talking about Trevor, the famous tap dancer, and how he had handcrafted his shoes for many years. Telling of Trevor's request, so soon before his death on the motorway, led to the time he had met Bradley and Annette, his mother, who had been Trevor's wife. A few aahs came from some of the family, as they began to see a connection. Oscar could see the way most were thinking and quickly explained his and Bradley's puzzlement when these tap shoes, now installed in Oscar's new flat, began to tap dance, on their own accord.

Skipping a large section of the story, Oscar relayed the time when the angels appeared, at the end of a stage show, telling those who were left tidying up, that God had passed a special dispensation onto the shoes, for the sole purpose of having them perform one night, on stage, at which time He intended to send a message, via the ordinary everyday object of these tap shoes, now named the 'specials,' to the world.

Oscar then told his family that following an early prayer meeting it was arranged for he and Bradley to speak to two onstage directors and managers of a theatre in which Bradley had been spotted for his first ever stage experience, in the background chorus, giving him an ideal opportunity to ask permission to have the 'specials' perform their own routine, now at the evening performance on New Years Day, two days before the current show called 'The Winter Special' is finally ending.

It's been a long-running dance organza, a prelude to 'The International Year of Dance' celebrating the common language of dance, without cultural barriers of tongue or politics and has been very successful. Annette and I went to see the first performance. That is all I can tell you, at this moment continued Oscar, as there were murmurs of disbelief. How God will use this occasion I don't know, but I felt that you should know about this, especially after yesterday's Christmas miracle and my privilege of being a part of His plan, all of which I believe was a prelude, for us as a family, before His message on New Years Day.

For a long moment, the family was speechless, then a deluge of amazed comments began, to each other, why they, as a family, should be given this knowledge. Oscar listened to these incredulous comments, making a point that we don't know how many other families already have this knowledge and we can't begin to explain how God chooses to impart His revelations and to whom, which was accepted as truth by the family. Instead, finished Oscar, we should be praying for a deeper faith filled with a resolve to tell others what has happened to us and the change it has made in our lives and how that change would be seen as real.

The following prayer time was earnest and being real before God. As sincere confessions were made and forgiveness received, Oscar was thrilled to see many of his family released from fear, anxieties, jealousies and even long-held resentments. Faces were filled with new peace and joy, whilst hugs were spontaneously exchanged.

Shortly afterwards Priscilla disappeared into the kitchen, with others offering help, for supper to be prepared. Once everyone was seated and the usual cold meats and salads served, it was all a little too much for Dillon, who had been persuaded to be quiet for far too long, before making a statement, at the table, that this had been the best Christmas ever. This caused a long burst of laughter, breaking the unusual silence, now releasing cheerful chatter, with the occasional joke being cracked by Michael, who was the comedian of the family.

Fresh Christmas crackers were pulled with the jokes, giving rise to ripples of mirth around the large farmhouse table. The atmosphere was returning to normal, with lightened hearts. Priscilla had made one of her delicious sherry trifles and with coffee, Christmas cake or chocolate log being indulged afterwards the family admitted they had dined well and once more were ready for bed. Several needed to head for home the following day, as some businesses needed to be opened up again, ready for sale time after Christmas. Dillon needed a little persuasion to clean his teeth, ready for bed and a story from his mum.

The next few days seemed to fly by, once those who had travelled quite away from home, were waved safely away by the remaining guests. The next time they would all meet up again would be in Thailand for the marriages of Mary and Martha to Karin and Steve respectively, in February. Oscar had planned to leave on the day before New Year's Eve, fully intending to catch a fast train to London, then a taxi home, which wasn't very far, but Michael had other ideas and refused to allow his father to journey home alone.

"Dad, you are not going to catch a train to London, on your own," protested Michael, when he heard of his father's plans. "Patrica and the children will, I am sure, have packing to do and one less person in Timothy and Priscilla's hair would be much appreciated. They've worn themselves ragged looking after us all this Christmas. What a brilliant job they've done too and deserve a break, at least." Besides, he continued, "I haven't given the car a long run, since we decided to bring it with us with all the presents and us to carry, so a good long trip will do it good. What do you say, dad? Will you trust enough in me, your youngest son, to drive you home?"

"Of course I trust you, Michael," laughed Oscar. "You've all looked at me so well that I thought I would give you all a break and get myself home, but if you really want to make the journey, then who am I to say 'No thank you,' so 'Yes please,' you can make sure your old dad gets home safely."

At this point the entire room filled with laughter, with the 'boys' protesting that their dad wasn't old at all, despite a distinct smattering of white hair, producing a rather distinguished appearance.

Dillon had immediately pricked up his ears at the mention of his great-grandpapa going home, begging to be allowed to go along too, but Charlotte had to say a very definite 'no,' as Michael was intending to drive back again, after a break for something to eat and drink and it would be far too late for a young man of Dillon's age to be up. After pulling a mock face of disappointment, Dillon decided that perhaps his mother knew best, after all.

Shortly after this discussion, Oscar withdrew to a quieter area where he called Annette to tell her of the change of plan, that Michael would be driving him home after all, so no need for her to meet him at the station, which was something she had proposed doing, when he had discussed coming to London, by train.

Annette was pleased that Oscar would not be travelling alone back to London. They chatted for a while about their Christmas' apart, promising each other that next year, they hoped, would be different. Her family had been entertained very well, by the chef, who had opened up his restaurant for a fabulous feast on Christmas Day, with Bradley being able to join them for dessert and after-dinner drinks, leading onto spiced hot coffee or chocolate, much to everyone's delight.

He had looked tired, she said, as the 'Winter Show' was still proceeding with a great deal of interest, which was why it had been extended into the New Year. Almost without stopping for breath, Annette said how much she was looking forward to the New Year's Day, evening performance, when the 'specials' would be introduced by Oscar and Bradley and God would give a message to the world. What would He say, she wondered and how it would be received by the first audience to be privileged enough to hear it? She was obviously worried by that first response.

Oscar could not answer that one, of course, but reassured her that what they were about to hear would have long-lasting consequences for everybody. A long hush fell over the air, then Annette was urging Oscar to hurry home, as she was a little scared. Whatever else we are, encouraged Oscar, we are not to be afraid. I will telephone you when I'm home, my darling, he promised. In the meantime, if you need to, speak to those we know at 'Merryfields' church, but please don't be frightened. You know how much we are loved by Him and this could be a wake-up call to mankind Annette. With that, he blew a kiss along the phone and rang off.

The final couple of days were spent seeing more guests leave Timothy and Priscilla's, heading homeward, each with their thoughts on the forthcoming event that Oscar had told them would happen on the evening of New Year's Day. It was both thrilling and exciting, tinged with a healthy fear of the Almighty, especially what they themselves had experienced on Christmas Day and the expectancy that was in all their hearts. This was an entirely new way of thinking for them.

Michael wanted to leave fairly early on the day he was taking his father home. Although cold, the day promised to remain dry. Most of the goodbyes were said the night before after another short Bible Study and prayer time in readiness for the journey, if nothing else, but ended in a time of singing some of the few Christian songs that Oscar had attempted to teach them and a spilling over of some tears, in appreciation of all that they were learning and how grateful they were.

Up and ready the next morning, Oscar slipped quietly into Dillon's bedroom before the little boy was fully awake to kiss him goodbye. Dillon's arms slid around Oscar's neck and with just a tiny sob, told his great-grandpapa how much he loved him, which was heartily reciprocated by Oscar returning the compliment into Dillon's right ear, before tucking the covers back over a still sleepy young man.

Tiptoeing out of the bedroom Oscar picked up his luggage, gave a hearty thank you and hug to Timothy and Priscilla, Selina and Rosemary, before joining his son Michael in his silver Mercedes'.

The journey to the motorway was quiet, with only a short queue to join this main route through to London. There wasn't the hectic rush of traffic at this time of the morning, but further on towards the city, it might be a different matter. The pair drove in silence for a while, each engrossed in their own thoughts until they both felt the need for a short respite and a welcome mug of hot coffee. A motorway service area was featured as being the next place to take a break and pulling off the motorway, they found a large parking area with an inviting array of shops to be seen within the complex.

Very soon Michael and Oscar were sitting in a replica of a woodland setting, hands comfortably warming on mugs of fresh percolated coffee and indulging in small talk, when they were aware of a group of about ten to twelve men and women carrying placards, approaching an area of a walkthrough, a short way from where they were sitting. Reading the placards, Oscar began to wonder who they were. Some were announcing that God loved them, whilst others read of the dangers of times ahead.

The group was not making themselves obviously known to the many visitors to the motorway service area, but out of curiosity, car drivers and passengers, also obviously lorry drivers were stopping to hear what was being said. When any of the group were asked who they were, they replied that they were Christians from various local churches in the nearby town and were there to remind people of a New Year's beginning and what people's expectations were for the coming year.

Some turned and walked away, whilst Oscar and Michael noticed that several did stay to discuss their secret ambitions for the coming year, mainly a desire for better paid work, others a better political scene at home and overseas. Yet others revealed a need for the country to become Christian again, with Christian values and still others proposed a better deal for an ageing population, whilst some, particularly women, wanted more security from the police, to guard against women molesters and killers.

All these objectives were considered worthy, by the group, but did people understand that when Jesus spoke to the people, when on earth, He had said that today there would be trouble and how much more these troubles would increase, before Jesus returned again, to this broken world, to administer justice, receiving to Himself those who professed His name.

Michael and Oscar listened as the gospel of Jesus Christ was proclaimed. Some of those that were listening and there were quite a few, began to look anxious and faces showed a disinclination to believe what they were hearing. Oscar then grinned at Michael and whispered that maybe they could be of use here, so getting up, with Michael reluctantly following, Oscar made his way over to the group, told them briefly that he and his son had heard what the group had to say, proceeding to tell of the Harrison families experience on Christmas Day, in their local Anglican Church.

You could have heard a pin drop, then a bevy of questions followed by the Christian evangelical group and those listening in the crowd, now gathered. It was amazing how eager people were to hear every detail. Oscar uttered an arrow prayer, to know whether he should share about the forthcoming show of the 'specials,' with these people, listening to every word spoken by both him and then Michael's affirmation of the events completely changing his life, with a surety of future issues that had been troubling him.

The answer to his prayer appeared to be a 'No,' so Oscar obediently declined his first instinct to tell of the future event coming. Without any suggestion, small groups of listeners began to congregate together, many of them offering simple but heartfelt prayers to a God that most of them did not know until challenged perhaps by the church group, which had now moved on and some who were persuaded by Oscar and Michael's testimonies. It was a quiet respectful time of intimacy with a higher power than themselves. One that was brought about so unexpectedly.

After another mug of coffee later, Oscar and his son were back in their car en-route to the motorway and so on to London, later than they had bargained for, perhaps with a further change of plan, with Michael staying overnight with Oscar. A very early morning start should allow Michael to return to Fareham, collect his family and still make it to the airport for their night flight to Singapore, with the inevitable stopover to refuel, before continuing the through flight, to Singapore and home.

A call from Oscar to Timothy and Priscilla came as a bit of a surprise when Oscar told them of the church's team at the motorway service stop. Patricia came to talk to Oscar, who could only relay Michael's assurances that by starting off very early tomorrow morning he could still be back to collect them all and make it to the airport in time for their flight. Patricia could only convey to Michael her concern at cutting it so fine but was equally delighted at Michael's confidence in speaking out his testimony. She sent her love for safe travelling and said she and the children would be ready to load the car as soon as he had arrived safely back in Fareham.

As expected, the closer Oscar and Michael approached London, they did meet with more traffic than they would have liked, but then Michael spotted a chance to avoid some of the traffic pouring into London. It had pared off some time and they weren't as late getting back to Oscar's flat as they had expected.

Annette had already been told of the delay, so wasn't anxious when eventually Oscar telephoned her to say they had arrived home safely. Not wanting to delay the pair from getting a meal and refreshments together, with an early night for them both, she refrained from asking questions about the reason for their delay. Tomorrow she and Oscar had planned to meet for lunch together and that would be time enough.

There wasn't a lot of food in Oscar's fridge, after Christmas away from home, but with careful forethought Oscar had prepared for any possible emergency and had cooked some meals for himself or Annette, if the need arose, using his limited freezer space for storage, plus with some cartons of milk that could easily be defrosted, he and Michael were able to enjoy a less Christmas rich meal together.

Talking for a while after eating, Oscar left Michael listening to a radio programme whilst he made up the bed in his spare bedroom. After a mug of hot chocolate, each of the pair were soon in their beds and asleep. Michael intending to be on the road leading to the motorway before Oscar was awake. He could always pick up a bacon sandwich somewhere along the way. Oscar though had anticipated this, so setting his alarm for an extra early awakening he was up in time to send his son back to Fareham, with a cooked breakfast inside him. Michael gave his dad a warm hug, thanked him for a bed for the night and breakfast and was soon making good headway.

Driving on his own now, Michael had the next few hours in which to mull over, in his mind, the whole incredulous happenings of this Christmas and the far happier future that lay ahead, for them all. Making good time and not being so tired, after the overnight stay with Oscar, he gently sounded his horn, outside Timothy's and Priscilla's, to announce his arrival, to have a harum-scarum bundle of little boy, open the passenger seat and hop in beside him, quick on the accusation that he was not supposed to have stayed overnight with his great-grandpapa and why had he, without really listening to the answer?

Laughing, Michael dragged him out of the car and set him on his feet, to run back indoors to tell everyone that Uncle Michael was back. His four cousins came running downstairs with Patricia, their mother, following behind. Luggage had been stacked just inside the front door, with the rest of the family hurrying up, in time to hug and kiss goodbye to the last of the Christmas guests, on their return to Singapore. It had been a happy and amazing time for constant reflection.

Once Michael had been waved on his way, with a firm assurance that they would let Oscar know of their safe return to Singapore and the beginning of the next stage in their lives, Oscar sleepily made his way back to the kitchen, to clear away the remains of breakfast. Glancing out of the window, he was rewarded by a cheeky little face peering back at him. No matter what time—early or late—that Oscar made an appearance, Cocky was always there ahead of him, waiting patiently for breakfast.

Oscar wondered how the little fellow had fared whilst he was away. Worms, that morning, had still to be collected and Cocky watched interestedly whilst Oscar dug, managing to find a few juicy worms, in the cold ground and with the warm milk was readily acceptable. Making himself another mug of coffee, Oscar waited impatiently in his lounge for the hands of the clock to creep around to a reasonable time when he thought Annette would be awake or possibly up, making breakfast for herself in the kitchen. Her sister and brother-in-law would already be on their way to work.

Deciding it was probably the right time, Oscar picked up his mobile, dialling Annette's number. She answered immediately pleased to hear his voice and the two chatted animatedly about the 'happenings' in the motorway service complex. Interested as she was, Oscar detected a note of anxiety in her voice. She had already expressed to him that she was scared, wanting him to hurry home from Timothy's and Priscilla's and he wanted more than anything to hold her in his arms, to reassure her that he was here now and there was nothing to be afraid of and that just a little fearful anticipation of the unknown was perfectly understandable.

Soon, Oscar was dressed and on his way to Annette's, where he found her composed and on her knees by the kitchen table, asking Jesus to forgive her for her fear and lack of faith. Oscar entered quietly, so as not to disturb her communing with her Heavenly Father, then, as she got up, surprised to see him, he then took her into his arms, lovingly kissing her cheek, saying that now they were together again, they would be in this as one being, in the Lord.

It was a moment of pure love and joy in each other's company. Anita, he felt at that instant, was in full agreement with their love for each other, wanting only their happiness, as he and his dear wife had been happy. Trevor had been as much one with Annette as he had been with Anita and Oscar felt them very close, rejoicing that their loved ones were finding hope and love again, for the future.

A taxi took the pair into a London district, where a small restaurant, tucked away among a less glamorous parade of shops and offering Oscar and Annette a choice luncheon menu, had been discovered by them entirely by accident one day and which they had since frequented several times. The two chefs welcomed them into the warmth and brightness of their domain, seating them in an appealing alcove, presenting a special menu for a New Year's Eve lunch.

The city, they could feel was in a constant buzz today with many people already coming in by train, coaches or car from surrounding locations in anticipation of the firework display taking place later that day, to welcome in, at midnight, a New Year. A year that could and would change many lives, following what God was going to reveal tomorrow evening.

During the course of a delicious lunch, Annette's mobile uttered its melodious call signal. Not expecting a phone call from anyone, she nevertheless answered, a little surprised to hear Bradley's voice, cheerfully asking whether Oscar had returned alright from Fareham and as there wasn't a performance that afternoon, he was hoping he could visit him later that afternoon to talk over the timing of the 'specials' role tomorrow.

"Hello Bradley," Oscar spoke into Annette's mobile. "It's great to hear from you. I fully intended to call you today, but I'm pleased you have this afternoon off for even just a short rest. Mum says you've been working very hard, but managed to have some time with them over Christmas, which was very good. We're having lunch in 'The Brig' today, but, I think—smiling questioningly at Annette—we shall be our way home very shortly and I'll call in at the bakery for rolls and bread, with some delicious home-cooked ham and anything else you would like, if you've got time to stay for an early tea?"

"Yes please, Oscar," replied Bradley, "fresh rolls and ham sounds good. I shall be onstage this evening, so can't eat a large meal. I'm just emptying the washing machine to dry some costumes I shall need tomorrow and then I'll come over in a couple of hours if that's alright?"

"Fine by me," smiled Oscar. "I'll see you then and can't wait to hear all your news about the show."

Finishing their meal in a leisurely way, Oscar asked the waiter for the bill, but not before Annette had forestalled him, announcing it was her treat today, as he had paid the taxi fare to come here.

It was a generous gesture, one Oscar knew she could ill afford, but thankfully tickets for the show tomorrow evening had been purchased well in advance. Thanking the chefs for the patronage privileges they always received, when eating there, the pair adjusted their jackets for the cold winter afternoon. Squeezing her arm to say 'thank you' he escorted her to the nearest taxi rank, to take them back to where they could purchase the items in readiness for Bradley's arrival. Soon they were home in the warmth of Oscar's flat and no sooner had they unloaded the shopping, than Bradley was on the doorstep, giving Annette a warm son's hug and welcoming Oscar also with a mutual hug.

Enjoying their hot beverages, the three sat companionably by the instant heat from the fire, in Oscar's lounge, Bradley obviously appreciating his half-day of relaxation, before once more treading the boards in The Blackbird Principle Theatre for the final few days of showtime. Much as Annette would like to stay on for tea, she and Oscar had enjoyed a lunchtime together and she now needed to be in her sister and brother-in-law's home, where she and Bradley were invited to live after the death of Trevor.

Bradley is now, of course, at Jonathon Tate's Dancing Studio and living, thanks to Jonathon, with his son Terence with whom he shared a flat. It was a good arrangement giving both boys a chance to be self-sufficient, but Annette did miss Bradley being around, also her eldest son was married with his own children.

Quite happily Annette offered to keep house and cook for her small family, so now it was time to get back, so there could be a meal on the table when Simone—a busy community midwife—and Rupert arrived home from work. Arranging a time to be ready for the theatre tomorrow took a moment or two, after which Oscar called a taxi company to take her home and Bradley affectionally kissed his mother goodbye until they would meet again tomorrow evening.

Tea had to be an early affair for Bradley, as he needed to leave in good time to get to the theatre—for which Oscar ordered another taxi—and change into the costume ready for the first troupe to perform. Being in a background chorus meant that he was often needed for more than one troupe, therefore involving a change of costume between acts. Bradley revelled in the life he was leading, but admitted to feeling very tired, needing plenty of rest before the next day's shows began.

Before Bradley left, he and Oscar discussed the timed appearance of the 'specials,' which had been agreed upon, would be after the finale for the evening, Both of them would be in the left-hand wing of the theatre, from where one of the stage directors would introduce Oscar and Bradley, asking them to announce a final very exceptional act given by a pair of tap shoes, with an extremely personal message for everybody.

After Bradley had left and the washing up completed Oscar was relaxing in front of the television searching for a suitable channel to watch, to herald in the New Year, if he managed to stop from falling asleep, when his phone rang. Over the airwaves came the sound of voices singing "A Happy New Year Grandpa" and realised, with a delight that it was Michael, Patricia and the children, ahead of British time, in Singapore. It was a joy to hear their voices and know that they were home safely.

Michael explained that neither he or Patricia were expected back at work until tomorrow and as schools weren't back until the day after, they were going to enjoy a very hot day out, maybe taking in the zoo, but certainly a visit to Sentosa Island for a spell of sightseeing. Oscar thought of the warmth of

Singapore and how cold it was in London, then sent them all his love for a lovely day out. Michael then asked Oscar to keep him posted about tomorrow night's presentation of the 'specials,'

He readily agreed, but equally felt that Michael and Patricia would know the results for themselves before many more days were past.

By now, it was only an hour or so before the throngs that were massing on the embankment would have their expectations realised as they watched this year's firework display, welcoming in the New Year, at midnight. Oscar began his New Year messages by ringing Annette, to tell her that Michael, Patricia and the children were safely home, having telephoned with his first New Year's greeting. He sent his warmest love to her, wondering if either she or him would make it up, to see the New Year in for themselves.

Annette did admit to feeling ready for bed, but as the countdown had almost begun, she had decided on a hot drink in her nightclothes, raise her mug to the New Year, with all its possibilities, then 'night nights' until tomorrow. By now the fireworks were being lit, the crowds roaring their approval and Big Ben gave the countdown to the hour of midnight, with Auld Lang Syne being sung, if not by the younger generation, but certainly in Scotland and those perhaps of an older generation.

Saluting each other with their mugs, at either end of the phone, Oscar and Annette praised God in all that He was going to do tomorrow, then kissed, over the air, before making their separate ways to bed.

Drawing back the curtains the next morning brought, with the sunlight, a sprinkling of snow on the grass outside his bedroom window. Although he knew it would be cold out there, nevertheless it did look very picturesque. His mind roamed to how nice it would be to have Annette with him, to be able to exclaim together, how pretty it looked. His line of thinking about asking Annette to be his wife was decidedly drawing towards its zenith or time scale, and, although marking time he was coming to the conclusion that after the marriages of Mary and Martha, in Thailand; once just the family remained after the reception, then he would finally ask for her hand in marriage.

The family knew she was attending as his guest, by which time they would have been introduced and hopefully getting to know her. He knew there had been much speculation over their friendship already, so to put everybody's mind at rest, he would make the proposal. He loved her dearly and amazingly, in spite of their age differences, she had reciprocated that love many times over, but he needed to be completely sure that this was what her family would like to see, for both their sakes and with so much in common.

Cocky, he knew, would already be waiting for his breakfast, feathers plumped up to protect him from the cold. Thankfully, shivered Oscar, dressing gown dragged over his shoulders, he had remembered to dig up a few worms, before his phone call from Singapore last night. Yes, there he was perched comfortably in the cherry tree, awaiting Oscar's arrival in the kitchen, but this time his feathered friend wasn't alone, but another sat close to him on the same branch. Could this be Cocky's lady friend, wondered Oscar, the one he flew off to see when he left Oscar's garden?

The pair seemed quite amiable together. Oscar had always assumed that robins liked their own 'patch' and was fiercely territorial, but this bird looked happy enough to be with Cocky. Taking the saucer of warm milk and the worms into the frosty garden Oscar was intrigued to watch the role-play between the two birds.

First Cocky flew down onto Oscar's outstretched arm, ate a worm or two, then turned as if to invite the other bird to do the same. Soon, two plumped-up robins were enjoying the same food and drink, from the same utensils as each other, then, having had their fill, without any 'by your leave,' flew off over the rooftops together, leaving their benefactor wondering what the bird world was coming too. No experienced ornithologist would ever believe his story!

Breakfast was a solitary affair for Oscar and already he was feeling edgy and unable to sit still. He needed a walk, he decided, to relieve his restlessness. It was going to be a long day, he thought to himself and it wasn't fair to seek Annette's company as soon as he felt unable to cope on his own. He knew, of course, he was never alone now, but somehow he needed to speak to a fellow Christian, as, when two or three are gathered in my name, Jesus had said, then I am there with them' was a piece of scripture that Oscar had recently learnt and was in need of applying.

Oscar found himself walking resolutely in the direction of Merryfields Baptist Church, where he knew other members of the family would be there, engaging in one of several activities that took place in the church most days. Pastor Stephen was likely to be there and Oscar did need to tell him of the arrangements he and Annette had made, to pick up him and his wife, to arrive in good time at 'The Blackbird Principle Theatre' that evening.

As expected, Pastor Stephen was in his office about to contact Oscar himself regarding this evening's performance. They greeted each other warmly, exchanging greetings for the New Year, which was beginning with such high expectations. Stephen could sense the restlessness in Oscar, which was only to be expected at this eleventh hour when Oscar's task was to announce perhaps the most important moment of his entire life. Here was a need for a special kind of prayer request.

Asking Oscar to wait for a moment, Stephen went into his church to find specific kinds of prayer warriors to join him and Oscar in his study. Those who were leading groups immediately recognised the necessity, by the intensity in Pastor Stephen's voice and quietly managed to hand over the leadership of the group to the next most competent person there, who willingly stepped into the role, unaware perhaps that a mini-crisis was being dealt with in the Pastor's office.

Altogether four experienced prayer warriors joined Pastor Stephen and Oscar, in the church office that morning, unused by the secretary that day, sitting expectantly around Stephen's office table and who spoke of spiritual warfare—something that Oscar, in his newness as a Christian—hadn't heard of before.

Explaining the need for prayer today, especially regarding the event that was to happen that very evening, he said he was very aware that the enemy of Jesus—namely Satan, the evil one—was attempting, even now, to try and disrupt proceedings, causing unnecessary unrest, to the extent of stopping God from speaking this evening. Oscar was shocked by what he was hearing, understanding that this indeed was the cause of his restless behaviour, but greatly encouraged by Pastor Stephen's, Holy Spirit given words, that now was the time for prayer and stop the enemy from causing more harm, than he had already done so.

With Stephen leading, they worshipped the living God first, before demanding that Satan leave now—in Jesus' name—never to return to harm God's people. It was powerful and intense praying that Oscar felt completely at home with. Once finished, the six hugged in a Christian bond, with the four prayer warriors returning to the church hall to continue their duties. Oscar also left soon after, assuring Stephen that they would collect him and his wife in good time for the start of the evening performance, tickets already purchased by Oscar.

Walking home Oscar felt considerably calmer, firmly convinced that God had been in charge, this morning and that tonight would go ahead without any interference. Clearing up after his rapid exit from the flat, this morning, Oscar had some lunch, made two calls to Bradley and Annette to ascertain that all was well, giving them a brief overview of the necessity for urgent prayer, at the church, this morning.

A short while later, Oscar spent a lengthy period of time, in the garden, clearing a few tenacious weeds. The early morning snow had gone and wintry spring sunshine gave him an opportunity to enjoy his small garden for a while. As the afternoon began to mellow into the still sunny but chill of evening, Oscar abandoned the garden for the warmth of the lounge indoors. A couple of letters later Oscar was ready for a short snooze, so setting his alarm clock, careful that he wouldn't oversleep, a warm comfortable feeling overcame him, his eyes closed, where sleep was waiting in the wings.

The gentle but insistent ring of the alarm clock woke Oscar at the appointed hour. With plenty of time before getting ready for the already booked taxi to collect him, Annette, Pastor Stephen and his wife, to arrive at the theatre, getting them into their seats well before the evening show started, there was still time enough to put on some classical music, to allay, he had to admit, a touch of anxiety, soothing him immensely and he soon found himself relaxing, thanking God for the gift of music.

Oscar then cooked himself a modest early dinner, as he wasn't very hungry, but knew he must not neglect eating, giving in to the fluttering in his stomach. Annette then telephoned to give him the extra boost of confidence, that she was sure he would be grateful for, as the time approached the hour when the world would hear, receiving the word or not, a revelation from the Holy God. Oscar felt humbled by the thought that he and Bradley would be instrumental in this, so every certainty of someone praying filled him with gratitude and he thanked Annette for her call.

The taxi driver knocked on Oscar's door promptly, as ordered. Taking his warm winter jacket from the hook in the small entrance hall, Oscar followed the driver to his car and after reviewing the addresses for passengers to be collected, sat back in his seat with a sigh of relief. The waiting was over, from now on out of his hands, as if it had ever been, but he had felt a certain responsibility as he had known Trevor, handcrafting these special tap shoes for him and now this!

Escorted to their seats by the ushers, Oscar and Annette waved to Jonathon and Terence, already seated at the far end of the row behind. The orchestra was seated and tuning their instruments for a perfect pitch and behind the slight gap in the curtain drapes, Oscar could see the stage managers making sure that the first background stage scenery was safely in place.

Bradley, he knew was behind the impressive stage, preparing for his onstage role, making certain the 'specials' were in a closed cupboard, ready to be launched onto the stage, at the appropriate time. Pastor Stephen and his wife Danelle had not visited this theatre before and were interestingly taking in the size, ornate ceiling and complicated-looking lighting, demonstrating the need for skilled electricians.

Seats were rapidly filling and soon the orchestra would call the audience to an alertness that the 'Winter Special' was about to begin. Smiling quietly to himself, Oscar had just spied a small inquisitive face, scanning the audience. It was Bradley, of course, confirming to himself that his 'partner' was very definitely where he should be, to be able to get himself to the left-hand-side wing of the stage, when given a prearranged signal from a stage director. The scene was set.

All was silent in the theatre, as the audience waited in anticipation for the orchestra to strike the first chords and the curtains to be opened. There was hardly a breath in the filled theatre as the first scene was revealed with the dancers in position, ready for the dance to be executed. The melody expanded throughout the great heights of the walls and ceiling; the dancers giving a tremendous display of their abilities, finally giving rise to a loud clapping of approval, as the dancers completed their presentation, exiting the stage into one of the wings.

Humming could be heard as the audience once again waited for the curtains to be drawn back, this time a completely different style of dance being performed for their pleasure. A roar of approval arose, this time as the dance ended, with a short interval between dances to allow for props and scene changes. This could be a challenging time, but the audience tonight was lenient and composed, waiting quietly during the pauses.

Oscar could see Pastor Stephen and his wife Danelle were suitably impressed with the performances so far. On occasions a lone performer would take his or her place in front of the closed curtains to give a recitation from a well-known poet, for example, or often announce a national dance originating from their own country and joined by fellow dancers would perform their own routine, which was always well received. As the show progressed Oscar pointed out Bradley to Pastor Stephen and Danelle, performing excellently in the many background choruses' in which he had a part to play.

Halfway through the evening, an intermission of half an hour was announced, with the audience being asked to return to their seats as soon as the bell rang, as they had a lot to accomplish this evening. Ices and drinks were on offer, in either the foyer or less time-consuming, in the theatre itself. Oscar, sitting relatively close to the stage, so he could get to the left-hand wing, when called, offered ices, easier to consume, to Annette and Stephen and Danelle, which were gratefully accepted.

Oscar could see Jonathon in the queue, gave him a thumbs-up sign, that was received with an emphatic nod. No sooner had his friend sat down, offering an ice-cream tub to Terence, than the bell rang for the short intermission to be over and for the audience to resume their seats.

The second half of the show proved to be just as entertaining as the first half had been, with the now fully hyped up audience asking for an encore after encore and then came the cue Oscar had been waiting for, as he squeezed Annette's hand and made his way to the left-hand-side wing, on the stage, to join a rather nervous looking Bradley, Touching his hand Oscar whispered 'God is in control,' seeing calmness appear on Bradley's face. The curtains were pulled together and the director of the theatre strode in front to face the audience.

Clearing his throat, he then announced that although the show, for this evening's performance, was technical over, there was however a very special treat for the audience. Calling for Oscar and Bradley to join him in front of the curtains, he addressed Oscar, who he knew God had chosen to first announce the 'specials,' with Bradley—still in final costume—to reiterate the story that Oscar was about to tell. Handing him the microphone the director made to move offstage, but Oscar signalled for him to stay.

Asking the orchestra to remain silent Oscar told the full story to an incredulous audience, then invited Bradley to have the curtains reopened, allowing the tap shoes to have the freedom of the stage.

Without any instruction from either Oscar or Bradley—of their own volition—the shoes performed impeccably whilst a hushed audience could hardly believe their eyes or their ears, as a rich, warm but firm voice was heard emitting from the shoes themselves. Some rose to complain it was a hoax, whilst others told them to be quiet and sit down until the end and then they could have their say. Obediently, the protestors reluctantly sat down, muttering to themselves that it was a trick and they would prove it.

The audience sat open-mouthed, as THE VOICE echoed throughout the building, emitting from the depths of the very tap shoes themselves. A warm, strong but firm VOICE that said;

DO NOT BE AFRAID. I AM THE LORD, YOUR GOD—THE HOLY ONE—YAHWEH.
I AM SPEAKING TO YOU AS THE GOD OF HEAVEN, AS WELL AS THE EVERYDAY.
HENCE I AM USING THESE TAP SHOES, TONIGHT, AS MY MOUTHPIECE.

OSCAR AND BRADLEY, HERE NOW, WILL VOUCH FOR ME.

YOU HAVE BEEN LIVING IN VERY DIFFICULT TIMES, AS PROPHESIED IN MY WORD.
COME TO ME ALL WHO ARE WEARY AND HEAVILY LADEN AND I WILL GIVE YOU REST.
TURN TO ME WHILST THERE IS STILL TIME, AS THERE ARE EVIL DAYS AHEAD,
AND MY ENEMY, SATAN, WILL SEDUCE YOU WHENEVER HE CAN, TO COMMIT EVIL DEEDS, YES, EVEN IN MY NAME.
COME MY PEOPLE, COME AND BE WASHED CLEAN FROM YOUR SINS, MANY UNIDENTIFIED BY YOU.
AS YOU ARE FORGIVEN, KNOW FORGIVENESS IN YOUR HEART, FOLLOWING MY LAWS, GIVEN TO YOU FOR YOUR OWN PROTECTION.
IN MY EYES YOUR FILTHY RAGS ARE GONE, REPLACED BY GARMENTS OF WHITE.

REMEMBER, THAT MY SON WILL RETURN TO EARTH AGAIN and THE TIME IS SHORTENING.

With the end of the message, one could metaphorically speaking, hear a pin drop, then, after a gasp, the inevitable eruption burst, shattering the silence.

"Who are Oscar and Bradley intoned a bemused audience. We need to speak to them, to explain."

Yet others were rejoicing in the message, raising their arms towards heaven in silent and not-so-silent prayer. Calling even louder, the people were in a state of extreme flux.

"We are here," quickly announced Oscar, coming, with Bradley to the front of the heavy stage curtains. "I am Oscar and this is my dear friend, Bradley. We can indeed vouch for the God most high. Your eyes and ears have not deceived you, my friends. We are privileged to be here to tell you all you want to hear. Let the questions come one at a time, we aren't going anywhere until you are all satisfied."

Although a sense of shock was apparent on the faces of many of those in the audience, there was also a sense of profound awe and Majesty. Nobody was inclined to speak, until a voice from the orchestra pit calling whether this was the God of the Patriarchs, the God of the universe and the maker of all life on earth, from the very beginning—the Alpha and Omega—and no end.

Oscar confirmed that what the oboist (who plays the tuning note in an orchestra, before a performance begins.) had called out, resonating deeply with the audience. Even the scoffers and those who wanted to disprove the voice of God using the tap shoes to relay his message through the tap shoes were silent, all animosity wiped from their minds, as they allowed God's word to enter their hearts with instant changes taking place.

Bewildered, they staggered to their feet, but the Lord, in His graciousness, had prepared for even this, and, as if from nowhere groups of people gathered, offering Christian hope and future advice, from the message they had just heard.

In the meantime, to those still sitting and happy to listen, Oscar told the story, yet again, of the part he had been given in God's plan, the request from Trevor, the tragic accident, the revelation by God of his planned use of the shoes. Stopping then, Oscar turned to Bradley, introducing him to the absorbed audience, as Trevor's son, now having dedicated ownership of his father's tap shoes.

It was Bradley's opportunity to speak of his father, his dedication to the art of tap dancing and the skill that he so obviously possessed and the fact that these very shoes were specially designed by Oscar, made in his skilful way, which would have catapulted his father to world recognition. Now, he said, he felt like Oscar, extremely privileged to be used by God, in such a way that his own life had changed completely.

Devoting himself, he said, he would continue to follow in his father's footsteps, also available for any service desired for him, by God, his Heavenly Father. At this, a ripple of applause began, but Bradley although still in costume, wanted only applause for God, breaking through with His warning and message of hope, so signalled a stop. By this time, queues were forming to talk to God's evangelists in the three aisles of the theatre. Some had already left the building, walking as if in a trance.

Pedestrians walking past the hastily opened doors of the theatre marvelled at the strong sense of something very special had occurred there, that evening and many remembered that once before a special event had taken place in a theatre not so very far away, but even then had not prepared the people for these earth-shattering revelations that had been on everyone's lips, as they mingled with the passers-by, telling them of all they had seen and heard, this very evening.

By the time the theatre had emptied of the audience, orchestra, electricians, performers, stage directors and theatre managers, Oscar and Bradley were still in the building alongside those who were ministering to many hundreds of people eager to understand more.

Offering to be responsible for locking up and security details, many of the staff were thankful to Oscar and Bradley, but needed to make their way home to their families, not before though prayers of thanksgiving had been made, the now silent tap shoes recovered from the stage where they had been subjected to many inquisitive hands examining them for batteries, hidden wires, even remote control evidence, but none, of course, had been found, leaving only one other option—it was an entirely God-given act, equally, the message was real—the interpretation of which was followed up by God's people, leaving Oscar and Bradley weak with Holy fear.

The following days were rather tumultuous, as reporters, camera teams and disclaimers (who had found not a shred of evidence for their predictions), headed for 'The Blackbird Principle Theatre,' desperately wanting a story, any story, true or false, with many a scuffle breaking out for prime viewing and discussion time, hastily calling together theologians from differing backgrounds, well-known and respected Christian authors and speakers, themselves unable to be sure of what really happened, but with varies theories being aired, disputed by others, all in opposing turmoil.

The one sensible thought, which was quoted from the Bible, was given by a presenter of a Christian radio show and went as follows, "Forget the former things. See, I am doing a new thing." It was thought to put things into perspective, by some authors.

Oscar and Bradley met up with Jonathon and Terence, as well as Annette, including Louisa, who had been present when the angels had spoken. Immediately they vowed to resume the prayer group, adding in Bible Study, of which Jonathon, Terence and Louisa had no experience of attending.

Oscar contacted Pastor Stephen to see how busy he was and if he could lead a group for them with the intention of including those who wanted to learn more about the Christian faith, but when Oscar heard what was happening in the wider world, he was astounded but thrilled. So many people had contacted Stephen and his wife, following the national press accounts of the 'specials' performance and more importantly God's message, through them, consequently had been inundated with anxious telephone calls and text messages asking to speak to him.

In answer to these requests, he and the Bible Study leaders had offered to hold several meetings, in the near future, for genuinely interested members of the public and he had heard of similar happenings in churches across the land. Pastor Stephen did agree with Oscar that he and Annette were not perhaps experienced enough to lead an in-depth Bible Study, therefore he would make sure of keeping one evening a week free to assist in the studies, which would obviously be needed.

Fired up with enthusiasm, urgent needs and those seeking safety and hope for the future, the first Sunday following the 'specials' impressive solo performance, used powerfully by God to awaken the lethargic and those given up on hope, to a strong warning to those opposed to God's ways, with unhealthy decisions being made, resulting in hate attacks, gang rivalry, fear and basic greed, unravelling the darker side of mankind's desire for control, not only of his, but other's commodities that he could use for gain, whether it be personal or attacks on neighbouring countries by rival nations.

The list is endless, with civil wars predominant in many lands as well as entire world wars, each inflicting massive losses of human life and whilst humans have the capacity to rise above grief and torment with a certain resilience, others are defeated human beings, apathetic and without hope, saw, on that first Sunday, an almost unimaginable number of the human population flooding into the churches of all denominations.

Timothy had telephoned Oscar no sooner than the national papers had published the events of 'The Principle Theatre,' causing a mass eruption of either glorious praise and thanksgiving for God's timely message to the nation or a great deal of great consternation amongst those who thought otherwise.

"It's amazing here, dad," exclaimed Timothy rather breathlessly. "There is a huge spread of publicity in the local papers, with, as you can guess, a large number of questions being asked, mostly in the churches. Priscilla and I have offered to assist where we can, now being the right time to tell of our experience on Christmas Day in St Andrews.

"The Reverend Greg Wilson has convened with the members of the congregation who feel led to lead Bible Study or chat groups, in their own homes, where they feel enquirers would feel more at home, ready to perhaps challenge their own fears, following what they had heard or read. Many, we know will come to faith, but will need, like us, a period of just being loved and shown Christian behaviour in daily action.

"I really wish you weren't so far away, dad, as your new knowledge and understanding in your new life as a born-again Christian, would be a big encouragement here, although I understand this momentous happening has caught the attention of all people, responding in very different ways. Many are calling this a revival, but I feel it is much, much more than that. 'Wow' to actually hear God's voice must have been such an incredible, almost speechless experience."

"Yes, son," responded Oscar with a slight sob of sheer ecstasy in his voice. "His voice, we heard in the theatre won't be the last we shall be able to hear His wonderful message. In His graciousness, God has revealed to Bradley that he will be asked to dance in theatres, at first in Britain and then around the world. The training Bradley will need to follow in the experienced footsteps of his father will be given partially by Jonathon—Bradley is learning his skills at Jonathon's studio at the present time—then to polish the high standards needed, a more experienced tap dancer than Jonathon, if that is possible!

"At these venues the managers of the theatres will be made aware, in plenty of time, that Bradley would be performing or even competing—if that is the case—in these 'special' tap shoes, once belonging to his world-famous father, for every performance.

"Here comes the really exciting piece of news Timothy, God will be speaking on every prearranged occasion, through his mouthpiece, these shoes, that Bradley will announce and set in motion on the stage. Everybody who books in to see the shows will be fully aware of God's intention to reveal His love for His creation, by reiterating His message of hope, given by His servant Isaiah—the prophet—whose words from God can be found in the pages of the Old Testament of the Holy Bible, in whatever, carefully produced translation you prefer."

"It sounds as if we are all in for a busy time ahead," replied Timothy. "The girls and I have taken some leave until things have settled down a little and we are more in a state of preparedness. By the way, dad, knowing you would be very tied up initially, Priscilla and I have telephoned most of the family, including Michael and Patricia, in Singapore, explaining the situation here, your heavy involvement and said I knew you would be in touch as soon as you could. Was that alright?"

"Thanks, Timothy. That was thoughtful of you," answered Oscar. "I've tried several times to attempt to make some calls to the family, but then an urgent request for assistance may come in and I feel obligated to help.

"It's a wonderful but busy time and I'm thrilled that the occurrence on Christmas Day, your finding of faith, has somewhat prepared you for this phase of God's plan and maybe—the doing of a new thing, as spoken of in scripture—has been initiated for us in these last few days. We cannot and should not go ahead of God, but He's had plans for each one of us, even before the beginning of the universe. What a marvellous God we have Timothy and the more we see of His actions and means, the more we come into a deeper relationship with Him."

With Timothy agreeing wholeheartedly, Oscar sent his love to Priscilla and the girls, then each said goodbye for now, with Oscar clarifying that if Timothy needed anything from him in any way, he could ring immediately.

Nationwide hope had been revived to an extent beyond any human imagination. The nation was ecstatic with praise. No human being could stand in the presence of the magnificence of God, but to hear His glorious voice brought a great renewal of faith, also a stark warning not to give Satan a foothold, whereby destruction of body and soul was the result. It was difficult for many to assimilate.

The churches were well aware of their need to tread carefully, nurturing the newly converted, from their unsure early days of becoming a Christian through to a firmer mature footing, consequently, every church and Christian organisation were crying out for help, which was forthcoming in many miraculous ways, solving or helping to solve an overwhelming need.

Oscar and Annette were kept busy with this need for assistance in 'Merryfields,' willingly devoting their time wherever Pastor Stephen had a particular assignment for them. Bradley resumed his final performances on stage at 'The Principle Theatre,' with seats reserved well in advance and a complete sellout of tickets.

Such was the optimism of the way ahead, as the word spread to other nations eager to have God's reassurance. Bradley's show had finished, with clambering for further shows, leading to an announcement that this show had been a prelude to 'The International Year of Dance' bringing with it an enthusiastic response and requests for advance bookings.

Terence had begun rehearsing his title role as 'Rip Van Winkle,' a character in a dance show set against the backdrop of The American Revolution of 1775-1783, a long military struggle against Britain, for American independence. The venue had not been fully confirmed, yet rehearsals were well underway, with the remainder of the company rehearsing in their own country until, at the final few rehearsals, the entire trope would rehearse together, ready for showtime.

Bradley therefore had begun intensive workouts with Jonathon, reaching a peak of near perfection in a very short space of time, unheard of a year or so ago. His dedication, endurance and love of tap dancing increased with every practice performed under Jonathon's watchful eye. Their regular prayer meetings and Bible Studies continued on a weekly basis, happily including newcomers, often referred by Pastor Stephen from Merryfields Baptist Church.

It was a joy for anyone new to join such an enthusiastic group of people, praising God for every moment they spent together. Friendships developed, blossoming into strongholds of faith, proving it in many ways, of works of love and a growing dependence on their Heavenly Father.

The next meeting of the 'clans,' for the Harrison family, was in a few weeks' time in Thailand, for the marriages of Martha and Mary to Steve and Karin, respectively.

Frequent mobile and Skype video calls, if not Zoom, kept the couples very much in touch and as the amazing events of the past few days had reached as far as Thailand there were very mixed reactions from the animistic believers with their long-held traditional belief that everything from objects, creatures and places possess a distinctive spiritual essence—breath—spirit—life, declaring that this was a hard to understand an event that the voice of the One True God should have been heard, by an utterly astounded audience, in a theatre and the mouthpiece used, was of all things a pair of tap shoes—inanimate objects—already owning a spiritual essence, but not one claiming to be the God of Heaven and Earth, whereby everything would under His control.

Instantly, trickery was thought to be used to subdue and deceive the listening audience. Learning of the great numbers of people crowding the churches and places of spiritual knowledge (known only to a few particularly holy people, in the world, could be taken as an effrontery to their highly regarded, untouchable monks in their holy temples).

To Steve and Karin, their belief and way of life had never been questioned, but now, hearing of Martha and Mary's joint observation and subsequent conversation, in the Fareham church they had unexpectedly attended on Christmas Day, gave both the friends a reason to explore their family's long-held belief.

Martha and Mary had spoken to Oscar whilst they were still guests at the home of Timothy, Priscilla, Selina and Rosemary, wondering what to do with this new experience of allowing Jesus into their lives and hearts, knowing full well of Steve and Karin's belief's, but somehow that fact had not, in the past, given them any cause for concern. Now, they understood the big difference this could make to all their lives. Martha and Mary knew they were unable to live a lie in their married lives together, pretending that Steve and Karin's beliefs didn't matter, because they felt and knew strongly that it did matter, even if the boys thought otherwise.

Oscar had been concerned about the differing ways of understanding that Martha and Mary would eventually come across when they married, now being so firmly in love with Steve and Karin, that he had spoken to Pastor Stephen, who, although a little taken aback by Oscar's question, attempted to secure a hopeful solution to what could be a cause of division in these marriages, in later years.

The first suggestion was to carry copies of Bible translations, not of the first language, at least, until both partners are more conversant with the English language. This Oscar had considered a good idea, easily slid into Annette's and his luggage, but how to implant or at least prepare their hearts for God's life to enter and claim their attention.

As Pastor Stephen gave this some more thought, he suggested that the boys might be encouraged to see a side of God's personality in everything, for example, the wonderful colours, shapes, ecosystems as being so much of a higher entity than a vagueness about the spiritual essences expressed in the animistic view. A grand designer, giving purpose to all things great and small and how just the right amount of rain and sunshine caused the buried seeds to burst forth, send out roots to retain moisture and grow into the crops that Steve and Karin were familiar with seeing grow, ready at just the right time, for harvest, thereby feeding their families.

It was an interesting thought and one that Oscar could see perhaps working, for them to get to know the beauty to be seen and enjoyed, under the unique diversity of a creative God. This one majestic God existed before the beginning of the universe, bestowing life on humankind and all things that move and have their being. He flung stars into space, moons and suns were subject to His authority.

Science belongs to Him and thousands of archaeological finds and manuscripts dating back centuries ago have been found, adding to the immense knowledge of theologians, without the weighty proof of His word, in the Bible, given by God to many writers, including Kings, Prophets, His disciples who spoke of His miracles His son Jesus performed, when on this earth and who died in the place of sinners to draw mankind back to God. The evidence is endless Pastor Stephen had continued to say, so Oscar was more than happy to speak to Martha and Mary, repeating Pastor Stephen's offers of advice. They had come to similar conclusions themselves but were unsure how to even begin to talk to Steve and Karin.

Oscar's next thought came as a surprise to all of them. Being relatively new to even speaking to the family in Singapore, Oscar's suggestion was that they could perhaps set up a Zoom conversation between the five of them, with Steve and Karin leading the way with any relevant questions they may have or would like a little more explanation, for the startling events they were reading about and the corresponding discussions that had followed in temples across Thailand and beyond.

Martha and Mary, having told them of their experience in the church and their instant conversions, were longing to go through the facts again and again, if asked, to see a glimmer of hope for Steve and Karin to fully understand, beginning to get to know Jesus. What a wonderful start it would be for the newlyweds.

As Bradley's confidence grew with the extra tuition he was receiving, not only from Jonathon, but another master tap dancer skilled in encouraging healthy competition from among those aiming for world recognition, but for Bradley, of course, with a very different purpose in mind, that of service to God, with the use of the 'specials' in theatres both in the United Kingdom and around the world.

Many organisers of tap dancing extravaganzas around the country were watching Bradley's dancing expertise grow rapidly, arranging auditions for star performances. His level of skills were developing beyond anything they had witnessed before, from being a novice such a short while ago. Travelling from city to city for these auditions were very tiring and time-consuming when all he wanted to do was dance and train, but he also needed to learn the audition skills of fire, passion, creativity and individuality by wearing and appearing comfortable in the right clothes.

Annette saw very little of her son these days, as did Oscar, who was concerned that the large amount of travelling time was interfering with the time he could spend at the prayer or Bible Study meetings, so asked Bradley if he was prepared to have driving lessons, as he was now of age. Although Bradley hadn't anticipated this he realised was a good idea, so with a well-recommended driving school being found, there was time now to be allocated, for the lessons.

Taking to this 'like a duck to water' knowing it was a means to an end, Bradley very soon was able to apply to take the ultimate driving test, enabling him to drive a car on the road, thus joining many other motorists. Nervous as he was on the day of the test, Bradley's efficacy in what he had made his mind up to achieve, paid dividends, with the examiner declaring a pass status, already having achieved the question and answers part of the completed test. Getting rid of the L-plates was a tremendous boost to morale.

With the coveted driving licence in his hand, the search was now on for a suitable car. Quite quickly a small, good on petrol car was found and, with a little help from the family, saved an enormous amount of travel time between auditions.

Competitions for excellence in the skills of tap dancing proved to be more difficult than Bradley had imagined, but with a lot of training, practise and encouragement from both Jonathon and 'Spike' his other tutor, himself an expert in achieving competition accolades, of credit distinctions. With a determination to have his father's name remembered throughout the dance world, Bradley worked harder than he had, in his life before, rapidly gaining recognition as a rising top-class dancer. Underneath all his devotion to attaining the highest merits he could, he constantly desired his service to God as being of overall importance.

His astonishing rise to popularity brought some stardom roles within his grasp, with his own show-stopping skills and the 'specials' amazing performances, through which God gave his message of hope to the nation. Despite being away from his flat, sharing with Terence and Oscar and the family, he tried to get home as often as he could, to attend prayer and Bible Studies. Wherever he was performing next, Bradley would attend a local church as regularly as possible.

Meanwhile, the Harrison families were preparing for their attendance at Martha and Mary's marriages in Thailand. Hearing from Clive and Annabelle, Oscar was delighted to be told that his gift of two homes for the newlyweds had virtually been completed. Annette had been responsible for stocking the kitchen areas with requested equipment from a delighted foursome. Flights were booked and finally, only a few days were left before departure.

Oscar carefully included the engagement ring for Annette, in his luggage, plus both of them took the Bibles suggested by Pastor Stephen. It was a crucial moment of decision-making for the pair, who were still unaccustomed to speaking to others, who did not know Jesus, but who wanted some decree of rationale when Oscar and Annette were so enthusiastic about knowing their Lord, so it proved to be as much their behaviour as their words that gave credence to their beliefs, thereby sowing the seeds for sharing the gospel.

The conversations held on Zoom, between Oscar, Annette, Martha, Mary, Steve and Karin, had been an instant icebreaker with great interest being shown by Steve and Karin and personal testimonies given to the boys were well received.

The day of departure soon came with suitcases crammed into a hired car, to take Oscar and Annette to the airport, arranging a collection on their return journey in ten days' time. Oscar had plans for a short holiday for him and Annette, as an engagement gift, if she accepted his proposal, of course.

After the first initial flight to their destination of Chiang Mai—capital city of Thailand—Oscar and Annette were prepared for a stopover, at which they needed to board a connecting flight that would take them on the final leg of their journey to the International Airport of Chiang Mai Province—a gateway to the north of Thailand, where the guests attending Martha and Mary's marriages, would be transported by coach to the village whereby the senior elder would be licensed to perform the double marriages.

Arriving at Chiang Mai International Airport following two long flights, ahead of British time was a little confusing, but Clive and Annabelle, having flown out two days earlier, had already given the guests instruction to book a car to a proposed meeting place, where a reception would be held, once everyone had safely arrived. It was an exciting drive through the centre of Chiang Mai, with a driver keen to show them the highlights of his city, before expertly taking them to the arranged venue.

Clive had explained that a tip would not be expected, as the company had already received a gratuitous fee, in advance, in recognition of the drivers being diligent in meeting their customers. This was a new one to Oscar, who, automatically offering a 'thank you' tip, was surprisingly, politely refused, with a broken English greeting to Chiang Mai.

Making their way into the rather imposing hotel, Oscar and Annette were immediately welcomed by Clive and Annabelle with a hug for Oscar and a warm handshake for Annette, who had yet to be introduced. This long-awaited meeting of their father's long-standing close friend, of whom they knew about, but had not had the pleasure of meeting. Annette was as delighted to meet Oscar's family as they were to meet her, with an almost instant friendship beginning between her and Annabelle.

Oscar squeezed Annette's hand, understanding she was slightly nervous about meeting the remainder of the family, many of whom had already arrived, eager to greet Oscar and meet Annette.

Taking Annette's arm, Annabelle guided her into the main lounge, where the room had already been set for the reception. Only Michael, Patricia and the family had yet to arrive from London, from where their incoming flight had been delayed due to a luggage mix-up in the hold of the aircraft, but a brief telephone call to Clive a little later, revealed they had landed safely and were on their way, having been met by the driver of the prearranged car service.

A family reunion was a great occasion for all of them, since they had not been together since Christmas and there was much catching up to do, especially the voice of God having been heard by all those in Britain, each making certain they booked seats for Bradley's shows, thereby assured of hearing God speak directly to the audience, through the amazing tap shoes that Bradley wore for each performance, allowing them their own routine, with the calm, but firm voice of the Father, evident for everyone to hear.

Michael and Patricia, now conducting their arrangements for the move to Britain, where they would hear God's voice at a theatre close to where they would be setting up home. Internationally, the shows hadn't been announced as yet, but Bradley was anticipating a move to California towards the end of the year. The entire family was actively involved in speaking out their testimonies wherever possible, learning more and more about the trustworthiness of God through their own individual experiences.

Already the crime rate was reported as dropping and although there were still scenes of racial violence, they were less, as were domestic violence and abuse.

Apart from the immediate family some other guests—friends from Martha and Mary's place of work, Steve and Karin's family and friends, plus locally known villagers, especially the house builders—would meet up tomorrow morning, in a village called Bantu, where Steve and Karin had lived, respectively, with their parents, prior to attending college together and where the double ceremony would take place, towards the middle of the day, officiated by the village senior elder, whom Clive and Annabelle had met on previous visits to Bantu.

Traditionally, in Thailand, the groom would pay for the cost of the wedding, giving a dowry to his future wife's family, but in this instance, Clive and Annabelle, knowing that neither family were wealthy and to spare the groom's family any embarrassment, by attempting to meet the full wedding expenses, had offered to take a large proportion of the costs, especially as it was their two daughters marrying their sons.

It had been decided by all concerned that the weddings would be relatively sim*ple, as that had been the wish of the two couples, with the presentation being similar to British custom, but with a Thai flavour so as not to offend their in-laws Martha and Mary had both wanted the traditional white dresses for themselves, with Steve and Karin electing to wear the traditional groom's clothes. Although it would have the necessities of a Buddhist wedding, paying respect to the culture and tradition, the ceremony would appease both sides of the family.*

The reception, that Clive and Annabelle had organised for the family was very much appreciated, as it had given the family a chance to be introduced and begin to get to know Annette, before the marriage ceremony the following day. Martha, Mary, Steve and Karin would meet her the next morning, as the girls were staying with friends in the village of Bantu, having flown to Thailand with their wedding dresses two days before and with Steve and Karin were making final preparations for their 'big' day tomorrow.

Caterers, in Chiang Mai had been found by Clive and Annabelle, at the time of their last visit to Thailand the previous year. They were happy to supply a selection of Thai wedding finger foods with more sit-down dishes, including appetisers of chicken satay with peanut sauce or fried tofu, for example, followed by fish curries, green chicken curries, parang beef curries, with vegetarian and English options of smoked salmon with lemon and Thai vegetables, that would suit most palates.

Desserts were not usually supplied at the wedding breakfast, but those that were served, had a long-held belief of conveying special blessings on those that ate them, hence Clive and Annabelle had a delicious dessert called Khanom Karean, a sweetbread woven tightly together, symbolising a blessing for bride and groom to be joined together forever. A wedding cake would be made for the two couples depicting the four figures on the top of the four-tiered cake, surrounded by garlands of Thai flowers, finishing with a love knot centrally.

The reception would be partially outside with chairs and tables arranged informally, whilst a more formal seating would be erected in one of the far larger homes of a senior elder and where the two married couples with their corresponding bride and groom families would sit and be attended by their groom's and bride's servers. Beverages of Thai tea or Chang beer would be served by relatives or those living in the same village.

A formal photographer had agreed to take and present the couples with an album each, while family members offered their own services. Altogether it had been an enormous undertaking for Clive and Annabelle, Martha and Mary, making many of the arrangements from England, but now it was all coming together and tomorrow Oscar would propose to his precious Annette.

With allocated hotels, the Harrison families made their final good nights to one another and having been shown where they were staying, had been waved off in their taxi, by Clive and Annabelle, who, by now, were feeling pretty exhausted, yet delighted to have had such a successful start to the festivities tomorrow.

The coach company supplying the means to reach Bantu would collect the ongoing guests from their designated hotels, at prearranged times, so with a two to three hour journey ahead of them, they would need an early morning start. At their hotel after a refreshing cup of English tea each, Oscar and Annette went their separate ways, until the early morning wake-up call, making sure they wouldn't be late for the coach to Bantu.

February weather in the north of Thailand is usually hot with balmy evenings and a lower humidity was just about right for the visit of the Harrison families for an intimate family double wedding. No sooner had the coach parked in the village of Bantu, than it was surrounded by laughing, inquisitive Karen children, eager to meet the visitors who they knew were coming for a very special occasion. Gently brushing them to one side, Martha and Mary, radiating happiness and new inner vitality, enveloped their parents and the family, in welcoming hugs.

Although Clive and Annabelle had warned everyone to expect Thailand to be hot at this time of year and to dress accordingly, but with certain colour restrictions that were kept for funerals, most of the guests felt a little overwhelmed, even in their carefully chosen summer attire. Martha and Mary guided them all to a covered veranda area, where they were asked to be seated and cold refreshments would be served. Introductions were then made to Steve and Karin's parents, dressed magnificently in the traditional Thai long silky dresses of the Mother, to loose-fitting traditional trousers of the Father.

Introductions were made on either side of the families, with rather difficult, stilted conversations starting. Clive and Annabelle had learnt a smattering of Thai to enable them to approach the groom's families with a little more confidence. When Annette was introduced to Martha and Mary, both girls discovered an instant liking for their grandfather's long-time friend, joining them for this special day in their lives.

Apologising to those who had so recently arrived, Martha and Mary had to leave shortly after the drinks had been served, as they were due to return to their friend's home, to have themselves dressed and manicured, by their bride's server, intent on getting the excited girls ready for the midday ceremony. Slipping into their long white, nearly matching, wedding gowns, Martha and Mary were too impatient to sit still for long, peering through the half-open door in an attempt to see the arrival of Steve and Karin, their grooms.

Finally, their servers, themselves beautifully clad as bridal servers, in the traditional Karen dresses, complimenting the white gowns of Martha and Mary, were satisfied that they had accomplished the final dressing of these beautiful brides. Fully opening the door of their home, designed to protect them from the intensity of the sun, their friends Meo and Asika led Martha and Mary to meet Annabelle, who was to escort her daughters to meet Steve and Karin at the front of the veranda, attached to the side of a home and now used for village weddings.

As mother and daughter approached the two pairs of white silk-swathed kneeling stools, alongside which stood Steve and Karin, themselves dressed in the traditional clothes of a Karen groom, there was an instant intake of breath, showing approval, from the many invited and uninvited guests sitting in close proximity to one another under the covered veranda, Steve and Karin turned their heads to watch these lovely brides, each moving to stand beside her intended husband, smiling happily into their eyed. Their bride servers took up their position behind each bride they had a responsibility towards on the day of their marriage.

At the same time, resplendent in his Karen robe of respect, as the senior elder conducting the marriages, Renet took up his position in front of the two couples, behind which stood a white-shrouded table, that, when uncovered would reveal the official documents from Chiang Mai, that would be signed by the couples, their witnesses and the official himself who would carefully convey the documents to the safety of the registration offices, confirming the marriages legally binding.

Leaning forward, Renet placed a white twisted silk cord onto the heads of each pair thereby looping them together, fashioned in the centre of each by a cluster of white flowers. It was a beautiful and significant means, in Karen tradition, of investing the pair in a long and fruitful marriage. The kneeling couples conveyed loving looks to each other.

Oscar and Annette, sitting near the front of the invited guests, turned and smiled intimately at one another, at this point, the gesture not having gone unnoticed by quite a few members of the family, who wondered just how close the pair were, pleased to see the happiness they radiated together.

The marriage service was as conveniently structured, as near as possible to one conducted in Britain, with a number of traditional cultural ceremonies performed, that applied to an animistic wedding and to satisfy Steve and Karin's families, still containing the essential words to declare the couple husband and wife together.

One almost essential part of the Thai marital process is called the "Sin-Sod" dowry, which is traditionally given by the groom's family to the bride's family as a mark of respect for the good upbringing of their daughter, also as compensation for the loss of that daughter and all they could provide for their parents. This had been discussed when Clive and Annabelle had sat down with Steve and Karin's family, on the previous visit to Bantu, to decide on many things, one being the cultural dowry that the boy's families were anxious to continue with and warmly received by Clive and Annabelle.

As the final ceremonies were being concluded, the two, now married couples turned towards their guests and hand in hand walked, poised and dignified, to the rear of the veranda, where they were escorted into the home of the village elder, whose home was being used as the indoor seating area. Clive and Annabelle, both flushed, with a hint of tears in their eyes, smiled at their guests indicating for them to follow, for the formal presentations of the married couples, before being seated by the servers.

With the formalities being over, chattering and laughing, the Harrison family, together with the families of Steve and Karin, sat, to be served their preferred meal of a traditional Thai meal or a British option. Whichever one was chosen the guests kept up a sparkling conversation about the significance of the marriage ceremonies, remembering to include the groom's family, in their excited chatter. It wasn't long before they were toasting one another as if they had known each other for a number of years instead of having only just met.

Outside, the remaining guests were heartily enjoying the delicious selections of food, on the menu, with the village children being thoroughly entertaining. It was certainly a happy, joyous occasion, but for one guest there was a desire for many to leave, so that he could make his planned proposal to someone he hoped would become a lifelong partner and who was taking up a good proportion of his thoughts. Glancing to one side, bringing her profile into view, he knew he would have to wait patiently until, at least, the uninvited guests, had retired to their homes, anxious to get young ones to bed, before returning to the village, to continue the celebrations.

Once the meals had been served to all the seated guests and those outside were beginning to drift away and chat amongst themselves, it was time for Martha and Mary, to return, with their servers, to Meo and Asika's home, where they had been staying prior to their wedding day, to be helped from their white wedding gowns into comfortable daytime dresses, to signify that they were now married.

Steve and Karin were waiting patiently for them, as they hurried from the home to join their husbands, to continue with the evening entertainment, to be given by the older children of the village who had been practising, with their instructor, for many weeks. Seats were rearranged, by eager tribal villagers, in the centre of the village, where the newlyweds joined the families ready for the young people to present their offerings. The evening was balmy, with a much lower humidity—a truly romantic setting, with the dusky shadows of the forest trees forming a backdrop to the stage.

Truly a night to remember, thought Oscar, as taking one of Annette's hands in his, he rehearsed to himself, his words of proposal, whilst dutifully watching the intricate dancers perform typical Karen dances portraying their way of life. He had enjoyed the conversations he had been able to have with both Steve and Karin, who expressly wanted to thank him and Annette for their wedding gifts of the two homes, also supplying most of their culinary needs.

They had very much wanted to take him and Annette to see the homes in Suay, but time, they thought would not allow for it, so both were surprised to hear Oscar say that he and Annette would be having an extended holiday in Chiang Mai and surrounding areas, hopefully for an engagement present. Both Steve and Karin were intrigued, questioning Oscar about this and in a conspiratorial whisper he told them of his intentions later on, although keen not to divert any undue attention away from their wedding day.

Playing along, Steve mischievously suggested he and Karin take their wives for a quiet but undetected walk, whilst he got on with the proposal. Thrilled that he didn't have any opposition, but collaboration from Steve and Karin, who would tell Martha and Mary when out of earshot, Oscar was satisfied that he could pick the right moment to propose.

Gradually the dancing and small chorus of songs to the bride's and groom's came to an end with the children receiving well-deserved applause and with their instructor acclaimed also, before she shepherded the youngsters away from the guests and back to their homes. Out of the corner of his eye, Oscar saw Steve and Karin take hold of their brides' hand to lead them away for the invented walk. Now was the moment, before the chairs were removed and the Harrison families were taken by coach to a locally built bridal accommodation, where they were to stay that night before being driven back to Chiang Mai, in the morning.

Before any of his family moved from their chairs, Oscar gently pulled Annette to her feet to stand with him, facing the family. Surprised and a little startled Annette smiled a question at Oscar, when to her utter amazement Oscar knelt beside her, having withdrawn the box containing the beautiful engagement ring, from his breast pocket.

Feeling nervous and almost forgetting his planned speech, Oscar took Annette's left hand, deftly slipping the ring onto her ring finger and openly, in front of his children, their wives and his grandchildren, he asked for Annette's hand in marriage. A small choking sound sprung from Annette, as she responded with, "Yes, oh yes please, I thought you would never ask."

Laughing out loud with joy and with the applause of the family ringing in his ears, he held Annette close to him, whispering in her ear how much he loved her and thanked her for consenting to be his wife. Hand in hand, the pair walked towards each son and their families, thanking them for their trust in them, in turn welcoming Annette into the family and God's blessings go with them.

Afterwards, Michael, Clive, Timothy and Adrian remarked that they hadn't seen their father so happy, since losing his beloved Anita—their mother. Annette, they knew, would understand that special bond that sealed the marriages of their first loves, which would never be lost, but now the couple would have a friend and partner for, hopefully, many more years to come.

Oscar was surprised at how well Martha and Karin and Mary and Steve had managed to conceal the fact that they had left the village for a short while, to give Oscar the freedom to propose. He felt deeply indebted to them, as he and Annette spoke to them when they returned, as inconspicuously as they had left. Late as it was the evening was still pleasantly warm, but the two newly married couples had an unexpected surprise waiting for them, of which none of the Harrison family had any previous knowledge.

Steve and Karin's family, still present in the village, obviously knew, as small significant smiles were exchanged between the parents, at which point Oscar and Annette decided to start boarding the coach, whilst the others followed, after saying warm 'thank you's' to Steve and Karin's parents for the welcome received, into their village. The parents graciously accepted, conveying warm thanks of their own, waving happily to the departing guests.

The Chiang Mai driver was ready and waiting to drive them to the accommodation that Clive and Annabelle had arranged for the overnight stay, before the next leg of the journey back to Chiang Mai in the morning, with a number of the family guests having flights home in the evening.

The marital beds for Martha and Karin and Mary and Steve had been arranged at individual friends' homes within the village of Bantu, although the couples themselves did not know who had been allocated to which friend. Unknown to them an old traditional custom was about to be played out!

Accompanied by both sets of the groom's parents they were escorted ceremoniously to the first home, allocated to Martha and Karin and whilst Mary and Steve were kept occupied in another part of the village, Martha and Karin entered a highly decorative bedroom fully expecting privacy and for their parents to withdraw, instead of which they found an elderly frail-looking couple occupying their bed space.

Taken aback, they turned to leave thinking there must be some mistake, when an explosion of firecrackers sounded from within the room followed by laughter and clapping. The elderly couple removed themselves from the bed, as it was explained to Martha and Karin that the old couple had been married for a long time and were giving the newlyweds an example of the long married life that was expected of them.

Retreating from the room and the home, the groom's parents were escorted to where Mary and Steve were asked to receive them, with the ceremony being repeated for the second time, to an equally surprised Mary and Steve who had reacted in exactly the same way as Martha and Karin. Such was the beginning of a long and happy marriage for the Thai twins adopted as babies by Clive and Annabelle Harrison and the start of a new pathway for them, as they meet with Oscar and Annette during the next few days in Chiang Mai, before the honeymoon formally begins, after which, their new homes waiting for them in Suay were ready for occupation.

Tired, but contented, the families who knew and loved Martha and Mary from the time they came to England, as tiny babes in arms, from a country that only a few had ever visited, but had been enthusiastically educated by Clive and Annabelle, a childless couple who found it impossible to resist two tiny waifs desperately needing a home and someone to love them in their growing years, albeit not in their country of birth, welcomed this time of giving them back to their own country, so to speak. They could all see how much Karin and Steve loved their beautiful wives and knew they could be trusted to take care of them.

God was indeed at work in all this, preparing and sowing seeds for them to come to know and trust Him together, for their future, themselves placed in the right soil to sow their own seeds of spiritual truths, so others may live to follow the God of the Bible, they would soon share, with family, neighbours and friends of the Pwo-Karen tribes.

Tumbling into their single beds later that night, after a nightcap during which the coach driver announced he didn't have to be back in Chiang Mai until early afternoon, so they wouldn't have to leave until ten thirty in the morning, Oscar and Annette had discussed the intention of them both, to have their marriage as soon as reasonably possible, so they wouldn't have to be alone for very much longer.

As a married couple, they felt their strength could be made stronger for any future work God had prepared for them, but also understood their relationship with Him was of the first primary importance. Even at their advanced ages, they were still only infant Christians and were to reach maturity during a period of time.

Sleep didn't come easily for either Oscar or Annette that night. Neither were prepared for the wave of emotion that had nearly overwhelmed them both, at the response they had received from a family that had only begun to know Annette, during these two marriages in Thailand. Oscar had to ask himself whether he was asking too much of his family, too soon, remembering Timothy's words to him, before the happenings of Christmas Day and more recently, God using the 'specials' as His spokesmen. So much had occurred too quickly to filter it through his mind, so he laid it to one side, gave it up to God, drifting into a deep and peaceful sleep.

Not so Annette who had been taken completely unawares. It was a wonderful gesture this evening and so like Oscar to leave the proposal to a time like this, but was it the right time, as the family was already captivated by two wonderful marriages today and was their response genuine?

She found her eyes gradually closing in sleep, lulled into a gentle sense of having a comfortable warm blanket lightly supporting her body. Giving herself to the lightness of the blanket, she slept peacefully until a ray of sunshine roused her, not too early in the morning. Stretching slowly, not unlike the awakening of a slumbering feline, Annette gazed at the gorgeous ring, her birthstone in the centre, surrounded by a ring of pearls, that would match her necklace to perfection.

Blinking quickly she was momentarily overwhelmed to think of how much thought Oscar must have given to this day, the times he could have asked her to marry him, but hadn't, always thinking of others' feelings above his own. She loved him for his propriety of good moral character learnt long ago in defining his skills as a master craftsman. Raising herself onto one arm, she pretended he was beside her, to feel her arms around him. Sighing softly, she performed her morning tasks, eagerly waiting to see him before joining the coach to take them back to Chiang Mai.

Joining the others for a late breakfast, Oscar and Annette chatted for a while, Annette enjoying the opportunity of getting to know so much more about Oscar's son, their wives and his grandchildren, not forgetting the young scamp Dillon, his only great-grandchild.

After a while a few wandered off for a walk, suspecting rightly, following further congratulations, that the newly engaged pair would welcome some time alone. Once again, the weather was cooler, just right for a walk along some hidden pathways in the forest jungle. Hand in hand, they couldn't be happier. Their lives had taken a huge turnaround in the last eighteen months that it almost took their breath away and now the future lay open ahead.

Arriving back at the nighttime accommodation, just in time for a refreshing drink, before the driver was welcoming his passengers onto the coach, Oscar felt a small speech of thanks to his family was in order, not just for attending the marriages of Martha and Mary, his dear adopted grandchildren, but for their welcome of Annette into their hearts, giving him every confidence to take her to be his wife, laughingly saying they would give them a little time to replenish their purses before another marriage was announced.

Returning to the same hotel where the family had met on their arrival in Chiang Mai, they were surprised but delighted to find the newlyweds had already arrived for the honeymoon and were pleased to be able to say a big 'thank you,' for coming all this way to Thailand for the marriages, but another enormous 'thank you,' for the wedding gifts and their generosity in the many cheques they had received, enabling them to start a savings fund towards the elephant venture that Steve and Karin wanted to investigate.

In the meantime, they would make their homes in the village of Suay, where, with a huge thank you to grandad Oscar and his lovely fiancée, two homes had been built and stocked with the necessary homewares. Hugs and kisses followed as many were taking their flights home to England and Michael and Patricia to Singapore via London, soon to be returning to England and finding a home with the girls, leaving the boys to finish their education in Singapore. Cars had been called and were waiting outside, taking their passengers to Chiang Mia International Airport. Oscar and Annette were sad to see them go but promised to get in touch as soon as they returned from their extended stay in Thailand.

Before Martha and Steve and Mary and Karin left to book into a less expensive hotel in the city, Oscar offered to drive them there, in a car he had hired for his and Annette's stay. Oscar wanted to show her other areas of Thailand, having contacted a Municipal Tourist Board, in Chiang Mai showing some exciting places to visit, not long drives from the city. Having accepted the invitation, the six comfortably seated themselves in a large hired car that Oscar drove to their hotel.

Carrying their luggage inside, it was expected that Oscar and Annette stayed for an afternoon tea selection of delicious Thai delicacy, too good to resist. The following morning, Martha and Steve and Mary and Kevin were flying to Bali, in Indonesia, for two weeks, a honeymoon gift from Clive and Annabelle. Disappointed as they were, not to be able to show Oscar and Annette their new homes, it was suggested that they return to Thailand for their honeymoon, being welcomed to stay in Suay for a part of the time. This was a splendid idea, received gratefully by Oscar and Annette.

The opportunity to talk freely to the two couples, who were themselves eager to talk through what had been discussed during the highly successful Zoom calls they'd conducted, since Christmas, could not be delayed. Putting aside the thoughts of refreshments for the moment, Oscar asked Steve and Karin what their immediate responses had been when Martha and Mary had told them of their experience in the local church, in Fareham whilst staying at Timothy's and Priscilla's for Christmas.

Steve rolled his eyes and admitted his first thought had been, that a trick by the church people had been played on them, but listening to Oscar's account of the mighty wind they had also heard, thoughts started to enter his mind more and more, until he was convinced that it had to have been real, especially following the newspaper's reports of the amazing happening's with the 'specials,' being used as God's mouthpiece.

It was all too much, he continued, to be coincidental, but if this voice was really the voice of a Holy God, then their thoughts on many things, they had taken for granted and factual, whilst growing up, would have to change. Martha and Mary's faces were displaying the joy they were experiencing at hearing these words from Steve, then both looked at Karin to see his reaction. He too claimed to have come to the same conclusion.

It was at this point that Annette asked whether either of the boys had seen or read from a Christian Bible, to which both replied they had not seen one before, but knew that Martha and Mary were using them daily to find out more of God's word and had been told that at least two had been brought over in Oscar and Annette's hand luggage. Laughing, Annette drew one from a handbag she was carrying, showing it to Steve and Karin, who stared at its cover with a mixture of fear and awe.

Glancing behind him Oscar was of the impression they were being overheard and not wanting any susceptible undercurrents of concern or even hostility to be staged against the newlyweds, explained quietly that recently he and his fiancée had come to understand and be able to get to know, the Word of God, written in the Holy Bible—holding the book aloft—and the world has been hearing so much just lately of the Almighty Holy God speaking words of comfort and warnings through these special tap shoes, that we wanted to understand how these dear friends of ours felt.

Nodding their heads Oscar realised the waiters in the hotel were as puzzled by the 'happenings,' as many had been, who had yet to hear the incredible messages given by the creator of the world for themselves. That, Oscar knew would soon be remedied once Bradley's 'specials' accompanied him in shows around the world, putting God first, in these last days, months or even years, His message, to mankind, whom He had never left, but who needed Him now, more than ever.

Laying their Bibles on the table in front of them, Annette and Oscar invited Steve and Karin to take one each, turning the pages slowly to read the words—of these Bibles translated for those of which English was not the first tongue—and with both the boys had attended a college where English was learnt as a second language, they had little difficulty in pronouncing most of the words. Martha and Mary would be of great help here. Oscar was only sorry there wasn't time to even read from Genesis, the first book, about the creation of the world and much, much more.

Leaving to book in at their own hotel, later that evening, Oscar and Annette felt exhausted but exultant that a possible clash of interests had been diverted and had, in fact, resulted in an interest being shown in what was being discussed Oscar and Annette were claiming, with Martha and Mary ready and willing to share their new belief and testimony.

True to his word about seeing God, in so many things, made by Him or a painting perhaps, inspired by God shining out an example of God's character, to all who might view it, Oscar wanted to impress that point on the boys. In one corner of the hotel was a large pedestal on which stood a white vase showing off to perfection a beautiful arrangement of many of the abundant flowers that are at their best, as seen in February, in Thailand. These included damask roses—only found in Chiang Mai—dendrobium orchids, daoruang, lotus, jasmine and chrysanthemums—of differing colours—against a backdrop of wood panelling.

It was a stunning display and Oscar took great delight in having the newlyweds closely look at the perfection of each bloom, able to see a mirror image of a bountiful unconditionally loving God, in each petal, bloom, perfume and sheer mastery of beauty. Man would have planted the bulbs, seeds, corms or tubers but God supplied the sunshine and rains in equal quantities to enable the buried seeds to burst, sending out roots to absorb nourishment through the soil, thence growing and displaying the lovely blooms we can enjoy today. This seemed to be a revelation to the young husbands, who stared in fascination.

The knowledge that everything had a spiritual entity, therefore being greatly feared if there was a word spoken that could anger that spirit, was a culture the boys grew up in and didn't question, but the thought of a single God of love who made the universe with everything within it, had them look with fresh eyes at the beauty of each individual flower. A God who didn't demand retribution, now displayed so perfectly in every bloom, seen in the white vase, brought wonder and hope to their young faces. Oscar could see love expressed, in that moment and his heart leapt that God had proven Himself to be found, that special evening on the brink of the newlywed's honeymoon.

Having booked in at their hotel Oscar and Annette only had energy left to enjoy a nightcap of Thai tea, before making their way upstairs, promising to meet early for breakfast, then take a look at some of the places to visit, whilst taking a welcome vacation in the sun, for the remainder of the time that Oscar had booked to stay in and around Chiang Mai, as an engagement gift to Annette.

Prior to booking their flights to Thailand Oscar had undergone some research into interesting sites for himself and Annette to visit whilst in Chiang Mai and he had certainly come up with some novelties on the itinerary, the first being a manmade beach alongside a flowing river, complete with sun chairs, artificial sand, beach toys for children, even supplying light dishes, coffee and drinks at a café, in this 'out of city' resort.

For a genuine beach resort by the sea, a two hour flight to Phuket, Krabi or Koh Samui would be the only way of obtaining this, thereby missing many of the worthwhile sights, the city has to offer. With many Buddhist temples built very close to Chiang Mai, the pair were spoilt for choice, picking two close by that they thought would be interesting.

Oscar asked Annette if she would find a shopping trip to Bo Sang umbrella village a good start for the first day, with perhaps a well-recommended opportunity to taste Khai Soi at lunchtime, consisting of a curry-based soup with both fresh and dry crunchy noodles with your choice of meat or tofu? The noodles can be of rice or egg and in Thailand, this soup has a base of coconut milk.

Having eaten in several different nationalities of restaurants, in London, both Oscar and Annette enjoyed a variety of curries, but today were in for a special treat. Leaving the hotel for the first day of sightseeing, the pair weren't quite prepared for the vast array of bicycles on the roads that day, as a seasonal parade was being held, each bicycle ridden by an exquisitely dressed Thai lady, delicately shading her head from the sun, by means of a colourful parasol. Children were looped around with flowers riding their own tricycles, closely watched by doting parents. Flowers, in profusion, lined the streets and a sense of well-being permeated this happy throng.

Oscar and Annette were soon on their way for their first experience of Chiang Mia's umbrella street market of Bo Sang, full of noise and colour with the local Thai happily shopping alongside tourists, visiting Thailand from countries around the world. The village itself was famous for producing umbrellas and parasols for every occasion imaginable, being extremely popular.

A few items took their attention as possible gifts to take home for family and friends, but Oscar and Annette decided not to buy so early into their holiday, in case they spotted something more appropriate later on, although paper and silk were predominantly seen and offered by the local smallholders.

Beginning to feel tired and hungry, the pair made their way to a restaurant advertising their version of Khao Soi so synonymous with Chiang Mai. Friendly Thai waiters, eager to display their hospitality, seated them at a table where they could watch the colourful business of Chiang Mai as they relished this delightful northern dish, famous for its rich flavour without being so spicy as to only appeal to some tastes.

A leisurely afternoon called for a visit to the Montha Than Waterfall's trailhead beginning an easy-to-negotiate trail of flora abundance, indigenous to Thailand. Hand in hand, Oscar and Annette delighted in the sight of the majestic waterfall and with the pleasant warmth of the day bringing a glow to their faces, they walked as far as they found enjoyable before returning to the car for the final drive of the day back to the hotel, where they had decided to eat that evening, with perhaps an early evening stroll before bedtime.

The list of possible attractions that Oscar had found via the tourist centre opened up an opportunity to investigate a fraction of the elephant culture that belongs to Thailand. With the Thai name of 'Chang' the elephant, here being the Indian elephant, is a symbol of Thailand's pride, being used in many ways such as royal parades, in times of war and logging.

They are revered to the point that a belief exists that walking under an elephant showers down good luck. As a status symbol, they represent strength, loyalty and longevity, but sadly can also be exploited for the benefit of tourist attractions. Most live in sanctuaries or national parks under the care of rangers and wildlife experts.

Within an hour and a half's journey from Chiang Mai was The Jungle Sanctuary, an ethical, viably sustainable eco-tourism project, developed as a means of a non-exploiting enterprise, safeguarding the precious culturally held elephant. Trained veterinary specialists took great care of these majestic animals, not simply as a tourist attraction, but as creatures in their own right.

Having booked in for a half-day tour Oscar and Annette thoroughly enjoyed the travel through both fertile terrain, farmlands and dense jungle areas of Thailand's best, before arriving at this well-advertised sanctuary, just one of many in Thailand. Making themselves known to the porters and staff on the half-day tour, they were amazed by what the sanctuary offered in ways of entertaining, with chalets for overnight stays, food complexes and numerous children's invitations to find out the habitat, food, lifeline and many other interesting facts about these wonderful creatures they were about to meet, apart from having seen them through high netting, at a zoo.

Fascinating as the tour was entertaining, Oscar and Annette were glad of a rest as the afternoon drew noticeably towards evening. Thanking the tour guides and those they had met along the way, exchanging nods and handshakes of greeting the pair finished off a perfect day with a meal, before driving back to the hotel for an evening of relaxing. They were even too tired to wander into the many nighttime street markets, marking them up for a definite later on in the week.

Almost every day another excursion was available, including the Mae Ping River Cruise, refreshingly cool but invigorating as it was bustling with activity. The Thai Farm Cookery School proved to be a great hit for both of them, especially for Oscar, as he was taking a keener interest in Asian cuisine. The days passed quickly as they explored the Queen Sirkit Botanic Gardens, again cool as the gardens were canopied throughout and the blooms magnificent, the Lanna Folklife Museum and even tried their hand at beginners golf on the Lanna Golf Course, ending in peaks of laughter as the ball never seemed to go where it was directed.

The nightlife of Chiang Mai was finally tackled a few days before their 'engagement' holiday was coming to a close and England was beckoning. On the last full day before their flight home, the Doi-Suthep-Pui National Park was a must—a gentle, slow down—after a wonderful holiday with a last evening's experience of a rocky venue where you could either boil or grill food in the sight of mountains and stunning valley countryside. A never to be forgotten experience for them both.

It was home time for Oscar and Annette and after returning their hired car, made their way by local transport on the final leg to Chiang Mai International Airport, carefully carrying the gifts and souvenirs they were taking home. Many items were light to carry, scarves and clothing of Thai silk. Some unique ornaments had caught their eye, but these were few and easily packed as hand luggage. A special edition of Thai recipes, from the cookery school they had attended, was a prize possession for Oscar who was determined to put his recently gained skills to the test, as soon as he had obtained the numerous spices he would need to prepare and serve to friends who wouldn't object to a mistake here and there.

For the male dancer's gifts, they had mainly chosen Thai printed tee-shirts. Passing through into the destination lounge, they had a short time to wait, during which time they reminisced on all they had seen and achieved from the longer stay they had in Thailand, following the two marriages of Oscar's adopted grandchildren. They had received a card from the honeymooners happily enthusing that they were thoroughly enjoying their time in Bali, visiting many places of interest, hearing a differing style of music and watching cultural dances.

Although Annette had flown many times to watch Trevor perform, since the children had been born, these times were less often. Having flown across several time zones, in the past, she was unprepared for the intense feeling of 'jet lag' that was obvious when arriving at Heathrow, followed by the train ride into central London, then a taxi to both their homes. Oscar was less affected by the body trying to adjust to a new time zone.

February in London, in the northern hemisphere, was rather damp and cold, a far cry from the temperatures they had left behind in Chiang Mai, but at least they were home safely and with superb memories, on camera and with their many experiences to remember. Oscar made sure Annette was able to have Simone or Rupert home from work when the taxi arrived at her home. Simone had texted that one of them at least would be there for Annette's homecoming.

True to their word, Rupert had arranged to be home early, in case Simone had an urgent call-out with any one of her expectant mothers. Opening the door to his sister-in-law, he welcomed her home with a hug and congratulations to them both on their engagement, whilst in Chiang Mai. He gave Oscar a friendly punch on the arm, at which they both laughed and Rupert was delighted to say that Oscar was certainly the one to choose the right location to ask for Annette's hand in marriage and not before time he finished up muttering.

It was a joyful reunion and Oscar knew that his darling Annette would be well looked after. Giving her a hug and a lingering kiss, Oscar relinquished her into Rupert's care reassuring her that after a good night's sleep and with her body clock fast forwarded, she would feel better tomorrow. Promising to telephone at a reasonable hour, in the morning, Oscar returned in the taxi to his own home, which seemed to have lost some of its warmth and charm, without Annette's presence. He was determined to rectify that as soon as possible.

Oscar's body clock suddenly alerted him to the fact that 'yes' he too was beginning to feel the effects from the flight home to England, having had a short delay for refuelling, before touching down on home ground. Before unpacking he sat in his kitchen drinking as much fluid as he could manage, prior to making that all important phone call to Bradley, also his neighbours Pete and Jayne who had very kindly taken on 'Cocky' whenever he was away. His little friend seemed none the worse to new feeding human beings, even bringing his partner now and then. Maybe, Oscar hoped, there could be fledglings this coming season. He reminded himself to watch out for signs of nesting behaviour.

Dialling Bradley's number, Oscar realised it was a little late in the afternoon and his protégée could well be rehearsing for a stage show or even a competition. Surprisingly Bradley spoke into his mobile, sounding slightly flustered, but recognising Oscar's voice, he welcomed him home cheerfully enough. No sooner had Oscar and Annette arrived back in Chiang Mai, getting a better signal than in the higher territories, they had telephoned Bradley, Simone and Jonathan to tell them of their engagement. Bradley had called Oscar a 'dark horse,' being thrilled to hear the news.

Now they could be a complete family and Bradley liked the feel of calling Oscar 'dad,' in no way diminishing that title from his natural father, Trevor. He was happy to know that the two most important people in his life, were going to grow older together in companionship and a love covering many aspects of their lives. Dare he ask the question of when the wedding would be? His own life was changing rapidly and rather than taking on a complete show, his manager Jonathan, had ensured a two day or night performance, at which time the 'specials' would be used by God in many more venues than before, drawing in huge crowds hungry for the 'Word from God'.

Churches were becoming full to capacity, ministry was in abundance, mental and physical healings were being seen, with testimony after testimony filling the airwaves. This was certainly a renewal of enormous proportions and plans to perform on stage, in America, were being made for the Autumn.

February quickly disappeared into spring and summer, with both Oscar and Annette helping out daily, in Merryfield's church, which had grown rapidly since the beginning of the messages from God, via the now famous tap shoes, diligent in their duties, performing exquisitely with Bradley's feet encompassed in their care. Even without his feet being in the shoes, Bradley's skills as a top professional tap dancer brought him acclaim after acclaim, well within competition standards, but time was limited for these and the need for the 'specials' to be used by God in His wisdom, was of overriding importance.

Another important event in Bradley's life was a fondness he was beginning to feel for an outstanding young dancer—at least in Bradley's eyes—whose name was Naomi. She was tall and slender with chestnut curly hair that fell deliciously over her face during her practice routines. Bradley found it hard to keep from watching her interpret the very essence of the dance with vigour and yet poise.

After these very intense rehearsal times, they only smiled at one another, but during the intervals, for refreshment, they sought each other's opinions, so with this deepening respect for a common passion and interpretation of the dance, the pair found themselves wanting more and more to be with each other, gradually falling in love.

This was Bradley's first real experience, that he had allowed himself to feel for someone of the opposite sex. It was a breathtaking emotion and one he hugged exclusively to himself, only showing his innermost thoughts to Naomi, whom he knew he could trust explicitly, so, as he shared the story behind the 'specials,' and his blossoming relationship with his Heavenly Father, he was excited to find that she begged to know more. In time, he would meet and be fully accepted by her family, but for now, their intimacy remained solely theirs.

Bradley met up with his mother and Oscar as soon as he could manage any spare time. Terence, his housemate was deeply into rehearsing for his role of 'Rip Van Winkle,' sometimes needing input from Bradley, in one of the many shows to represent the celebration of 'The International Year of Dance,' proving to be highly successful.

Britain was hosting this event, in many theatres in and around London, with visiting countries demonstrating their talent from pretty much around the world, whilst national and international directors plied their trade, as professionals, working together to enlighten non-theatre goers of the international language of dance, uniting nations together.

Behind-the-scenes nail-biting scenarios had frequently taken place, with, for example, a country needing to relinquish their performances due to political reasons. Complete replacements at the final moment were almost impossible to find, but from somewhere a show would be produced, from almost thin air, so avoiding disappointments from last-minute cancellations. There was a great deal happening in London, at this time, giving rise to a better understanding of each other's needs, with support and help given in the most unlikely of situations.

Oscar, Annette and Bradley had many things on their mind, some of which needed airing, whilst others didn't, at least for the time being. With the three of them in Oscar's flat, small as it was, there was warmth again, with a pleasant atmosphere of love and acceptance.

Bible study and prayer nights were resumed as soon as Oscar and Annette arrived home from Thailand, although sometimes time restraints had to be imposed, with so many new attendees arriving for help to see the way forward, needing time to talk after the scheduled meeting time, but rewards were plenty when so many came to faith, giving them an entirely new direction to their life and a sure and certain knowledge of a Father God, who loved them unconditionally, something many had not experienced before, therefore had lost heart, living life on a knife-edge.

Speaking to his son over the following few weeks, Autumn was almost upon them and although Oscar loved the changing colours of the season, it was tinged with a little sadness this year with the thought of Bradley leaving for America in a couple of weeks.

Annette, he knew would miss her youngest son immensely and was concerned whether the heavy responsibility connected with the 'specials' would be too much, but then she had to remind herself that whilst God was in complete control of events, nothing was impossible.

Jonathan had secured some interesting venues, with meetings with the stage directors, who were eager to see this young man in action, as word had gone ahead of his skilful abilities as a tap dancer. Shows that he was scheduled to perform in were becoming fully booked, but the most exciting moment for Bradley would be when the 'specials' were allowed free rein, giving God the opportunity to speak directly to the people. Already the world was preparing to hear God's message, given directly to them through these remarkable tap shoes that God had ordained to be His mouthpiece to a hungry waiting world.

Despite the busyness of imminent departure, Bradley and Naomi saw as much of each other as they could, either after rehearsal times for Naomi or visits for documentation purposes and churches keen to sponsor the forthcoming trip, for Bradley.

They both knew that their time together was short, but Naomi's deepening love for Bradley assured him that no matter how long he was away she would wait for his return and young as they were, both were certain they wanted to spend the rest of their lives together. Naomi had asked Bradley if she could come along to his Bible Study and prayer groups, at least whilst he was away, for support and encouragement, so that she could prepare herself to be alongside Bradley wherever God sent him.

So it came about for Bradley to spill the beans, so to speak and tell Oscar and Annette about his deep love for Naomi and their desire to share their lives together. This announcement didn't come as too much of a surprise to either Oscar or Annette who had noted Bradley's preoccupation at times, his embarrassment when a call was made to him and the simplest of excuses for arriving late, for example.

It all added up to something else, taking Bradley's attention, not just his departure to America. The urge to tell was strong in Bradley, as with growing excitement he described Annette to them, his love for her and the deep interests they shared. Annette hugged her son saying that as she knew of his love for Jesus, she was sure of his sound judgement in finding someone like Naomi to be his lifelong love and companion.

Oscar shook Bradley's hand, hugged him and said that any friend of Bradley's was a friend of his and he shared Bradley's joy in having such a person in his life, knowing that he had found that same joy in loving Annette, both blessings from God. Annette was naturally eager to meet Naomi as soon as possible, not to be the possessive future mother-in-law, but in a gentle way to befriend her whilst Bradley was away. To have her ask to come along to the Bible Study and prayer groups was an added bonus. From what Bradley had told them, she knew that she loved this girl already.

Another very important decision to be made was between Oscar and Annette, who were delaying their wedding until Bradley returned from America in the spring of the next year. Both wanted Bradley to be there with the rest of the two families, besides Oscar would like to ask Bradley to be his best man, an honour that Bradley was thrilled to say he was happy to perform.

Before any of this was decided, Oscar and Annette spoke to individual members of their own family. Michael, Patricia and the girls were home in Britain, having moved from Singapore shortly after they arrived back from Thailand.

The branch of the bank in Manchester that Michael had been asked to revive into a viable nationally known bank once more, was a tough job, but Michael being Michael and having been raised by Oscar and Anita to persevere in any worthwhile venture, this attitude was paying dividends. Extra staff for specific interests of the bank had been carefully selected by Michael and placed in posts, proving to be an asset and approved by the bank's regulators. This was apparently inviting to future customers, great or small.

Oscar was delighted by his son's success, with Patricia taking on the role of head Liberian in her local branch—a job that she loved dearly—His grandchildren Sally and Anne found places in their relatively nearby senior school, but didn't find the transition from Singapore as easy as Michael and Patricia, with none of the children having been born in Britain. Visiting family, from Singapore, was a somewhat different matter for them, than actually living in a new country, but the girls would settle soon, already bringing interested friends home from school.

The boys thankfully were lodging at their new school, still in Singapore, missing the family but buckling down to study for forthcoming exams, after which they were flying to Britain for the summer holidays, shorter in Singapore than in Britain. Oscar and Annette had plans to visit whilst the boys were over during the summer.

As Oscar spoke to each of his boys, catching up with events in their lives, he was encouraged to hear that most were involved in their local churches and serving God in any way that had opened up for them. A question on all their lips was whether he and Annette had set a wedding day. Interested to follow Bradley's progress in America they all agreed that to wait until his return, was preferable to an earlier wedding, without him being there and unable to be best man.

Pastor Stephen had set aside a Saturday in early April, not long before Easter, which seemed about right for Bradley to be home by then. Finding out from Michael that the school in Singapore would be closing about then to allow for Easter and that the vital exams would have been completed, so his grandsons in Singapore would be home for good, keen to be ushers at the wedding.

Simone had volunteered herself to be matron of honour and was certain she could find a replacement midwife for the special day. Rupert was enlisted to draw up a guest list, seating plans once they had found a venue and generally make himself useful—which he would thoroughly enjoy doing—Victor was the obvious choice for Annette to ask to give her away, as in a traditional church wedding.

Terence, not to be outdone, as his father Jonathan was in America with Bradley, leaving the running of the studio in Terence's capable hands, as he had now qualified as a junior instructor to work alongside his father, said he would give his right arm to be allowed to make the wedding cake, as his skills as a chef were well publicised. He had also given some thought to erecting and advertising the studio as 'Jonathan Tate and Son Dance Studio,' a handsome name and one he knew would make his father proud, adding too, one more title to his family joke name of Rip Van Winkle, a role that had brought the house down, setting him even further on the road to future stardom.

The year had almost come to an end with Christmas once more hovering on the horizon. It had been an extraordinary twelve months with thousands of people on very different pathways of life from what they had been a year ago. According to national and international news the Americas, which comprises most of the Earth's land mass in the Western Hemisphere, with twenty-three countries in North America and more than two dozen non-sovereign territories, including Bermuda, Aruba, the Cayman Islands, Greenland, Puerto Rico of which the most spoken language is English, followed by Spanish and French.

These were not on the itinerary for Bradley and Jonathan, with the 'specials,' but other countries that Bradley and the 'specials' HAD been able to visit, were being transformed in the same way Britain had been on hearing the powerful, all-encompassing voice of Almighty God issuing from the very soles of the tap shoes. Amazing stories and testimonies were on the lips of ordinary people like you and me, ready and willing to reach out with the transforming gospel of Jesus Christ.

Bradley had been consistent with his reports of where they were at any given time. Theatres were block booking wherever he and the 'specials' were dancing next. Excitement rapidly spread after every performance, when Bradley explained the role of the 'specials,' to watch them dance of their own volition, then to hear the voice of Almighty God, being relayed directly through these remarkable shoes, speaking intimately into the hearts of all those who were fully ready to hear and believe.

This was always the moment of truth, reported Bradley. Hecklers, prior to Bradley's introduction of the 'specials' were themselves heckled by the remainder of the audience, who told them to sit down and hear something that might change their lives. Mostly they begrudgingly complied, but, not surprisingly they were stunned into silence, rarely making any further comments, some even stopping to talk to the groups of counsellors sprinkled in the exits of every theatre they performed in.

Newspaper reporters in every State of America were silenced from reporting any form of ridicule or suspicion, by the true factors of what was being experienced daily and by the very people themselves, a large number whose lives were dramatically changed for the better. Sadly wrote Bradley, neither he or Jonathan would be unable to make it home for Christmas, which had been expected, although many had remained hopeful, especially Terence, who was planning the newly worded boarding, at the front of the studio.

Jonathan's mobile was red hot from frequent calls to Terence, making sure that his son was not finding the responsibility of the studio too much, although another professional had been employed specifically to teach the new intakes, leaving Terence with a little more spare time to attend to the ever-mounting paperwork. Unknown to Jonathan, Terence was, in fact, in his element, enjoying both teaching and the general running of the studio.

He did admit to missing his dad being there, but probably more so, Bradley, as the two of them had formed a firm friendship over the years. This had not gone amiss to Oscar, who, on Annette's request invited Terence to join him and her families for Christmas, which had been arranged for a London venue this year, much to the delight of the younger members of the family, living in very differing parts of the country. Dillon had a new second cousin—Christopher— another great-grandson for Oscar, only recently born and lovingly being shown off by his grandparents Adrian and Sue. Some handsome photographs had come Oscar's way, but a first meeting would probably be at Christmas.

Dillon was aware of this and reported on Christopher's progress as often as he could get hold of a phone to ring his great-grandpapa.

Wedding preparations for the great day in April were progressing well now that a firm date had been set aside, with Pastor Stephen, for the ceremony at Merryfields Baptist Church. Oscar, Annette, Simone and Rupert had compiled a guest list, of which Oscar's family had a larger proportion of guests than Annette's, but to even things out Oscar suggested more friends of the Braithwaite family to be invited, including Trevor's parents, as they had known of their daughter-in-law's engagement to Oscar Harrison and had responded eventually with a congratulatory letter saying they deeply regretted not keeping in closer contact with Annette, Victor and Bradley, but sincerely hoping that Annette would finally find happiness after her loss of their son Trevor.

It had taken some thought and prayer on Annette's part to forgive the snub she and Trevor had received, on the occasion of their marriage and that they had rarely spoken to her and the boys after the bereavement. Together with Victor and Bradley they had made a clear decision to forgive what had taken place before, and, in a return letter, invite them personally to her wedding to Oscar, which they regretfully had to refuse.

Neither Oscar or Annette were keen to overspend on a massively expensive reception, eventually deciding to approach a particular hotel specialising in a variety of exquisite culinary dishes from countries around the world. Their restaurant space would be enough to cater for the numbers on their guest list, with banquet-style tables for the guests to join the celebrations.

Sitting comfortably, in consultations with the chefs who would prepare and serve these national dishes, for example, was an eye opener for Oscar and Annette and the chosen menus would provide a choice of dish, to suit all tastes, including especially arranged children's meals that were impressive. With the reception safely booked, a myriad of smaller but equally important arrangements had to be made, including wedding photographers, printing of service booklets and maps, for the guests, not in prearranged taxis, to find the hotel where the reception was to be held, the florist for bridal bouquet, buttonholes, not forgetting Simone's flowers.

Dillon had been drafted in as a page boy, delighted now he was six and a half, but anxious not to be made to look babyish, of which Oscar assured him he would look the part of a soldier, in charge of looking after Annette. His breast had swelled at the thought of the special duty he would have, on his great-grandpapa and great-grandmama Annette's wedding day, but wondered to himself why they wanted to marry when they were both so old!

By Christmas, there was more exciting news from Bradley and Jonathan, so near in spirit, but so far away in distance and that was because so many evangelistic events were being held across the United States, touching deeply into the so-called fringes of society, with caring and counselling given with compassion to those who asked, combined with meeting the desperate physical needs of so many people.

They were sorry not to be celebrating with the family at home, this year, but the restoration of all these lives touched by hearing God's words, through the 'specials' was as great a reason as ever to stay, for God's work to go forward, staying where the greatest needs were. After the Christmas season, they felt sure, they would understand what their next moves should be. In the meantime, they sent their love and 'Christmas Blessings' to everybody.

With Christmas not far away now, Oscar and Annette had successfully completed their final lap of the family guest arrangement, putting the wedding to one side for the moment, as the only items to be purchased after Christmas would be the outfits for the bride, groom, matron of honour and the pageboys. As the pair wanted an informal wedding, the guests would not be required to hire expensive top hats and tails.

Having discussed where everyone would stay when coming to London, for Christmas, Annette had come up with the brilliant idea of speaking to her chef friend, who owned 'The Stag,' where Annette and Trevor had spent many a Christmas and Annette had been invited last year whilst Oscar was in Fareham. She knew he only entertained a few guests on Christmas Day, but the area going further into the building was much larger, enough, she thought to accommodate both sides of the family for a Christmas Day celebration together.

The sleeping arrangements were less easy to find, but when Annette approached Stanley with her request for him to open up his premises for them, he surprised her by saying there were plenty of bedrooms upstairs, that was used by London businessmen during the week to allow them to stay close to their offices, but who were not there during the Christmas season, therefore they were thoroughly cleaned and redecorated, if necessary, ready to reopen in the New Year.

Stanley, who was very fond of Annette and was deeply shocked when Trevor died, had been a strong friend, who gave her his time and support after the accident. Living on his own after his wife had suddenly left him, feeling very bereft, he had successfully opened his business, relying on the constant stream of customers to meet his need for companionship. His response to Annette's enquiry was a fervent 'yes,' giving him the chance, he said, of meeting Oscar's family prior to the wedding in April.

Oscar, he had known for some time, after Annette had introduced them shortly after Bradley had begun to attend Jonathan's dance studio. The rooms, he assured her, would be ready to be occupied by Christmas Eve and a cot would be arranged for Christopher, the new great-grandson that Dillon couldn't wait to introduce to Oscar at Christmas.

'The Stag' was only a short taxi ride away from Oscar's home, but as the small flat couldn't accommodate the entire families, Oscar gave them instructions, from the flat that they all knew, to where it had been arranged for them to stay, with Oscar and Annette meeting them there, making sure they were all settled comfortably, on Christmas Eve. Stanley had employed another chef and waiters for the occasion and was happy to oblige with a party of welcome in the evening.

Oscar wanted to arrive early as he had an important question to put to Stanley, who had always said he had thought Trevor deserved a medal for his reaction when, on the motorway that evening, he had taken the fatal evasive action, to avoid a far more tragic accident than had occurred. Even the police and investigators at the scene commended Trevor's bravery, that had sadly, though, led to his death.

It was this very thought that had occurred to Oscar four years on from then but had wanted to talk to Stanley first to see how feasible it could be, as a close friend of his had once served on one of the cabinets deciding panels for posthumous awards. Stanley was instantly interested and talked with Oscar out of Annette's hearing, who was having a conversation with Sue and Adrian, having only just arrived with Christopher—their latest grandchild—and his parents, who were being shown their room by none other than Dillon!

On coming downstairs to look for his mother, he quickly spotted Oscar, unceremoniously laughing at his great-grandpapa's serious face, then, as Oscar asked him to wait a moment, did so with a sense of injustice, before at last taking his hand to lead him over to greet Adrian and Sue who were holding Christopher. Oscar gasped his thanks to Dillon before peering into the bluest pair of eyes he had ever seen, in a baby so young, reminding him of the infant Jesus' eyes that he had seen in the crib, on Christmas Day, last year.

With the welcoming party going well, introductions were being made and for long afterwards friendships were formed that night. Long after everything was cleared away and preparations were ready for tomorrow, being Christmas Day, Oscar thought long and hard about his talk with Stanley. It would need a carefully worded letter to the government's cabinet, detailing the accident, which would then need a full report from the police and investigators that had been at the scene, on that fatal day, that had robbed the dance world of one of their star and most loved performers.

The George Cross, an award instituted in 1940 by King George VI, seemed to be the most appropriate, presented to the military or civilians usually, for outstanding acts of bravery. Resolving to talk with Stanley, after Christmas and perhaps together put forward a proposal, Oscar, not disclosing any thoughts of awards to Annette, had kissed her tenderly at her bedroom door, before climbing wearily into his own bed with little thought of sleep, for a while at least.

With Christmas morning rousing Oscar from a deep slumber, remembering nothing of having fallen asleep the night before, Oscar grabbed his bathrobe, almost running along the corridor to Annette's room rapping done too gently on the door to wake her up with a hearty 'Happy Christmas' hug and kiss, presenting her with a daintily wrapped gift box. Opening the box carefully, Annette gasped with delight as, nestled in pretty coloured tissue paper, was an exquisite handmade Rhinestone and Pearl bridal hair clasp. Her dark shining hair, now sprinkled with a few grey sparkling stars, felt warm and soft as she snuggled up alongside him, exclaiming with pleasure.

"I have a confession to make," admitted Oscar as he positioned the clasp on her dark curls. "I hope you don't mind, my darling, but I spoke to Simone about a Christmas present for you and asked her how she thought you would wear your hair on our wedding day. To be fair, she was a little unsure, but giving it a little thought she felt you may like to put it up, in a delicate way, she said and thought a diamanté clasp could be a good idea. It's up to you how you want to wear your gorgeous hair, but you can wear this whether it's down or up, so a friend told me of a personal jeweller friend of his, who handmade the clasp to my own instruction. The pearls, I thought, would match your necklace and earrings. I do hope you don't mind? I've been so worried that I've done the wrong thing?"

Placing her hand over his mouth to stop any more confessions or awkward explanations, Annette kissed him soundly on his lips, as she quickly removed her hand. "Please, darling, don't worry so much, I think your idea of asking Simone was lovely and this clasp is a beautiful piece of your friend's workmanship and I'll tell you now, I am going to wear it on our special day and treasure it forever, thank you."

"Now I have a confession," smiled Annette. "I hope you don't mind either, but I asked Ollie and Abby if they would sing at our reception. They have a great repertoire of songs like 'amazing grace', ' ava maria', 'can't stop loving you' and with the combination of their voices, should be a wonderful entertainment. What do you think? Are you a little annoyed that I asked them without asking you first and I promise I won't do it again?"

"That's unfair, Annette," responded Oscar in a mock angry voice, rolling her over onto his chest. "I think it's a brilliant idea and thank them both for me, please."

Thinking the rest of the family would be up and about and could hear them in the bedroom, he rapidly moved away from her. Blushing at his impertinence in coming into her bedroom, Oscar kissed her quickly, grabbed his bathrobe and fled out of her room as quickly as he had come into it.

Once back in his own room, Oscar breathlessly settled his breathing, showered and dressed as quickly as possible, then appeared to amble carelessly downstairs, greeting Annette with a kiss, at the bottom of the stairs, as if they had met for the first time that glorious Christmas morning, even so, deliberately avoiding some of the grins from the family. His new metal framed glasses, finally doing away with the familiar pince-nez, hurt his face, but he didn't care. The day was off to a fine start and he was looking forward to meeting with members of Annette's family, plus enjoying his own and celebrating the birth of Christopher Oscar Harrison.

Circulating around the two families Oscar and Annette enjoyed bringing the relatives together, some having already met the evening before, gifts were exchanged with heartwarming thanks expressed, especially from Dillon who, as usual, was thoroughly spoilt, when finally aperitifs and small bowls of appetisers were served by Stanley, his new chef and waiters, who were achieving great results in the kitchen, judging by the delicious aromas that were wafting in their direction, causing everyone to feel hungry and pick at the tiny bowls of appetising food selections.

Oscar remarked to Annette that Stanley must have been here all night to rustle up such amazing food. She laughed, pulling a face as she watched him devouring the nibbles, saying he wouldn't enjoy his main meal if he ate any more, at which point he stopped and grinned at her, agreeing that 'yes' of course she was right, but he was so impressed by what the chef's had conjured up.

As soon as the guests had taken their seats, Oscar proposed a toast for all who were here to help celebrate this Christmas Day, together, remembering friends such as Bradley and Jonathan, Martha and Steve, Mary and Karin, so many thousands of miles away doing a mighty work for God, but here in our hearts as we think and pray for them. He also called a special toast for Stanley and his team, for giving up their time to prepare and cook this special meal today.

Glasses were spontaneously raised and the toasts drunk, whilst the waiters busied themselves with placing the food on the tables, from where they served each guest with a selection of either the traditional turkey and all its trimmings, roast pheasant, roast beef or poached salmon for those who were vegetarians.

Sumptuous Christmas puddings were on offer for dessert or a selection of fruit sorbets, followed by the traditional after-dinner mints and coffee or any other preferred beverage.

What a feast was eaten at 'The Stag' this Christmas. Oscar making sure that Stanley and his team were well provided for, with his four sons insisting they chipped in as well. There was a positive response to the family celebrations being held in London this year and certainly seemed to be enjoyed. It was later in the evening when Bradley telephoned Annette on her mobile phone and instantly putting him onto her loudspeaker relay, every person in the room was able to hear her son sending greetings from America.

The whole room responded loudly to Bradley's greeting, waiting avidly to hear what he had to say next. He and Jonathan had apparently seen a tremendous healing mission established, following innumerable dance shows, where God had magnificently used the 'specials' to deliver His word to America and the America's bringing about repentance after repentance, followed by changed lives. It's remarkable, mum, he said, to witness such an act of love and compassion for humanity.

"Good to hear you Bradley and all you have to tell us," replied Annette. "Have a great Christmas Day and our same greetings to Jonathan. Hang on a moment, I think Oscar wants to have a word with you," as Annette handed her phone to Oscar, switching off the loudspeaker as she did so.

With the volume of chat and laughter in the room intensifying, Oscar had to move to a quieter area in which to continue the conversation with Bradley. At last, he could question him more deeply on how he and Jonathan were coping with the tours. Bradley admitted to feeling very tired but enormously encouraged by God's love and compassion, released so dramatically in the hearing of His voice, relayed through the 'specials.' Jonathan, he said, was well and doing a magnificent job of arranging venues and accommodation. They were not in need of financial assistance, as at every venue they were adopted as a family into many homes and travelling expenses were paid for by arrangements with the theatres.

The final question Oscar wanted to ask Bradley was the likelihood of them both being home in time for his mother's and his big day in April. Bradley said nothing would stop him from being Oscar's best man and was looking forward to the day immensely. The matter of the posthumous award to his father, Trevor, could wait until Bradley was home again, planned for early February. Saying farewell to his future stepson, Oscar moved back into the noisy but happy atmosphere of the main room, where relatives of both Oscar's and Annette's were getting to know one another.

Stanley and his team were busy clearing tables, rearranging yet more food of slices of Christmas cake and mince pies for those who had room for any more food. Annette joined Oscar and together they saluted each other that this Christmas Day had been a great success.

Making their way their way to where baby Christopher was being plagued by Dillon, Oscar offered Annette a seat, before sitting himself, to apologise for his lack of attention to them and hoped they had found some of Annette's family to converse with. Simone had apparently made herself a surrogate mum to Christopher, getting his attention and his parents, anything from the tables, making herself a lifelong friend of Adrian and Sue's. She knew almost all she could know about babies, offering her help in any unexpected circumstance.

The best Christmas Day ever, according to Dillon, was drawing to a close. Mums and dads were taking their children upstairs for bed, whilst Oscar and Annette thanked Stanley and his chef and waiter's for this most wonderful day. Stanley beamed with pleasure as he was extremely fond of Annette, her son Bradley and now Oscar—the future bridegroom. He wished them all the happiness in the world, as he proposed a toast to the pair.

As the day wound down to a close, families disappeared to bedrooms for their final night, before preparing to return to their homes in the morning. With the 'The Stag' pretty much retuned to its normal business, Oscar had breakfast prepared for his guests, for those who wanted to stay on before, for some, a long drive home. As Annette and Oscar waved each carload on its journey across country to Home Counties and beyond, their thoughts pivoting towards those far away, that had been unable to attend these Christmas celebrations. Boxing Day would be a good time to catch up.

Collecting their luggage and Christmas gifts, Oscar made a point of thanking Stanley once more, making sure he was well compensated for the efforts he had unstintingly given to Oscar's and Annette's families the previous two days. He was to be found, unremarkably, in his kitchen, amongst sparkling work counters and even sparkler utensils, which was way this small restaurant was so popular, being a pleasure to eat in. Nothing was too much trouble for Stanley, who prided himself as being named as one of the top smaller restaurants in London.

Their final hug before Oscar and Annette drove away and with an invitation to the wedding in April, resting in the pocket of his chef's apron, he promised

Oscar he would send him a draft copy of his request to the cabinet, regarding Trevor, in time for the New Years honour list. Knowing the full story, Stanley was fully aware of how his application should be worded.

The New Year growled its way in with torrential downpours alternating with thicker and denser snow storms causing havoc on the roads. Oscar had his groceries delivered, whenever possible and made Annette stay put in her sister's and brother-in-law's home, so she wouldn't risk a fall by coming to his flat each day.

Soon, very soon they would be together for good, bunking down together when the weather was poor. Zoom sessions—a revelation to Oscar—had to take the place of meeting with their church Bible Studies and Prayer gatherings, keeping new Christians in constant touch with all the churches who had reached out to new converts since the beginning of the new wave of God speaking to the world.

An amazing, but equally impressive way of—see, I am doing a new thing—do you not perceive it—now it springs up—I am making a way in the streams and wilderness in the wastelands. To have a God who cared so much for lost mankind was a bountiful blessing that more than compensated for the years the locusts had taken away, bringing newly found hope, joy and an inexpressible peace.

January soon passed into oblivion and the much awaited time for Bradley and Jonathan to return home from America approached. The weather finally conceded defeat and a weak sun begun to brighten the days ahead. Once out from the confines of being housebound because of the weather, the pace of life gathered momentum for Oscar and Annette as they began once more to arrange their wedding and a suitable location for the reception.

In central London, it was difficult to avoid the number of hotels offering bridal suites and large expensive receptions. Motoring into likely areas the pair came across a delightful function room with elegant panelling and charming walks outside and on enquiry found that a cancellation had only just been received for the exact same day as their wedding at 'Merryfields,' with enough space to accommodate their guests and a reasonably priced menu catering for any known diagnosed diet, plus an interesting children's menu that Oscar knew would please Dillon especially.

With the booking firmly made and deposit paid, Oscar and Annette drove home to draw up maps for their guests to find the venue, not too far out of

London. Starting as late as they were into the New Year, they were thrilled to have found such a lovely place, already and available. Place settings would be drawn up when Oscar submitted their guest list. Flowers for decoration would be handled by the management, allowing for selection specials.

With Simone free one day and with Oscar knowing Dillon's size, it was time to make the final, but large chunk of the occasion, on selecting the bride, matron of honour and pageboy outfits that would complement the menswear, yet be relatively easy to find. Annette had a very clear idea of what she would like to wear, again to compliment the beautiful pearl necklace and hair piece that Oscar had presented to her. To her, they were very precious symbols of their love and she cherished them.

After discussing colours and styles with Simone and with Oscar reluctantly in tow, their first visit was too a bridal parlour. Although the choice was enormous and there were some beautiful gowns, they were however not to Annette's liking, being rather heavy, not flowing enough. Eventually, down a small side street, a single fronted shop caught Annette's eye, with simple but perfect gowns displayed in the window.

Off the shoulder styles were tried on enthusiastically, the perfect colour of a long flowing silk and lace gown in an oyster shade, with a styled cape, for Annette and just right for Simone, a maxi length silk and lace dress in a subtle shade of mint green, full necked and without a cape, doing justice to both sisters who gazed at each other with joy in their eyes. Oscar, meanwhile, was sitting alongside the manageress, gaping in awe, until Annette gently told him to close his mouth. What a beautiful bride she was going to make, at the same time muttering a 'thank you' to his personal friend Trevor for allowing him, Oscar, make himself and Annette, so happy.

Carefully carrying their purchases home to Simone's, where the gowns would hang in Simone's large wardrobe ready for the coming wedding day. Gasping with tiredness the three sat in Simone's kitchen, whilst Annette put the kettle on for a refreshing cup of an Asian tea that she and Rupert enjoyed and Oscar had got to eventually enjoy, as well.

Still under discussion when Rupert arrived home, giving him and Oscar to escape for a while, was the pageboy colour and style, that Annette fancied a three quarter length pair of trousers in the same shade as Simone's gown and cream shirt with matching piping, long socks and buckled shoes, for Dillon, sporting a medieval pageboy haircut. This sounded good to Simone who suggested that

Oscar and Bradley have the same colour cravat's and pocket handkerchiefs, as Dillon's outfit, then the young pageboy would feel more in tune with the men.

Sauntering into the kitchen, with the chief aim of closing more wedding discussions Oscar casually suggested that he cook the evening meal, as, he said he had done little that day, except approve the gowns. Thankfully Simone relinquished her role of head chef, allowing Annette and Oscar free rein, in the kitchen, hoping there wouldn't be any urgent delivery complications to deal with, at least until the family had enjoyed their supper together.

A deliciously cooked ham and vegetables later, followed by a crème brûlée— a dessert that Oscar had mastered only recently—weddings were still the topic of the conversation, to which Oscar and Rupert gave in fairly graciously. It was finally decided that Dillon's outfit, plus shoes for the bridal party could be purchased during the next few days.

Come the day when Bradley and Jonathan were expected home was a rapturous occasion, not only for 'Merryfields' Baptist Church, whose welcome committee organised a magnificent reception, inviting many churches along, but across the country church bells announced their arrival home and prayers of praise and worship were given for their safe journey to and from America, with many places of worship asking for a personal appearance and specifically the 'specials' with their intimate message from Almighty God.

It was a hectic few weeks, but eventually, Oscar managed to have a heart-to-heart talk with Bradley, who was by now writing his best man speech. He had two very important pieces of news for Bradley—the first being that Trevor had been nominated and awarded a King George VI gold cross for bravery—in recognition of his action on the motorway, preventing a more fatal collision— bringing Bradley close to tears.

Annette had only just been informed and would receive the posthumous honour at Buckingham Palace a little later on in the year, after the wedding, to which Annette, Oliver, Bradley and Oscar had been invited. It was indeed a time for great jubilation, of which the tabloids, once more, pivoted the success of Bradley and Jonathan's overseas tours, which finally covered the world.

The second piece of news for Bradley was that Naomi was now a born again Christian, that Bradley was thankfully aware of, during their long discussions, on their FaceTime mobile calls whilst Bradley was on tour. Bradley, in fact, had further news for Oscar and that was that he and Naomi had become engaged to be married during this period, much to Oscar's delight. Another marriage, surely made in Heaven.

April—the second Saturday of which was Oscar and Annette's wedding day. There was little left to do now, except wait, in anticipation for the big day, which finally arrived in the fine style of a warm early spring morning with the promise of a beautiful day ahead. Lambing time had come and there was new life everywhere one looked. Even 'Cocky' had arrived one morning with a new chick and happy mother, by his side. Annette was as thrilled by the sight as Oscar had been.

9 AM and Oscar's small flat threatened to become overwhelmed with his children and their families, eager to send their father and grandfather off, into blissful matrimony. A buzz of excitement filled every nook and cranny. Bradley arrived looking every part the groom's best man, resplendent in a new narrow pinstripe suit with the requested mint green cravat and matching pocket handkerchief.

Dillon had arrived at Simone's and Rupert's mincing around cheerfully in his new pageboy outfit, determined to play his role of pageboy, to the full, by taking care of grandma Annette, for the whole day, unintentionally tripping others up, in his desire to be close to his charge. Simone's and Annette's hair was dressed by a professional stage hairdresser, who was a close friend of Annette's and the all-important hair clip adorning a piled-up hairstyle with soft curls encircling her face.

When both Annette and Simone were declared ready for the church, the official car had arrived and with radiant waves from their neighbours, at last Annette was able to join in beloved, at 'Merryfields' in readiness for a future of married life to the man, whom she knew would make each other complete.

Brilliant, but slightly chilly, rays of sunshine greeted Annette's arrival at the church. As the bridal party groped together in preparation for the procession to the altar, so The Trumpet Voluntary in D Major echoed through the building bringing an instant exhilaration of pure joy to the proceedings, so Annette joined Oscar at the altar of God to be united with him until death parted them on earth, to continue into eternity, with their Jesus, in glory. It was a triumphal moment for both families to witness such a match, thoroughly endorsing the union.

The reception was a smooth, unhurried affair, with happiness encapsulated in every aspect of the day, to be retrieved in the years to come, bringing enjoyment over and over again. Bradley, although on the bridal party table, had

Naomi sat very near and following the rather hilarious speeches, they danced close together, almost nonstop, into the twilight, when they wandered into the peaceful grounds, in partnership with one another, not gone unnoticed by Oscar and Annette. It would be their turn next, they dreamed.

What a wonderful emotional day it had been and with especially prepared wedding duets, sung by Oliver and Abby as poignant as they were embracing of Oscar and Annette's love for each other, truly reflected Bradley and Naomi's love too.

"Mr and Mrs Oscar Braithwaite, your car awaits," announced a joyful Jonathan, who had arranged beforehand to drive Oscar and Annette to the airport, for a flight to Paris where the pair were taking a few days in which to view the attractions of the city and seek out new and refreshing restaurants. It would be a pleasure, he had said, to drive such a devoted couple to the airport for their flight to France.

He also wanted to tell them how thrilled he was, on his and Bradley's return from the States to see the new sign, that Terence had erected stating, 'Jonathan Tate and Son Dancing Studio.' He said that it was his and Margot's dearest wish that Terence would love dance as much as he and Margot had and to see his son's name on the fresh billboard was a thrilling and unexpected surprise, awaiting him on his return home.

His one prayer was that the studio would produce new and exciting young dancers to grace the London stage and beyond, qualifying in an exceptionally high standard of dance, especially through the stages of tap dancing to a professional standard, where lay the pinnacle of Trevor's success.

Oscar and Annette's ears prickled with excitement, as they were both in awe of this investiture at Buckingham Palace, in recognition of Trevor's selfless act. The honours would be declared by the Master of Ceremonies and the award conferred to Annette by either the king himself, or, if unable to attend, a member of the Royal Family. They both wanted this honour to be remembered in a very special way and for Trevor's name to be upheld in the world of dance or for example a lasting legacy, for generations to come.

Following on from Jonathan's prayer of, he and his son producing highly skilled ballet and professional tap dancers, led to a train of thought forming in Annette's mind and once on board their flight to France and their honeymoon in Paris, she laid her germ of an idea in front of Oscar, who, having picked over the bare bones, was as excited as his adorable wife was, on touchdown in Paris. Her idea would indeed be a lasting legacy for Trevor and a substantial role in assisting underprivileged children, to obtain some form of stability in their lives.

Oscar's thoughts ran along the lines of deaf and blind children, with only the sense of touch to enlighten their lives, that through the rhythm of the taps, a resonance of sound could be produced by contact with a surface such as wooden studio dance flooring. This made a great deal of sense to Annette, but how to aid a deaf/blind child to hear, let alone even see the keys of a piano, the beats of a music accompaniment, in the first place? Mulling this over during their few days in Paris, before the investiture, gave Oscar and Annette a fresh God-given purpose to their newly married lives.

Flying home to England, from Paris, after a sublime holiday of beautiful memories, the question uppermost in both their minds, was how to develop this new and exciting idea and how to put it to Jonathan, in a practical and efficient way. He seemed the most appropriate person to approach, in the first instance, but it would require a great deal of investigation and debates with government policy, within their hierarchy or organisations, set up to address the isolation of these children, from the world around them, although dearly loved and cared for by dedicated parents and their careers. There could be no margin for error, the idea must only succeed or fail in the attempt, with no child used in an experimental way. All governing bodies must be dedicated to success.

Jonathan, as promised was waiting for Oscar and Annette's flight to arrive at Heathrow, expecting a full and glossy report of their brief honeymoon. It came as no surprise to hear them say, they had a specific idea to discuss with him, when he could spare a few hours away from the dance studio obligations. Intrigued by their positive attitude and to hear what they had come up with, Jonathan arranged a day for the following week, allowing the newlyweds to settle back into domestic bliss now they were safely home.

Warmly welcomed home at Merryfields the next Sunday, Oscar and Annette found themselves the centre of excitement for the coming investiture, to receive Trevor's King George Vl bravery award, at the Palace. They found themselves recounting the events leading up to this decoration and with Oscar beside her Annette, bravely answered concerned questions regarding her son and his tremendous skill as a world-famous tap dancer.

This award, they knew, would make world news, but, as yet, it was too early to announce any furtherance of their plans for deaf/blind children in the world of dance. Jonathan had initially been uncertain how to begin the investigation into the possibility of progressing with the plan, but was greatly encouraged by the enthusiasm generated by nominal groups and, indeed, parents.

Determined to endorse and encourage what Oscar and Annette were planning, Pastor Stephen was keen to put a trust fund into operation. He didn't know much about the world of dance, but he could well understand methods such as using vibrations in the body to stimulate nerve responses. With careful controls in place, used only with trained and highly skilled technicians, he felt sure a breakthrough would be found.

In the meantime, the investiture was only a few days away and as the excitement grew so Oscar, Annette, Bradley and Oliver regaled themselves in suitable clothing for their visit to Buckingham Palace to receive the coveted award. An especially commissioned car drove Mr and Mrs Harrison and Oliver and Bradley Braithwaite to the Palace where they were cordially welcomed, then escorted to the reception area where many people from all parts of the country, were gathered, to receive specific honours from His Majesty, the reigning monarch, during the two hour ceremony, culminating in a grand reception.

After a short wait, whilst others collected their awards, Annette was announced by the Master of Ceremonies, proudly being called forward to receive Trevor's posthumous award for bravery from His Majesty. Curtsying, once the award was in her hands, Annette rejoined Oscar, Oliver and Bradley for official photographs to be taken, assured that she would be sent a formal photograph with documentation, as a keepsake.

The reception, often held outside, was for being held inside the Palace that year, as weather prospects were of showers during the afternoon. The obligatory mingling of the guests was facilitated by stewards and at one point in the afternoon Annette found herself being addressed by the king himself who enquired the nature of Trevor's public valour of bravery, to which she responded somewhat nervously, but supported by Oscar, she told the complete story, engaging His Majesty over and above the official time allowed.

His interest knew no bounds as she outlined their plans for a permanent reminder for Trevor, by the building of a special residential dance school or academy for under privileged, namely deaf/blind children. The king offered every support, already having knowledge of the 'specials' message from Almighty God, from which he himself had responded. Bravely donating a significant sum the trust fund set up in Trevor's name, the overawed family returned to civilian life with a deep gratification in their hearts, both to God and the reigning monarch, who, true to his word boosted the Trevor Braithwaite trust fund to an overwhelming amount.

Research had shown that with intense skills available for these children, the project was given special government approval and a dream was born. The Trevor Braithwaite's Residential School of Dance gave the project a name to be proud of and premises were found, in a rural district just outside of London. Building, to very specific designs began in earnest with everyone with tap dance above standard skills and a very real role to play in giving these children another sense, so allowing confidence and 'yes' budding talent to shine into otherwise restricted lives, were employed, having undergone exhaustive interviews.

These specialised experts would be residential, with the children, in their care, as could be parents of the children, admitted to the ever-growing interest, in one of two homes, fully equipped and active.

By the time this brave initiative was up and running smoothly, only then did Oscar and Annette take a step backward. Several years had passed, Bradley and Naomi were married with two children, a son and daughter as eager to see Trevor's legacy become a standard household name and with many, many young deaf/blind children, gaining, not just a love of dance, particularly of tap, but a confidence to take on the world whatever it meted opt, as, were their parents. God was definitely in total control of every situation and the country knew without a shadow of a doubt that nothing could have been achieved without His name being held in adoration in everyone's heart. 'Praise God, in whom all things are made new.'

THE END